CINDER
&
GLASS

DISNEY DESCENDANTS SERIES

The Ring and the Crown
Something in Between
Someone to Love
29 Dates
Because I Was a Girl: True Stories for Girls of All Ages
(edited by Melissa de la Cruz)
Pride and Prejudice and Mistletoe
Jo & Laurie and *A Secret Princess*
(with Margaret Stohl)
Surviving High School (with Lele Pons)

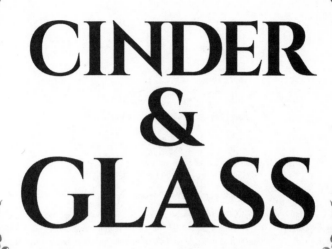

CINDER & GLASS

MELISSA DE LA CRUZ

putnam

G. P. PUTNAM'S SONS

G. P. Putnam's Sons
An imprint of Penguin Random House LLC, New York

First published in the United States of America by G. P. Putnam's Sons,
an imprint of Penguin Random House LLC, 2022

Visit us online at penguinrandomhouse.com

Library of Congress Cataloging-in-Publication Data is available.

Printed in the United States of America

ISBN 9780593326657 (hardcover)
1 3 5 7 9 10 8 6 4 2

ISBN 9780593463086 (international edition)
1 3 5 7 9 10 8 6 4 2

LSCH

Design by Marikka Tamura
Text set in Kis Classico

For Mike & Mattie, always,
and
for all the princesses in my life:
Marie de la Cruz
Sophia Evans
Dagny Hartman
Christina Hossain
Caitlin and Whitney Jones
Lois and Bonnie Robinson
I wish you all the most magical happily ever afters

Versailles, 1682

I believe that the histories that will be written about this court
after we are all gone

will be better and more entertaining than any novel,

and I am afraid that those who come after us

will not be able to believe them and will think that they are
just fairy tales.

—*Lady Elizabeth Charlotte, Duchesse d'Orléans,*
sister-in-law to Louis XIV, King of France

LIGHT

O happy childhood! Blessed youth!

But once we know thy potent power;

But once we live all careless free;

No cross to mar our love-lit bower.

—*Pablo Neruda*

I WAS MEANT TO BE listening to Claudine explain how best to pack for the move to Versailles. Instead, I was staring out the window in Papa's study, watching Elodie and Marius clamber about in the orchard at the edge of the lake behind our château. Marius was hoisting Elodie up so she could reach the branches of the gnarled little trees. My friends picking cherries without me. I couldn't blame them. The most wonderful cherries grew there, sweet and fresh, with just a hint of tartness. And it was a beautiful early summer day, perfect for cherry picking. I wished I could be out there with them, but I was already fifteen years old, no longer allowed to just do as I pleased.

My feet itched to run out of the room and join my friends, and I tugged impatiently on a lock of hair that had escaped my chignon. My long, wavy golden-brown hair was no longer allowed to flow freely down my back. Now that I was getting older, it had to be styled and set every day.

"Cendrillon. Are you paying attention?" Claudine said sharply. "Cendrillon?" She looked down at me with a disapproving frown.

1

Our housekeeper used to scare me, as she was tall and towered over everyone else in the château. I wasn't sure how old she was, maybe Papa's age or even older. Her hair, always worn in a tight bun at the nape of her neck, was slate gray, and her face was lined with wrinkles around her eyes and mouth. But they were mostly from laugh lines, as Claudine could never be mad at me for too long. She was devoted to my family and had been with us since before I was born.

I turned away from the window to face Claudine and the curious gaze of the footman, who was awaiting my instructions.

"I'm paying attention. Of course I am."

"Were you? Because the footman needs to know how to pack up Monsieur de Louvois's study. You *are* the lady of the house."

For so long, lady of the house had been Maman's role, and every time I tried to grasp those words and apply them to myself, they slipped through my thoughts and fluttered off into the wind. Maman had been gone for four years, and though it was hard to believe, her role was now mine.

We were moving to Versailles at the end of the week, and much more would be expected of me there. If I wanted to earn a place as lady-in-waiting to a member of the royal family—perhaps even to the queen herself—I certainly needed to be able to handle something as simple as the management of my own household.

"My father's desk can remain here," I said to the footman. "He has another waiting for him at Versailles. The same can be said for the rest of the furniture in the study. But do empty his desk of all effects and pack them up."

"Yes, Lady Cendrillon," the footman said with a nod, turning sharply on his heels and heading over to Papa's grand wooden desk.

Claudine smiled approvingly. "Very good, ma chérie. Now we need to discuss what furniture we'll be taking from the bedrooms. Monsieur de Louvois has allotted us a budget to purchase new furniture, but only a few pieces, so we'll have to be thoughtful about what we bring."

Her words became muffled and hazy, as if I were eavesdropping on a conversation through a closed door. My chest tightened, making it nearly impossible to draw breath. How had it gotten so warm in this room? Sweat beaded on my skin. What if I couldn't do this? Be the perfect lady that everyone expected me to be? Maman died before she could teach me about court life, and Papa's distaste for it kept us away for so long that I never learned anything on my own. If I couldn't handle the packing of the château, how could I handle impressing the king and queen, much less any suitors Papa might choose for me?

"Will you excuse me, Claudine?" I blurted out, the words strangled and nearly incomprehensible. "I need a moment to . . . refresh myself. I won't take long."

Without waiting for a reply, I hurried from the study, letting my feet carry me where they wished. And where they wished to go was outside the château, to the wide lawn leading to the lake. As soon as my feet hit the grass, I started running. I needed to see my friends. Just for a moment. Spending time with them always cheered me up.

Elodie's mother had been our seamstress for many years, with Elodie taking over the position after her mother passed from the same illness that took Maman. And Marius came to us at a young age to be a stable boy after his parents could no longer care for him. We'd grown up together. They were the only constants in my life now that everything was changing.

They were still picking cherries.

"Marius, don't wobble so much! You're going to drop me," Elodie said, balancing precariously on the palms of Marius's hands.

"How am I not supposed to wobble? You're *heavy*, and I'm no strongman."

Elodie sighed loudly as she stretched into the tree, but she was

3

still too short to reach the fruit nestled in the uppermost branches. She was my age, with round pink cheeks and a messy ponytail. Marius liked to tease her for her fondness of sweets, but Elodie paid no mind and declared she liked how she looked and would continue to eat as she pleased.

"You have to lift me higher!"

"I *can't* lift you any higher," Marius said, grunting with the strain of holding Elodie up.

"You're not tall enough, Elodie," I said, smirking as both Marius and Elodie startled at my voice. "Maybe you should let me try."

"Cendrillon! What are you doing here?" Elodie asked as she awkwardly clambered down off Marius. "Claudine said you would be helping with the move today." She blew her dark hair away from her pleasant, ruddy face. "She said we weren't to bother you."

"I *have* been helping with the move. Now it's time for a little break."

Marius and Elodie glanced between each other nervously, as if I were doing something that I shouldn't. Which I was, but I didn't need them to point it out.

"You're going to need my help if you want those cherries," I said, tamping down my annoyance at their lack of enthusiasm. "Marius, are you going to lift me up or not?"

Marius backed up a few steps. "Do you really think I'm going to go against Claudine over a few cherries if she wants you up at the château? No, thank you." Towheaded and gangly, with freckles across his nose, he had grown taller over the summer and loomed over us now, though he used to be the shortest of us three. Two years younger than us, we both babied him and bossed him around.

I turned to Elodie, but I could tell from her frown that she wasn't going to take my side. She put her hands on her hips. "Is there a

4

reason why you're so reluctant to leave? I thought you wanted to go to Versailles."

"I *do* want to go to Versailles," I said far too defensively.

I wasn't being untruthful. At least not about all of it. The palace of Versailles was said to be the one of the most beautiful palaces in the world, dripping in luxury and large enough to house the entire court. I wanted to walk through its grand halls and mingle with lavishly dressed courtiers while being wooed by a handsome prince.

Before Maman married Papa, she had been a lady-in-waiting to the king's sister-in-law, Lady Palatine, Duchesse d'Orléans. So many of Maman's bedtime stories featured the wonders of court life, from being honored with attendance at the king's and queen's daily rituals and meals, to the fabulous midnight balls and garden parties that featured the best food in France and the most talented musicians. Maman had dreamed of this life for me. But I was scared to embark on it without her guidance and support.

"Are you not going to let me pick cherries with you?" I asked. "Why can you do it and I can't?"

I knew I sounded childish, but I didn't care. When I got to Versailles, my blissfully simple country childhood would be over. Couldn't I be a child until we left?

"Because you're a *lady*," Elodie said with an eye roll that she'd never give to anyone but me or Marius. "A noblewoman. Lady Cendrillon de Louvois."

I opened my mouth to protest, when I heard a loud voice coming from the direction of the château. "Cendrillon! Marius! Elodie! Come inside this instant!"

Claudine was standing at the back door, all the way up the hill.

"Come on," Elodie said, snapping me out of my thoughts. "We should go before she gets mad."

Marius, Elodie, and I ran back up the lawn toward Claudine's imposing figure.

Her imperious stare was in full effect as we reached the château. She thought we were all too old to be climbing trees. Slowly, she stepped to the side, allowing us inside, and followed us, shutting the door with a decisive *whoomph*.

"Marius, the stables won't clean themselves. Elodie, you need to start packing your fabrics into the empty trunks. They're downstairs in your chambers," Claudine said.

My friends ran off, and Claudine and I were left alone. I turned to face her, waiting for my reprimand. She opened her mouth to speak, but her eyes fixed on my face, and with a few tuts she licked her thumb and began vigorously rubbing at my cheek.

"You had a spot of dirt," Claudine said, her expression lightening as she tapped me on the cheek. "I remember the day your maman gave birth to you, and now here you are, about to go off to the royal palace to be a lady of the court."

My throat felt tight and sore. I wanted to tell her that being a lady of the court was exciting but also terrifying, but Claudine wouldn't entertain such a notion. She would tell me that it would be good for me, that Maman had excelled at being a courtier, and that I would too.

The moment passed, and Claudine went stern again. "Now, I won't have you putting off packing your things anymore."

"Hello, hello!" a man's deep voice called.

"Papa!" I said joyfully.

My father walked into the kitchen, a wide smile on his face. He kept coming and going between the château and our new home adjacent to the palace, both to prepare for our move and to perform his duties as the king's closest advisor.

When Maman was alive and Papa was home, the three of us would spend every evening together. Maman would read to us from one of the books in the library, or we would play card games in Papa's study, maybe go for a walk in the gardens or visit the village.

After Maman died, Papa tried to keep up our old rituals, but it was hard not seeing him when he was away.

"Happy to see your old papa?" he said, chuckling.

I smacked him gently on the arm.

"You're not *that* old. You won't be needing a sedan chair for at least a few more years."

"Thank you, ma fille. Your confidence in my abilities warms my heart, truly."

Laughing, I sat down on one of the stools at our heavy oak kitchen table. I didn't like to think of it, but my father was getting older. His hair was more gray now than the caramel-brown color that used to match mine exactly.

"Good evening, Claudine," he said. "How goes the packing?"

"Good evening, Monsieur de Louvois. The packing is going well, apart from a certain someone's procrastination."

Claudine fixed me again with her stern gaze before bustling out of the kitchen. This was the only room in the château that wasn't half-empty, with sheets covering up the furniture.

"You haven't started packing yet? Why not?" Papa asked.

"I don't know." I squirmed in my seat.

"Aren't you excited? We're leaving in less than a week." He looked worried, a frown emphasizing the redness of his eyes and the dark circles underneath. Telling him how nervous I was would just make him feel guilty for keeping us away from court for so long.

"Of course I'm excited. I just— I— I can't decide what I want to bring with me. There's only so much room in my trunks."

"I'd like for you to have your trunks packed by tomorrow. The coaches are filling up quickly." Papa paused and then smiled, his eyes lighting up like they did when he had a surprise. He looked the same

7

way when he'd bought me my lovely mare, Rose, for my twelfth birthday. "Perhaps a certain visitor coming later today can help you decide what to take to court."

"Who's coming for a visit? Lady Françoise? It has to be!"

We didn't get many visitors other than my godmother. He tapped his nose and continued smiling but stayed silent.

"Papa! Is she here?"

"Patience, patience. You'll just have to wait and see." He got up and gave me a quick kiss on the forehead. "Now go to your room, please, and start packing."

CHAPTER TWO

My room was on the second floor, up the curved wooden staircase and tucked away in an alcove at the end of the hall. The task went slowly, but I made progress in the next few hours.

And the first thing that would come with me was Maman's mirror.

The mirror had been my grandmother's—my mother's mother—given as a gift to Maman on her wedding day. Its frame was inlaid with painted wood pieces in the shapes of intricate flowers that curled around one another with birds perched within them.

When I was small, I would lie on her bed and watch as she prepared for a ball or social outing. Claudine would be there, curling her hair, pulling it into intricate knots, and adorning it with flowers or pearls. Sometimes when we were alone, as Maman applied a bit of rouge and powder on her face and dabbed red stain on her lips, she would put a touch on me as well. I don't remember much of my mother, but those moments are imprinted in my memory, how beautiful she looked in that mirror, how she would smile at me when our eyes met. Maman had soft brown hair and sweet brown eyes; everyone tells me I look like her.

After she died, Papa gave the mirror to me, and it's been hanging in my bedchamber ever since.

"Where is my sweet Cendrillon?" said a voice from my doorway, gentle and full of humor. "Oh, ma filleule?"

I turned to see none other than Lady Françoise de la Valliere entering my room, arms outstretched for a hug.

I ran into her arms. "I just knew you were the visitor. Hello, Marraine!"

Lady Françoise laughed and said, "Why? Your father has no other friends who come to visit?"

"Of course not," I said, but I didn't quite mean it.

I was sure that my father had other friends at court, but none of those friends ever visited us at home. Lady Françoise was the only one, which made sense, as she was Papa's oldest friend. They'd grown up together at court and remained friends to this day, rising through the ranks to become favorite courtiers of the king. I'd known Lady Françoise my entire life. She was my godmother and held me at my baptism. I don't know what Papa and I would have done without her support after Maman's death.

"Still, you're the best one," I said.

We linked arms, and I led her to the only settee in my chamber that hadn't been packed away. Lady Françoise looked beautiful, with glossy black curls piled atop her head. Her red dress was set aflame by the light streaming through the windows.

"Now that you're coming to court, we'll be able to see each other nearly every day! But I'm sure you won't want to spend *too* much time with me, not when you'll be making so many new friends."

My pulse jumped at the mention of court. I grabbed Lady

Françoise's hand. "That's not true—I'll be completely lost at court without you."

Lady Françoise squeezed my hand and peered into my face. "What's wrong, ma jolie belle? You look very pale. Are you feeling all right?"

"I'm nervous," I blurted out. "About going to court." The weight in my chest eased as the words passed my lips, even though my body tensed as I waited for her reaction.

"Nervous about court? Do you not want to go?" she asked, her expression frustratingly neutral.

"No! I mean, I'm excited to go to Versailles, to see the palace, the world that you and Papa live in, but—"

"But what?" asked Lady Françoise, her perfectly arched eyebrows raised in alarm.

"But I'm afraid too. Worried I won't be able to achieve what Maman had dreamed for me. She was like you—always so composed, so capable. She could handle *anything*. I'm not like that," I finished weakly, embarrassed by how immature I must sound.

Lady Françoise smiled softly and wrapped an arm around my shoulder, drawing me tightly to her side and enveloping me in the calming air of her jasmine perfume.

"Your mother was a wonderful person," Lady Françoise said, giving my shoulders a reassuring squeeze. "One of my dearest friends. And she loved you more than anything else in all the world. *Nothing* you do could disappoint her."

"But—"

"No. I won't hear any argument on the matter. I knew her longer than you did, and I am sure she would be happy as long as you're happy. You must not allow the fear of disappointing her cloud your mind, because it simply wouldn't be possible."

I opened my mouth to speak, to protest, to agree, to start crying. I wasn't sure. And it didn't matter, because Lady Françoise carried right on, as if she knew I needed further encouragement.

"I understand how you're feeling about court, though. It can be difficult to adjust when you're new. Adhering to the strict rituals, getting used to the meddlesome courtiers, meeting the king and the royal family . . . It can be confusing and will take time to get used to. That's normal."

"Is it?" I leaned against her just as I had as a child.

"Of course! You've never been to court before, and your life here is very different from what it will be in Versailles. Why wouldn't you be nervous? Still, Versailles is more wonderful than even *I* could imagine. It's a marvelous circus of parties, and you will meet the most interesting people in France and from around the world! Perhaps you'll fall in love with one of the handsome nobles or even a prince! That alone makes it all worthwhile."

I slumped back into the cushions and released the breath I'd been holding. Lady Françoise laughed and leaned back next to me, without a thought for her hair getting mussed or her bodice wrinkling.

As much as I loved her, I wasn't sure I wanted to share the *other* reason I dreaded the move, the one that kept me up at night: becoming a courtier might mean my two best friends would be taken from me.

On the rare occasions Papa invited his court acquaintances to the château, they would see me playing with Marius or Elodie, smile condescendingly, and comment on how lonely it must be for me, having only the servant children to play with. They said an introduction at court would afford me a *whole* host of playmates befitting my station. Sometimes they said it in front of Marius and Elodie, and I would see Marius's cheeks burn red and Elodie's eyes fill with tears. Then they would pat me on the head and saunter off.

The injustice was frustrating, and there were bound to be even more people at court who thought I should not be so familiar with servants. Would Papa listen to them? Would Lady Françoise? While kind and gentle, she was a still a noblewoman, and I couldn't be sure that she would understand.

Instead of telling the truth, I chose a safer question. "Do you *really* think I'll do well at court?"

"You'll be wonderful. I'll be there to help you, and so will your father."

It was amazing how much better Lady Françoise could make me feel in the span of a few minutes. Whether I was fighting with Elodie, having trouble with one of my lessons, or missing Maman, I could always write to her with my troubles and she would come for a visit and try to help. Sometimes that help took the form of recommendations for a new tutor and sometimes it was a strawberry tart and a shoulder to cry on, sprinkled with a touch of advice. She had never let me down before, so I couldn't imagine that she would now.

"Do you live near court as well?" I asked.

"Yes, of course," she said as Papa entered the room.

"Ah, Michel," she said. "I was just telling Cendrillon to come to me with whatever she needs while adjusting to life at Versailles." She squeezed my hand again.

"Well, that's good. I'm afraid I won't be much help when it comes to dealing with courtiers and the like. Give me a private audience with the king any day and I'm fine, but balls and public suppers are things I'm still not comfortable with."

"Quite right. Do you remember when you made that comment about Duchesse d'Orléans hair at last year's state dinner?" Lady Françoise said, smirking mischievously.

Papa turned about as red as an overripe tomato. "Bird nests are . . . are wondrous creations. I thought it was a compliment."

"Papa, you didn't," I said.

13

Lady Françoise giggled. The giggle turned into a full-blown laugh that soon had her doubled over, clutching her stomach.

Papa's face was still aflame, but he laughed as well as he dragged my one remaining armchair across the room to sit with us.

When she managed to get herself under control, she said, "Madame didn't get over that comment for at least six months. She still mentions it occasionally and says that she won't appear at any more dinners with the incomparably rude Monsieur le Marquis de Louvois."

"Oh, dear," Papa said, scrubbing at his face with his hands. "I hope the king hasn't heard about this." Madame is his sister-in-law and a favorite at court.

"He would probably think it funny."

"Yes, he just might. You clearly do," he said with a mock glare in Lady Françoise's direction. "Laughing at my embarrassment."

"Your embarrassment is a primary source of amusement for me, as you're mired in it so often."

I looked between them with a smile. There was so much affection and intimacy between them. They were meant for each other, I was certain. Maybe they would even wed before the year was out. That happy thought stayed with me as I finally finished packing.

CHAPTER THREE

"GO EXPLORE THE GARDENS. HAVE fun," Papa said, his words rushed as he helped me down from the carriage. "Stay out of trouble." Elodie and Marius hopped off from the platform in the back, where they had been riding. The three of us squeezed hands and grinned, thrilled to finally see the famous palace and its grounds.

The château the king had assigned to us was tucked away in a secluded forested area of the countryside just outside the town of Versailles. It was three stories tall, with a blue-slate roof and walls of bright white stone that were similar in style to the palace—a fact Papa bragged about to anyone who would listen. From the moment I'd seen it, I was struck by its simple, stately beauty and leaned my head out the carriage window so I could stare at it during the entire drive up the road.

Our household was mostly settled in the new estate. But we had only been there two days, and things were still somewhat chaotic as everyone continued to get comfortable.

Though the château and grounds would be considered small by

Lady Françoise's standards, and probably the rest of the court's as well, I didn't mind the size, and neither did Papa. Smaller houses were cozier, anyway.

At last, today was our introduction to the grandest palace in all of Europe. My godmother was supposed to give us a tour of the grounds, but she wasn't feeling well. And since Papa had been away from court for a while already, the king had requested his presence soon after we arrived. Papa wanted to bring me with him to Versailles so I could become acquainted with the palace and the many courtiers who lived there. I insisted that Elodie and Marius come along. They would never forgive me if I left them behind.

I hugged Papa goodbye.

"And stay out of the palace proper, please," said Papa.

Without another word, he hurried off, his black clothing a stark contrast to the brilliant colors worn by the other visitors to the sunny gardens.

Anyone could visit the palace if they followed the dress code, which meant wearing your best clothes. There were noble ladies in ornate satins and high heels, dukes with swords of gold hanging at their sides, also wearing high heels, and foreign royalty in fabulous finery. Even wealthy Parisians wearing the height of fashion stared enviously at the courtiers, for they had the ear of the king. Visitors from surrounding villages wore modest gowns of wool with only two or three petticoats.

As we watched these visions walk by, the din of different conversations going on at once made my head spin. I heard snippets of what sounded like German and Spanish and English and some languages I didn't recognize. Like every noblewoman of the day, I was educated in all the continental languages, but it was overwhelming to hear them all at once. I felt deluged by the many people wandering about the gardens, and I could tell that Elodie felt the same way. Her eyes were darting around to all the different people, and we not so subtly slid over to each other until our shoulders were pressed together.

Marius, however, was bouncing on the balls of his feet. I don't know if I'd ever seen him so excited before.

"Can we get going? I don't want to waste our two hours just standing here. I want to see the Latona fountain; it's supposed to be incredible," he said with a huff as he walked quickly away from us.

"Hold your horses," said Elodie. "There's no rush." To me she whispered, "He probably wants to see as many naked lady statues as he can!"

Marius grunted, but he slowed down.

The palace of Versailles was located on a hill above gardens that led to the Grand Canal. We walked through the geometric lawns and past many fountains that featured many naked women and men to a terrace that overlooked the king's famous Orangerie. Papa had told me that thousands of orange trees grew there, along with other imported trees and plants.

I hadn't eaten an orange in ages, and I'd never seen an orange tree. They were rare in France, and incredibly expensive. Sometimes at Christmas, Papa Noël would bring me one, and sometimes my papa brought one back from court. There were two sets of steps leading down to the Orangerie from the terrace. After descending one, we came across an open door leading into the Orangerie's indoor galleries.

"Should we go in?" Elodie asked, peering into the dim, shadowy room nervously.

"I don't see why not. The door is open. And Papa's been here before with other courtiers."

We went inside. The air in the gallery was humid and smelled of fresh soil. Small potted trees and bushes lined both sides of the gallery, leaving only a narrow path to walk on. I ran my fingers across the soft green leaves but couldn't tell what kind of plants they were.

I didn't see any oranges. It felt like we were walking through a miniature forest.

"It's lovely in here," whispered Elodie, stopping to inspect one of the trees. "Is that a pomegranate? I've never seen a pomegranate before! Only in books!"

Elodie reached for the red fruit and ran her fingers across it gently.

"Where's Marius?" I asked, realizing that he'd wandered off while we were examining the trees.

"Through here!"

I turned to see Marius up ahead of us, disappearing around a corner. We followed him.

"Come see!" he called.

It was an orange tree, my height or perhaps a little taller, and absolutely covered in huge oranges that hung heavy on the branches. A lonely little orange lay on the ground just underneath the tree. I bent down to pick it up. I would never dare pick one of the king's oranges for myself, but surely he wouldn't mind if we took one that had already fallen.

I turned to Elodie and Marius. "Should we share it?"

"Yes!" Marius said eagerly.

Elodie frowned at us. "You two are really going to steal one of the king's oranges?"

"It was already on the ground," I said. "It'll go bad if we don't take it, so I'm sure he won't mind."

She stared at me for a second, then shrugged. "That's a good point."

"We should find someplace to eat this that isn't here. It's . . . pretty, I guess, but far too hot," said Marius while he warily poked at the skin of the orange as if he expected it to burst.

"Let's find a quiet place farther out in the gardens. There might be less people there."

"What are you doing?" someone behind me said, loud and imperious.

I turned slowly, my heart jolting in my chest. The owner of the voice was a boy, maybe a year or two older than me, with dark brown hair and a sneer etched onto his face, standing on the path behind us, blocking our way back. He wore a golden embroidered justaucorps and a ridiculously lacy cravat at his throat. With him was another boy and two girls. The girls stood arm in arm, wearing matching green silk dresses with pristine lacy white petticoats. Both girls had silver-blond hair that glowed in the sunlight. They had to be sisters. Lady Françoise always cooed over baby sisters who wore matching outfits, but the mother of these girls had continued the style long beyond the age it was considered to be sweet.

"I said, what are you doing?" the boy said, taking a step toward us, his red high-heeled shoes crunching on the gravel path.

I took a step back instinctively. I wouldn't usually be afraid with Marius and Elodie by my side, but he was quite tall, nearly as tall as a full-grown man. He was also clearly highborn. By the state of their clothes, I'd say all four were highborn.

"Exploring the Orangerie," I said, glad my voice didn't tremble even though I nearly lost my grip on the orange.

"Who gave you permission to explore the Orangerie? No one is supposed to be in here."

"You're in here, aren't you?" I asked. "I thought it was open to the public."

"You thought wrong. And *I* don't need permission."

The other boy, who had been standing behind the rest of his group examining the orange tree next to him, stepped forward and put his hand on the mean boy's arm. "We received special permission from the king to visit the Orangerie. There really isn't supposed to be anyone else here. My brother is correct about that."

He smiled at me and shrugged his shoulders, as if in apology. His eyes were green and clear, and he seemed a little shy, glancing at me and then looking away when our eyes met. I was surprised that the boys were brothers, and much preferred the younger boy's shyness to his brother's rudeness.

"Yes, no one is supposed to be here but us," the shorter girl said, eyeing Elodie and Marius. "Is that an apron?" she asked Elodie with flagrant distaste.

Elodie opened her mouth to reply, her cheeks bright red, when the taller girl cut in, completely ignoring her.

"Of course it's an apron, Alexandre. She's obviously a servant. Which is why *you*," she said, directing her comments to me, "shouldn't have brought them here. The only servants allowed in Versailles are footmen or lady's maids."

"Actually, they *are* my footman and lady's maid," I said, my words short and clipped.

I was trying to remain polite, but the girl had upset me.

Her eyes widened. She glanced at the one named Alexandre and mouthed something to her that I couldn't make out. The tall boy in the golden justaucorps leaned in to listen and smirked at whatever they were saying.

The girl turned back to me. "They're your footman and lady's maid?"

When I nodded, she continued. "You must be new at court, aren't you? At Versailles, footmen and lady's maids don't wear . . . rags like those." The girl glanced disdainfully at their clothing. "Surely it's embarrassing for you to wander about with servants dressed so poorly."

I wanted to snap back at them, but there was nothing I could say that these girls would listen to, much less a defense of Marius's and Elodie's sturdy but simple clothing.

"Severine, please. You're being rude," the younger boy said.

He attempted to walk over to the girls, but his brother grabbed his arm and held him back.

"Severine is asking a perfectly valid question. Why is this girl wandering about where she shouldn't be with shabbily attired servants?"

"Based on what she's wearing, I'd guess she was from the country. That dress is positively rustic," Severine said, her mouth twisted up as if she'd tasted something sour.

Alexandre giggled and covered her mouth with her hand, and the tall boy laughed outright, hysterically, as though what Severine had said was witty or amusing instead of horribly inappropriate. My face was burning hot with anger now, and I had to bite my tongue so hard, it was sore afterward. I'd never been a combative person, but with Elodie shrinking behind me and refusing to even look at the four and Marius glaring but saying nothing, I fought to control my temper.

"I apologize for entering the Orangerie without permission. This is my first day at Versailles, and I am clearly unfamiliar with the customs. But I don't appreciate the judgment that you're casting upon me when we've only just met."

What I said didn't seem particularly offensive, but the girls gasped as if I'd slapped them, and the sneer on the boy in the justaucorps coat turned into an outright glare.

"You can't talk to me like that," he said, his voice rising with every word. "You're just an uncouth country girl whose parents never taught her any manners. People like you don't even belong in the vicinity of someone like me. I'm—"

"That's enough!" The younger boy stepped in front of his brother and held up his hands. "Let it go. We'll miss the boat race in the Canal if we don't leave now. You've been talking about it for weeks."

With a final glare in my direction, the boy stomped back down the path, the girls following him in a huff without even deigning to look at us again.

The younger boy turned to Marius and Elodie. "I'm sorry. Truly. Please, stay and enjoy the Orangerie for as long as you'd like. I'm sure the king wouldn't mind."

How would this boy know what the king would or wouldn't mind us doing? What a strange thing to say.

The boy ran off after the other three, leaving us alone in the Orangerie. I turned to Elodie and threw my arms around her. She was trembling.

"Are you all right?"

"Yes, I'm fine," she said, but her voice wavered and her eyes were watery. "I expected something like this to happen eventually. Servants among the courtiers and all. Most won't be like you and Monsieur le Marquis. I just didn't expect it to happen so soon."

"Marius?"

"I'll be fine," he said dejectedly. His dark eyes were mournful, and he looked like a little boy again.

"Let's get out of here, okay? We'll go to one of the little groves Lady Françoise mentioned."

Elodie nodded and sniffled. Marius took off ahead of us, weaving across the path. My eyes burned with tears. I wanted to cry, too, but that would only make Elodie more upset, so I held the tears back as we walked to the gate to find an exit.

I should have been prepared for the attitudes that Elodie and Marius would face at Versailles. I would have to ask Papa to get them new clothes so they could blend in better with the other servants. But if this was what Versailles was going to be like, full of snobbery and bullies, I didn't want any part of it.

CHAPTER FOUR

"YOU ALL KNOW THAT WHEN entering a room the king is in, lords must bow and scrape before him, and ladies must make a deep curtsy. But what do you do when the king enters a room that *you* are in?" Lady Celia asked as she paced back and forth at the front of the room, the swooshing of her gown and petticoats clearly audible in the silence.

I had absolutely no idea. I didn't know most of the answers to the questions Lady Celia posed during our etiquette lessons. My lack of knowledge put me at a severe disadvantage compared with the other young ladies in the lessons with me, who had been meeting for months already. But I had to attend; Papa said it was required of every young lady at court.

Because the entire royal court and advisors were in residence at Versailles, every room in the palace was already being used, so the twenty of us were shoved into a claustrophobically tiny wood-paneled room in one of the four corners of the Grand Commons, a quadrangular structure directly across from the south wing of the palace.

As the days marched well into summer, the heat in the room was becoming unbearable, so I sprinted to every class to make sure that I claimed the seat next to the window. Lady Celia appeared to wilt more every day, and I wasn't sure we would make it to the end of summer. Maybe if we were lucky, she would decide to hold the lessons in the garden.

"Severine, would you like to answer the question?" Lady Celia asked, snapping open her fan and waving it vigorously at her face.

Severine sat up straighter in her chair and smiled at our instructor. That was another downside to these lessons. Or more specifically, there were two additional downsides to these lessons: Severine and Alexandre. The horrid girls who had insulted Marius and Elodie in the Orangerie were also here. They had had the nerve to insult me for being "country" but were clearly new to court themselves.

Thankfully, the bulk of our interactions consisted of a few glares or smug smiles shot my way when they said something rude about me to another classmate. By virtue of attending classes together before I arrived, the other girls were already on their side, and while a few were almost friendly to me, the others were much less so and seemed to scare the friendlier ones away. I decided to stay away from all of them. It didn't bother me much anymore, but I couldn't deny that I was lonely, even in a stuffy room filled with people.

Severine answered, "If you are in a room that the king enters, you mustn't bow or speak or approach him. You must avert your eyes and retreat from him in silence. Only speak if he speaks to you first." Her ice-blue eyes glittered, and she was as beautiful as she was smug.

She was clearly far too pleased with herself for spouting off another one of the court's etiquette rules. Severine and her sister were thankfully not in matching dresses today, but they were still attired in much too many bows. They had bows on their sleeves, bows on their bodices, bows along the hemline of their skirts, and bows in their hair.

Bows were fashionable at the moment, and I enjoyed them on occasion, but this was going too far.

"Very good, Severine! Only those who have the closest relationships with the king may approach him. And always remember to remove yourself from the king's path as he walks about Versailles. You don't want to be the person who gets in his way."

"Now, Cendrillon," Lady Celia said, turning her gaze to me.

I froze in my seat, completely unprepared for any question. All I wanted was for the lesson to be over with.

I missed Marius and Elodie. While I was at Versailles learning rule after rule after rule about how to behave at court, they were home at the château in relative freedom. Versailles might have balls and fêtes and a theater where I could finally see an actual play, but I'd never heard of so many rules in my life, and nearly all of them were absolutely ridiculous.

Last week we'd spent three hours talking about the etiquette of seating in the presence of the royal family. Only the king and the queen are permitted to sit in armchairs, and only members of the royal family can sit in chairs with backrests, but only on certain occasions. Everyone else allowed to sit could only do so on little stools. There were entire procedures about who could sit and when based on rank. In the presence of the king, only members of the royal family, duchesses, and princesses of the blood were allowed seats on stools. Everyone else had to stand. The further down in rank the royal family member was, the more the rules changed for them.

I couldn't keep any of it straight. The one thing I knew was that since I was neither a princesse nor a duchesse, I would always be standing in the presence of royalty.

Courtiers at Versailles were obsessed with etiquette. They immersed themselves in it because breaking the rules could lead to scandal. I had to stop myself from rolling my eyes when Lady Celia mentioned that, when the king wasn't in attendance at Versailles, his royal portrait represented him, and we must bow or curtsy to it as we did to him.

Papa was never one for overly strict rules or enforcing etiquette at home, and Lady Françoise never mentioned anything like this when she spoke of Versailles. They were both very easy and familiar with each other when she visited us, dining together and walking arm in arm around the grounds, which wasn't done at Versailles especially by unmarried couples. Coming from such a home, I was having a difficult time adjusting to such strict regulation of time and behavior. It might've been easier had I someone to commiserate with.

Lady Celia's gaze fell on me as, at last, she asked her question: "When attending the king's public suppers, what must one do when faced with the king's dishes?"

I was about to admit that I was unable to answer the question when there was a commotion at the door. All eyes were drawn to the front of the room as a boy with dark hair and bright green eyes walked in and approached Lady Celia. It was the kind boy from the gardens, the brother of the arrogant boy.

Hopefully, he wouldn't notice me tucked away in the corner. Having Severine and Alexandre here was already bad enough. They certainly noticed him, though, immediately pressing their heads together and whispering.

"Oh! Welcome, Your—" Lady Celia said, pausing at a strange look from the boy. "Welcome, Auguste! What brings you to our lovely little corner of Grand Commons today?"

The boy leaned in toward Lady Celia and handed her a letter bound in red ribbon, his whispered words too faint to make out. While Lady Celia read the letter, the boy's eyes darted around at all the curious faces staring back at him. I scooted farther down in my seat and tried to hide behind my fan, but it wasn't enough. Our gazes met, and he gave me a little crooked smile. It was so unexpected, I almost dropped the fan.

"Well, Auguste, you can tell Madame de Maintenon that I would be more than happy to arrange private lessons for you. *These* lessons are for the young ladies of the court. I should be able to arrange something for you tomorrow, but you can stay for today. As long as you don't tell anyone," Lady Celia said with a pointed look at him.

He nodded quickly, and Lady Celia continued. "There's no point in making you walk all the way back to the palace and miss out on valuable knowledge. Besides, I'm sure you won't mind spending time with the ladies. There's a chair for you in the back next to Cendrillon. Please take a seat and we'll continue."

Auguste picked his way carefully through the press of chairs and sat down beside me. Lady Celia went on with the lesson, forgetting entirely that she'd asked me to answer a question. Small blessings. I returned to staring out the window at the gardens, hoping Auguste wouldn't try to talk to me.

Though I tried to focus on the lord outside trying very hard to prevent himself from being thrown off his horse, I could feel Auguste's eyes on me.

"I'm truly sorry about my brother's behavior a few weeks ago," Auguste whispered. "He was terribly rude to you and your friends. Please accept my humblest apologies."

I tore my eyes away from the window to face him, relieved that at least there were no hard feelings from his end. When I looked at him, Auguste offered me a small, slightly nervous smile and glanced down, his cheeks pink.

"You have nothing to apologize for. You weren't the one being rude."

"I should have stepped in sooner. I know what my brother is like better than nearly anyone."

"Well, thank you for the apology. I accept. But I do realize that you can't control your brother and your friends," I said, nodding at Severine and Alexandre.

Auguste grimaced at the word *friends*. "I only met them for the first time that day, and I haven't seen them since. They were not very happy that I called them rude."

Auguste glanced at the girls, who promptly spun around and pretended that they hadn't been staring.

"You and me both. They haven't talked to me once since I joined the lessons a few weeks ago and—"

"Lord and ladies, please pay attention. There is far too much whispering going on," Lady Celia said, scanning the room.

I would've felt guiltier if we were the only ones whispering, but we weren't. In addition to Severine and Alexandre, whispers had cropped up throughout the room. Apparently, I wasn't the only one growing bored with the lessons. When all the whispering quieted down, Lady Celia resumed her pacing.

"Where was I? Oh, yes, the king's public suppers. If you are attending one of the king's suppers, you must bow or curtsy when the royal procession brings the dishes into the antechamber. If you aren't attending but happen to run into the procession elsewhere in the palace as it makes its way to the king, you must still bow or curtsy, as it is another representation of the king."

I sighed more loudly than I would have liked and quickly glanced around to see if anyone heard. Lady Celia continued talking, but Auguste was looking at me and smiling. Of course he had heard.

Auguste whispered, "It is a bit silly, isn't it? Bowing to the king's supper?"

"Just a *tiny* bit," I replied with a raise of an eyebrow.

"Okay, quite a bit silly," he said, laughing. "The king loves pomp and ceremony above all else. It's difficult to master all the rules, clearly. I find it's best just to go along with them while silently bemoaning their absurdity. Or making fun of them with someone who understands."

I smiled at Auguste. Maybe I wasn't so alone in my opinions as I feared.

CHAPTER FIVE

MY SHOES CLACKED LOUDLY ON the wooden floors, the sound echoing off the empty walls of the classroom. The rigaudon was a beautiful dance to watch, with graceful, energetic dancers leaping up into the air in a complex twist of quick steps. But that was the problem. Those complicated steps. I couldn't master them, no matter how much I practiced. And I'd been practicing for the last hour, and an hour before during the last lesson. As I stumbled and nearly fell for the twentieth time in a row, I started to realize that the rigaudon may not be the dance for me.

"If I'm not mistaken, I think those steps are meant to be for a rigaudon, but they're not like any I've seen before."

I jumped, startled, and turned to see Auguste standing in the doorway of the classroom, arms crossed against his chest.

"Please demonstrate how it's done, then," I said as I limped over to one of the chairs and collapsed, desperate to rest my aching legs.

Auguste shrugged, then claimed the empty chair beside me. "I'm too tired from my own dancing lessons to do any more today."

"Oh, really?"

"Yes." Auguste fidgeted in his seat a moment before saying, "To be honest, I don't dance the rigaudon very well either."

"I thought so," I said, leaning back in my seat with a sigh.

"Ouch."

I laughed, then groaned as I felt the ache in my arches. I was going to be sore for days. Thank goodness lessons were over for the week, but Lady Celia had said that noblewomen must know a variety of dances, and so next week would be more of the same.

"Why are you here all by yourself?" Auguste asked. "I was waiting for you on the Latona Parterre for a half an hour. We were supposed to meet. Did you forget?"

"I'm sorry. I didn't forget. My rigaudon was so bad today that Lady Celia made me stay after lessons to keep practicing."

Auguste and I had become something like friends and had taken to roaming the gardens and exploring the halls of Versailles after lessons. I'd told Elodie a little about him but not that she had met him in the Orangerie. All she did was tease me and ask if my mysterious friend at court was very handsome. I told her he was, but more than that, he was the friendliest person I had met at court so far. "I don't understand why we need to master every dance. My allemande and gavotte are more than adequate. Shouldn't that be enough?"

"If you've already mastered the allemande and the gavotte, you're far more advanced than me. My tutor is shocked by how bad I am."

I shouldn't have been surprised to hear that Auguste also had dance lessons. It was mollifying to know I wasn't alone in my labors, especially when the other girls seemed to pick up the lessons so quickly. Especially Severine, who didn't hesitate to point out when I made a mistake or stumbled over a step.

"At least your lessons are private," I said. "There's no one to see

31

you fail but your tutor. Everyone in class heard Lady Celia ask me to stay behind and keep practicing. It was mortifying."

"I am lucky in that regard," Auguste said. He sighed and for a moment looked almost upset as his green eyes clouded over and his perfectly square jaw set. Even the tone in his voice was strange. Like it hurt him to talk about it. I glanced at him to see his eyes fixed on the ground. But he must have felt my eyes on him, since he looked up and smiled shyly. I met his eyes and felt my cheeks burn.

"If you want," he said, "we could practice together. It might be easier to learn that way."

I sat up excitedly in my seat. "Yes, let's! That would be wonderful!"

But the responding throb in my side and feet and legs reminded me that it wouldn't be wonderful today.

"Perhaps another time would be best, though. I'm a bit too sore to do any more dancing over the next few days," I said as my skirts swished around me.

"Next week, then," Auguste said. "Dancing has exhausted me too. My tutor has been just as exacting as Lady Celia."

I laughed in disbelief and caught my reflection in the mirrors all around the back wall. "Does your tutor keep reminding you that perfect mastery of each and every step is the only way to make yourself an attractive prospect for marriage? If not, your tutor is most definitely not as exacting as Lady Celia."

I'd thought my comment was harmless, but Auguste seemed to take it poorly, turning his face abruptly and taking great interest in a painted cherub nearby. What did I say? I didn't mean to hurt him. "Auguste, are you all right?"

"Yes. Yes, I'm fine. It's just . . . marriage is a difficult subject for me."

"Why?" I asked, only afterward realizing how impolite I'd been.

Auguste turned back around and looked at me so intently that it nearly took my breath away. It hadn't registered to me before just how close we were, and the realization set my heart racing. I'd never been this close to any boy besides Marius. But he didn't count: Marius was like a brother to me. Auguste was something else.

"Cendrillon, I need to tell you something," he said, so seriously it made me nervous.

"I'm listening," I said, wondering why he was so grave all of a sudden. Perhaps it had to do with his parents; there was always so much pressure among the aristocracy to please one's elders.

"There's a reason I haven't told you what my family name is, and I appreciate that you haven't pushed me about it."

"I thought it strange that you hadn't introduced yourself fully, but really, the family you come from doesn't matter to me in the slightest."

"But this might." Auguste took a deep breath and exhaled the words in a rush of air. "I'm a bastard. My father was already married when he fell in love with my mother. I don't carry his name, and it's likely that I never will."

A *bastard*. I hadn't even realized that illegitimate children were allowed at court, but it was clear that Auguste was being treated like any other noble child—at least when it came to his education. I wondered if it was unusual, but I didn't dare ask. It seemed as though he expected me to get up and storm out, offended by his very presence.

Auguste fiddled with a button on his waistcoat, and I could see his hands were shaking. Impulsively, I reached out and took his hands in mine. That got him to look at me, and the fear I saw in his eyes made my heart ache. "What does it matter how you were born? You're my friend. That's all that matters."

Auguste's green eyes flashed, as if he hadn't expected that reaction, and then he smiled so brightly that my own lips curved into a smile.

Then he leaned toward me and I leaned toward him, but before I even realized what might be happening, he pulled away and jumped out of his seat, backing away from me slowly as if I were a wild dog.

"What's wrong?" I asked. I made to get up, to follow him, but it was too late. He sprinted from the room and was gone in an instant, as if he'd never been there at all. But he had been about to *kiss* me. I could feel it. He wanted to. But then he ran away, so something must have put him off. Did I do something wrong?

I put a hand to my lips, unsure whether this was an occasion that called for elation or concern.

CHAPTER SIX

"ARE YOU GOING TO THE ball on Wednesday?" Auguste asked.

He'd been waiting for me outside the lesson room. Our walks were a blessed reprieve from our stuffy tutors' endless drilling on proper behavior. Auguste made me feel less lonely in this strange, unfamiliar place.

We never talked about the almost kiss. I wondered if I should bring it up, but the right time never seemed to come. I wished he would say something, but he didn't. It stung, but if he wasn't going to talk about it, then neither was I. Nothing happened, after all, and I wasn't about to let it ruin our friendship. *There will be other boys to kiss*, I told myself.

After leaving the lesson room, we followed our usual path through the servants' corridor and ended up near the Grand Commons' interior courtyard. Auguste was going to give me a tour of the palace. Papa hadn't had time yet, and I'd been too nervous to go myself. Lady Françoise was away visiting her relatives in England.

"I wish I could go to the ball. My father says I'm not allowed until

I've been presented at court. Are you going? You're the same age as me, aren't you?"

"I am, yes. But my father is granting me special permission to attend," he said, tugging at the lacy sleeves of his waistcoat.

"How unfair! I've been dreaming of going to a royal ball for months!" It was all Elodie and I talked about, truly.

"I wish you were coming. It would be much more fun with you there," he said as we meandered down the garden path.

"I wish I was too," I said. "Where in the palace is the ball being held?"

"The music and dancing will be in the Salon of Mars, the food and other events in the Salon of Venus and . . . maybe Abundance, as well. I know it will be spread out across multiple salons."

That was perfect. A plan was beginning to form in my mind. Even if Papa wouldn't let me attend the ball, he might agree to let me remain at Versailles after class. It was a masquerade ball, and if I was masked, maybe I could sneak inside and then I could at least see what all the fuss was about.

Auguste and I made our way into the courtyard. Grouped together by the central fountain were Alexandre and Severine, along with Veronique, Diane, and a few other noble girls from my etiquette class who I didn't know well.

"I heard that certain ladies of the court have been visiting . . ." Veronique said, lowering her voice and leaning forward. "Enchantresses."

We slowed to a stop as we passed the fountain. Enchantresses? Marius said he saw an enchantress in the village once, but I'd never heard anyone talk of *magic* at court. Sorcery was outlawed in France.

"Why would they do that?" Alexandre asked, her blue eyes wide and her mouth agape.

"They want love potions." Veronique paused and smiled as everyone in the group, including me, waited with bated breath for her to continue.

"Potions?" whispered Auguste. "Poisons is more like it."

"Shh," I said. "I want to hear."

"Potions to ensnare the king!" Veronique, who was rather plain-faced no matter how many beauty marks she painted on her chin, declared triumphantly.

Shocked gasps erupted from the group perched on the fountain. Auguste had been a few steps ahead of me, but he froze at Veronique's words.

"Ensnare the king?" Alexandre's voice was shocked. "But the king is married! Oh! So you mean, so they could become his next . . . his next . . ."

"His next *mistress*," Veronique said, rubbing her hands together in glee.

More people gasped. A few laughed nervously. I wasn't sure how to react. As a child, I'd heard Elodie's mother and Claudine whispering about the king's many mistresses, but they always ushered me from the room as soon as they noticed me listening.

Auguste did not look intrigued. His face had gone pale, and his hands clenched into fists.

"How do you know all of this?" Severine asked Veronique, much more skeptical than her sister. Severine and Alexandre looked almost identical, but Severine had a crueler mouth, given to twisting in scorn.

"I have a source who knows one of these enchantresses."

"A source?" Severine demanded, crossing her arms in front of her chest.

"A source." Veronique frowned at Severine and pointedly turned her back on her, focusing on the rest of her onlookers instead. Severine snorted but made no attempt to leave. To be fair, Alexandre, who was sitting next to Veronique on the fountain, looked so enraptured that I don't think Severine could have dragged her away if she tried.

Auguste looked pale enough to faint, and I shot him a questioning look, but he just shook his head.

"My source said that someone close to the king himself has employed the services of one of these enchantresses."

Veronique paused again, the air crackling with tension. I stepped closer to the group, almost unconsciously.

"The queen."

A hush fell over the courtyard. Everyone seemed to freeze in time, the only sound the tinkling of water falling into the fountain's basin. I realized that I was holding my breath and released it in a rush of air.

"But *why* would the queen have anything to do with a sorceress?" I asked, my voice ringing out in the silence of the courtyard.

All eyes turned to me, and the spell was broken. Everything felt normal again when Severine fixed me with a snooty glare.

"Shh! You really are from the country, aren't you?" Veronique said in a low tone, her voice coated in disdain.

I opened my mouth to respond, but no words came. What could I say that wouldn't make me look even sillier than I already did? I *was* from the country and clearly knew less about the goings-on at court than the rest of my classmates.

"Don't be rude, Veronique," Diane said with a frown. "I was wondering the same thing. If I don't know, then surely Cendrillon wouldn't either."

I shut my mouth and smiled gratefully at Diane. I didn't know her very well, but she never made fun of me, which is more than I could say for most of the girls in my class.

Veronique snorted and rolled her eyes. "They say the queen wants a sorceress to cast a spell, or perhaps concoct a love potion, that will win back the king's affections so he'll banish Madame de Maintenon. Apparently, the queen wasn't happy when the king replaced his previous mistress, the late Madame de Montespan, with Madame de Maintenon, and thinks magic is the only way to be rid of her."

Auguste turned away and hurried toward the main gates. I tried to follow, but his legs were longer than mine, and he outpaced me considerably. I started to run after him, but my long skirt complicated matters.

"Auguste!" I said, calling after him when I couldn't catch up.

He briefly stopped at the threshold of the gate to wait for me.

"I have to go, Cendrillon. I'm sorry, but I won't be able to accompany you to the palace today. I'll see you after your next lesson," he said, his voice trembling.

Auguste walked through the gate and disappeared into the crowds bustling in and out of the south wing. I hadn't known him for long, but he didn't seem the type to be scandalized by a little court gossip. He did look quite upset and worried, though. Whatever the reason, I couldn't help feeling inordinately disappointed that we wouldn't be spending the afternoon together.

CHAPTER SEVEN

"THIS IS A TERRIBLE IDEA, Cendrillon. You've had terrible ideas before, but this may be the worst one yet. We're going to get caught!" Elodie said as she, Marius, and I crept up the Ambassador's Staircase. My plan had changed, and instead of staying after lessons, I decided we would just sneak back into the palace because I wanted Elodie and Marius to accompany me. There were so many side doors for servants that we just slipped through one easily.

The staircase was thankfully empty of courtiers because everyone was already at the ball. Muffled laughter and the faintest strains of violin strings echoed down the staircase as we climbed.

"We're *not* going to get caught," I said, but my words belied my jittery pulse.

"You were so confident that it was acceptable for us to visit the Orangerie, weren't you? And look how that turned out!" Elodie declared. She was in a pretty pink-and-gold mask that matched her pink-and-gold ball gown. She looked like a particularly delicious confection.

"But we didn't get in trouble, so does it really matter that things went a little sideways?" Marius asked, pulling at the lacy cravat of his borrowed clothing. Since Elodie was just a little bigger than me, it had been relatively easy to dress her, but I had to do some digging to find something for Marius. I managed to find an old outfit of Papa's buried in a dusty trunk in the attic, and Elodie tailored it perfectly.

"Yes, it does, because it was humiliating!" she said, stopping and glowering from her perch above us on the stairs.

"We're not going to get caught," I said again. "We're all wearing fancy clothes, with actual masks on our faces. You won't be questioned if you're in the palace and look like you belong. No one will be able to tell it's us, and we won't stay for very long," I said as I flicked my fan open. I had borrowed a dress from my mother's closet, a white one with blue ribbons, and found a matching blue mask as well. "I just want to take a fast peek, and then we'll go."

"Promise?" Elodie asked.

"I promise."

I took Elodie's hand and gave it a little shake. Her smile was small, but it was there, so we continued up the stairs. I'd managed to convince our footman that I'd left one of my necklaces at the palace and needed to retrieve it right away, so he drove us up to the palace in our spare coach. Thankfully, he didn't question why all three of us were dressed up. I hoped not to bump into Papa in case he demanded I leave immediately, but I also secretly hoped to see him in this environment. How thrilling to be part of the royal court!

I had never visited the king's state apartments before, but I knew from lessons that the room we were entering at the top of the Ambassador's Staircase was the Salon of Venus. If we started there, then moved through to the Salon of Diana and entered the Salon of Mars, where the dancing was taking place, we would be able to see the entirety of the ball.

Because of the risk of Papa spotting me, this would have to be a quick visit, but I didn't mind. A few minutes would be more than enough.

"We are *not* going to talk to anyone," Elodie said, stopping us before we entered the Salon of Venus. The massive white double doors were thrown open, letting a flood of brilliant light out onto the landing. "None of us knows enough about court life to pass as a courtier, so we stay along the walls and talk to no one."

Elodie's voice was firm as she stared straight into my eyes through her mask, as if she could hypnotize me into doing her bidding. I couldn't argue with her. Even with all my lessons, I wasn't skilled enough in etiquette to interact with people who'd been living and breathing court life.

"I have absolutely no problem with that," Marius said. "I just want to try the pastries."

"I'm not going to talk to anyone, I swear."

Elodie still looked nervous, but she nodded. "All right. Let's go in."

We walked through the doors of the Salon of Venus into a sea of light. Crystal chandeliers hung from the ceiling, along with dozens of candelabras placed strategically on sideboards, casting the room and its inhabitants in a warm glow. The walls were a speckled burgundy marble, glossy and highly reflective in the candlelight. Beautiful murals of frolicking nymphs were painted on the ceiling, and everything was bordered in gold.

Despite the room's elegance and beauty, it was smaller than I had imagined. There wasn't nearly enough room for the number of people milling about, chatting or sipping from the glasses in their hands. Perhaps *milling* wasn't the correct word to describe the movement of the people in the room. There wasn't enough room to mill. The courtiers were packed in and standing shoulder to shoulder. It was clear that there were no other options but to skirt the wall in order to move. Pushing through the middle of the salon seemed far too perilous.

"Ready to go?" I asked, turning to see Elodie staring wide-eyed at art on the ceiling while Marius stared wide-eyed at the tables running along the wall, covered from end to end in delectable-looking confections. Pyramids of oranges and lemons towered next to delicately tiered platters of glistening candied fruits. I spotted golden pastries and chocolate tarts, bowls of nuts, and intricate marzipan creations in the shapes of flowers and animals. Little chocolate-covered marzipans sat on a silver platter on the table right next to where we stood. I couldn't resist grabbing one and popping it in my mouth. The bitter sweetness of the chocolate and the nuttiness of the almond exploded against my tongue. It was so wonderful that I had to stop myself from groaning in pleasure.

"I'm staying here," Marius said, his eyes fixed on the desserts. "Find me when you're done."

"We are not leaving you," said Elodie, but Marius was already walking away.

"He'll be fine. How much trouble can he get into at the dessert table?"

Before Elodie could respond, I grabbed her hand and dove into the crowd of people. We couldn't afford to waste any more time. My cheeks were warm, and my hand slipped as I tried to hold on to Elodie, who bumped into me when I stopped to look at a painting of a pavilion that caught my eye.

"Keep moving. It's awful in here," she said, pushing me forward.

We made it to the door and hurried through, desperate to get away from the throng of courtiers. The windows in the Salon of Diana were opened wide to let in the air. A lovely breeze was blowing through, cooling the room considerably.

"The dancing should be through there," I said, pointing to the two sets of doors leading to the Salon of Mars.

I could hear the music more clearly now, something light and airy with violins and a harpsichord. Opening the door just a touch more, I slipped inside the salon and slid along the wall. Elodie called after me, but I didn't stop to respond.

I surged forward, very nearly bumping into a dancing couple. Then I saw them! Papa and Lady Françoise were dancing together. Papa looked distinguished and handsome in a blue justaucorps brocaded with gold—it was the first time in years he'd worn anything but black—and Lady Françoise was elegant and beautiful in a cream-colored silk ball gown draped in emeralds. She whispered something in his ear as they danced, and Papa tossed his head back and laughed. The way they looked at each other . . . I hadn't seen anything like it since before Maman died. They looked at each other like they were in love.

Tears pricked my eyes, but I blinked them away. I wasn't going to cry. I adored Lady Françoise, and she made Papa happy. I wanted him to be happy more than anything.

I was just backing away from the dance floor when a dark-haired boy seated on a dais at the far end of the salon caught my eye. Auguste.

He had told me that his father gave him permission to attend the ball, but why was he seated on a dais? It was only when I spotted who he was sitting next to that I realized what was going on. He was seated next to the king, who was leaning over to speak to the boy on his other side. Auguste's older brother, the horrid, rude boy from the Orangerie.

Only members of the royal family were allowed to sit with the king. Which meant . . . Auguste and his awful brother must be the king's sons. They were princes. Or at least the older one was; he was the Grand Dauphin, Louis.

Just a few moments ago, I'd been so happy, but now I didn't know what to feel. Auguste wasn't just a bastard; he was the king's bastard. High-ranking, regardless of the circumstances of his birth. Papa told me once that kings often legitimized their bastard children, especially bastard sons. I turned away and promptly smacked into a woman standing behind me.

"I beg your pardon, please forgive . . ." I said, the words dying in my throat as my eyes met hers.

The woman was wearing perhaps the most magnificent red dress I'd ever seen. The neckline was cut high and off the shoulder, the skirt cascading to the floor in waves of ruby-encrusted silk brocade. A gold-and-ruby mask covered half her face, with horns that curled delicately upward like a crown. She was stunning, but her cold blue eyes pierced right through me, and the scent of rose perfume, thick and cloying, wafted off her in waves. She had two matching beauty marks shaped like apples on her cheek as well, the very latest fashion.

I'd nearly knocked the contents of her glass all over her ball gown. The liquid still sloshed around the sides of the crystal.

"You're very lucky you didn't ruin my dress, ma chérie," the woman said. She looked me up and down with a calculating gaze. I was used to being appraised at court—people were intimately concerned with whether your clothes were laced with silk and if your fans were made of feathers or cloth.

"That's quite a lovely gown," she told me. "It must have cost a pretty penny."

"Thank you, Madame," I said with a curtsy. "It was my mother's dress from when she was at court. Our seamstress is skilled, and my father is a generous man. I am very lucky." It was a gorgeous gown of the finest Venetian white lace, with just a simple blue sash for effect.

"Your mother? Would I know her?"

"Alas, she is no longer with us." I bowed my head.

She clucked her tongue. "How sad. But your father is here, yes? Who is this wonderful man, if I may ask? I will have to tell him his daughter is a delight."

"Michel le Tellier, le Marquis de Louvois," I said with pride.

"The king's minister?" she said. "You truly are a lucky girl." The woman's voice was sweet and her tone friendly, but there was something unnerving about the way she studied me. And I suddenly realized I had told a lady of the court my name. If she told my father she'd met me at the ball, I would be in awful trouble. Papa did not take kindly to liars and sneaks.

I needed to find Elodie. We had to leave. The fear coiling in my stomach didn't make any sense. While the lady's words were nothing but kind, her cold eyes made me want to run as far from her as possible. "Excuse me, Madame," I said hurriedly.

"Elodie!" I said, spotting her standing at the door to the Salon of Venus, talking to a girl.

Elodie was smiling and laughing. The conversation appeared to be quite lively. Both girls turned at my call, and I got a clearer look at Elodie's conversation partner. It was Alexandre. Elodie, one of the shyest people I knew, was having a pleasant conversation with this awful girl, of all people. When Alexandre spotted me, the smile dropped from her face, and with a whispered word to Elodie, she left the room in a whirl of skirts. She and Severine were a year older than I was and not just out in society but actually invited to the ball. I envied that they didn't have to sneak in to be part of it.

"Was that Alexandre? When did you get to know each other?" I asked when I reached Elodie. "I didn't know you two were so chummy."

"And what if we are?" Elodie said defensively. "We met . . . I don't know . . . a while back. Does it matter?"

At my skeptical look, she said, "I know. It's hard to believe. But she apologized for her behavior at the Orangerie. She seems quite lovely."

Elodie blushed and smiled. Any other time I would want to hear more, but right now we needed to leave.

"You can tell me about it when we're back home. Let's find Marius and go."

"So soon?"

"Yes," I said emphatically. I wanted to get out of there as soon as I could. My only friend at Versailles was the king's illegitimate son. I'd heard a rumor that one of the king's other mistresses poisoned his mother, Madame de Montespan, for being the king's favorite. No one knew if it was true, but it was no wonder he'd been upset by all the talk of potions, poisons, and mistresses.

Elodie pressed her palm to my forehead. Her hand was cool on my flushed skin. Maybe I was sick, which gave us another reason for us to leave.

"I'll explain everything in the carriage, but for now can we please find Marius?"

Elodie's eyes scrutinized my face. She bit her lip but nodded and followed me into the Salon of Venus.

This night wasn't at all what I'd anticipated, and at the moment I wished I'd stayed home.

CHAPTER EIGHT

A FEW WEEKS AFTER MY disastrous infiltration of the ball, Papa sat me down in our kitchen, his face serious but his eyes gleaming. "Cendrillon, sit with me for a minute. You're always at your lessons or running about at the palace. I feel like I never get to talk to you anymore."

I took a seat at the worn oak table that we brought from our old house: its sturdiness and finish polished by the years always made me feel safe. But yes, I had been distracted lately. I hadn't seen Auguste since discovering he was the king's son, and I'd spent a lot of time asking around the palace to find out where he was, so I suppose I had been neglecting Papa. Lady Françoise hadn't been by to visit, so he must have been terribly lonely.

"Of course! Lessons have been taking up a lot of my time recently."

"I understand. You're growing up, becoming a lady of the court. My little girl will be leaving me soon enough."

"I'm not leaving you," I said, grabbing his hands and squeezing.

Papa patted my hands gently and smiled. His eyes were gleaming brightly, but they were also a bit red, and the dark circles under his eyes were more prominent than usual. A twinge of guilt needled at me. Was missing me upsetting him this much? Papa was always so busy with the king that I never thought he would notice.

"Yes, you will, and that's the way it's supposed to be. I'm not looking forward to it, but the day is coming when you'll marry and move on. That's partly the reason I want to speak with you. I've started making plans."

I gripped his hands tighter. This conversation was making me uneasy.

"Plans? What kind of plans?"

"Plans for the eventuality of you leaving me. After your mother died . . . you were all I had. I don't know if I would have made it through those first few months after she was gone without you."

"Nor I you," I said, trying very hard not to cry.

"Well, uh, yes, it's true. You've been a blessing to me since the day you were born, but I can't hold on to you forever. But I'm not the kind of man who does well alone either. Now I want you to know that I'm not replacing you—I'm just trying to ensure that I'm not hopelessly lonely when you're all grown up and don't need me anymore."

Papa's final words were rushed and a little breathless, and he looked at me with wide eyes, almost hesitant, as if he was afraid I would be angry with him.

"I don't expect you to think of her as your mother. You're far too old for that. But I want us to be a family."

"A family?"

Papa cleared his throat. "I've been preparing this speech for ages, and I didn't even tell you the most important part. I'm getting married, Cendrillon."

My mouth dropped open, and I couldn't muster the will to close it, no matter how uncouth it was. Married. Papa was getting married. When I saw him and Lady Françoise at the ball, gazing into each other's eyes, I could tell they were in love, but I wasn't sure anything would come of it. They'd been friends for so many years, after all.

I jumped out of seat and threw my arms around him.

"That's wonderful, Papa! I'm so happy for you," I said, my words muffled by the tears I wasn't able to contain any longer.

Papa held me tightly and patted my back.

"Are you crying because you're happy or sad?" he asked, a touch of worry in his voice.

"Happy! Absolutely happy! I love her already! You know that!"

"Good! That's good. I thought you would be, but I wasn't entirely sure. Lady Catherine will be thrilled that you're taking this so well. It took some persuasion to bring her daughters around."

I pulled back to look at him. "Excuse me? Lady Catherine? Wh-who is she?"

Papa laughed and said, "The woman I'm going to marry, of course. Lady Catherine Monvoisin. I'm so excited for you to meet her. And her daughters. You'll have sisters! Won't that be wonderful?"

I didn't say anything. I couldn't say anything. Not when the words coming out of Papa's mouth were completely incomprehensible.

"What about Lady Françoise?" I asked weakly.

"What about her?"

"Aren't you two still . . . friends?"

"Of course we're friends," he said somewhat impatiently, checking his pocket watch in his waistcoat. "But I'm not sure what that has to do with my marriage to Catherine."

Could I have misread the signals between Papa and Lady Françoise so badly? The way they danced together at the ball had been all but proof to me that they had feelings for each other. Friends didn't gaze into each other's eyes the way they did.

I managed to muster up enough conviction to ask, "When did you meet Lady Catherine?"

Papa was practically beaming as he said, "At the ball a few weeks ago."

"Oh," I said weakly.

"By the way, I saw you at the ball too! But I didn't want to embarrass you. You'll be out in society soon and will have no need to sneak into royal balls," said Papa.

I was too rattled to realize Papa knew my secret. Instead I was still reeling from his news. "You've only known each other for a few weeks and you're already getting married?" I said, my voice growing louder with each word.

I immediately regretted my tone when I saw the dejected look on Papa's face. He looked crushed above his white linen cravat.

"I don't mean to be unsupportive, Papa. I'm happy for you. I am. This is just all very sudden. I wasn't expecting such . . . wonderful news."

"I know, ma petite beauté. I know it's sudden. It's sudden for me too! But when I first talked to Catherine, she cast a spell on me. She felt it too—she said it was love at first sight. And at my age, I can't afford to drag my feet."

Papa looked so hopeful. Even though I was nearly sick with confusion, I couldn't take that happiness away from him by being difficult.

"When is the wedding?" I asked, pasting a smile on my face.

"Well, that's another thing," he said with a wince. "It's in two days."

My smile vanished. "Two *days*! But that's so soon!"

"I know. I know. We've been planning this since I proposed two weeks ago, but I put off telling you until the last minute."

I laughed despite myself and said, "That might be the least surprising thing you've said today."

Papa mock-glared at me but started to laugh when I hugged him again. I buried my face in his shoulder to hide the tears gathering in my eyes. I was a lady. Nearly fully grown. And that meant I had to give up the childish fantasy of my father and Lady Françoise falling in love.

And it wasn't all bad. Surely Lady Catherine would be a lovely person. Papa wouldn't marry her otherwise.

"Are you all right with this, Cendrillon? If I could have told you sooner, I would have."

"That doesn't matter. I'm happy for you. Truly."

Papa kissed me on the forehead. "I'm glad you're excited," he said. "That makes it all so much easier. I knew when I asked for her hand that she was the perfect person to bring into our family."

The morning of the wedding dawned bright and warm, far too warm for this early in the morning. The ceremony was being held at a little chapel in a town in the outskirts of Versailles. Papa sent me ahead while he went to pick up Lady Catherine and escort her to the chapel. I stood outside, anxiously staring down the little road and waiting for the carriage to appear. I was jittery, bouncing on the balls of my feet and pacing back and forth in front of the big wooden front door. The priest offered to let me wait inside, but I was too nervous to sit still in the dark, musty chapel. I hadn't seen much of Papa in the past two days, busy as he was preparing for his new bride's move to the château, so I was anxious to see him and meet Lady Catherine and her daughters.

I'd tried to reach Lady Françoise and even sent a message to her château, but none of my messages were returned. I wondered what she thought about all this. She was Papa's best friend, and it seemed odd for her to miss his wedding.

A cloud of dust kicked up farther down the road and grew closer every second. If I strained my ears, I could hear the faint clopping of hooves in the distance. They were here. I ran down the gray stone steps and stood in the little courtyard, waiting for them. Time seemed to slow as I watched Papa's coach get closer and closer, then finally pull into the courtyard and rattle to a stop on the cobblestones.

Papa hurried to open the door to the coach. I first saw a skirt of gold brocade with a matching golden fringe running along the hemline and multiple satin petticoats, then a gold high-heeled slipper dotted with pearls emerged. An enormous tower of pale blond hair, nearly silver in the sunlight, studded with pearls and adorned with a tall cap made of ruffled lace, tilted out of the door. Two curled strands of hair escaped and tumbled delicately to a woman's shoulders. That must have been the new fontange hairstyle Lady Celia mentioned in lessons. It was quite impressive, to say the least. Each wrist had a pearl bracelet, and around her neck hung a triple-strand necklace of pearls and diamonds. It looked just like the one in my mother's jewelry box . . . It was my mother's.

Lady Catherine started walking in my direction, but I was distracted by the people who exited the coach after her. Alexandre and Severine. When they saw me, they stopped abruptly, causing Papa to bump into them as he climbed down after.

I felt as though I'd been struck. Alexandre and Severine must be Lady Catherine's daughters. I'd been cautiously optimistic about the wedding, but the appearance of the two girls ruined any happy anticipation I might have had.

"Ah, Cendrillon," the woman said, fixing me with her pale blue eyes and smiling warmly. "We meet again! Your father has told me so much about you, I feel I know you already."

My mind was blank. All I could do was stare up at the taller woman silently. There were two dark spots on her face, one on the apple of each powdered cheek. When I looked closer, I realized they were beauty marks in the shape of hearts. This was the woman from the night of the ball, the one who had asked about my father after I told her he was a generous man.

"Lady Catherine," I said, my voice hoarse, as if I hadn't spoken in weeks. "A pleasure to make your acquaintance." I barely remembered to curtsy.

Papa approached us, escorting Severine and Alexandre. They were both as tall and beautiful as their mother, in silver dresses that matched their silver hair. Except Severine looked angry, her lips pursed into a pout as she alternated between glaring at me and her mother. Alexandre looked as confused as I felt, her mouth opening and closing as if she were trying to formulate a sentence.

"Isn't it a beautiful morning, Cendrillon?" Papa asked, beaming at me. His face was glowing as he took the woman's arm and squeezed her hand. "I'm so happy to finally be able to introduce you to Lady Catherine, my beautiful bride-to-be."

"Oh, Michel," the woman said fondly as she gazed up at him.

"I only wish I'd been able to introduce you two sooner, but everything happened so fast, there simply wasn't time. I'm happy that we are all together now."

I was sick with dismay at the thought of Alexandre and Severine becoming my stepsisters. My head had begun to pound, and I was starting to feel a little dizzy.

"And of course, we can't forget Alexandre and Severine," he said.

"We know each other." Severine's words were sharp, but the smile she gave my father was sickly sweet. "We're in etiquette lessons together. I adore Cendrillon."

"Wonderful! You three are already well on your way to becoming sisters. Now it's just you and Cendrillon who must become better acquainted, mon amour."

"I'm looking forward to it. I think you and I are going to be the best of friends," Lady Catherine said.

She ran her fingers through my hair and patted my cheek gently. Her hand was warm, almost hot against my skin.

"Monsieur le Marquis, we must commence with the ceremony," the priest said from the top of the stairs.

The cool darkness of the chapel's interior called to me. My thoughts were muddled and hazy, but I knew if I didn't get out of the heat soon, I was going to faint.

"Let's get inside. We'll have time after the wedding to talk more," Papa called over his shoulder, escorting Lady Catherine up the stairs and into the chapel.

Severine followed without a backward glance, but Alexandre stayed by my side.

"Did you know . . . ?" I asked, trailing off as I couldn't figure out how to string together a question diplomatic enough to not offend her.

I wouldn't normally trust Alexandre as a source of information, but there were no other options. And Elodie seemed to like her, so she couldn't be all bad.

"I had no idea," Alexandre said in a whisper as we walked side by side up the steps. "A few days ago, Maman told us she was getting married, but I had no idea it was to your father. It's all very sudden."

"Yes. Yes, it is."

It was dark inside the little chapel. Mismatched candles were jammed into sconces that dotted the thick stone walls, and while there was a window in each one, they were small and barely let in any light. The air was so thick with the scent of incense that it was hard to breathe. My head hurt, but the priest was herding our little group to the altar, so there was no time to stop and rest.

"Papa, should we sit in the pews?" I asked as we waited for the priest to fetch his missal.

I wanted to sit down, catch my breath as much as I possibly could in the hazy air, and think. Everything was happening far too fast, so fast that I couldn't wrap my head around it all. Not only was Papa marrying a woman that I was only meeting today, but her daughters were Severine and Alexandre.

"No. Absolutely not, Cendrillon," Lady Catherine said, linking her arm with mine and pulling me forward to stand next to her. "I want you, Severine, and Alexandre by our sides while we wed. We're a family now. It's important to us that you share in this moment."

I glanced nervously at Papa, but he just smiled encouragingly at me. I wished he could say something to guide me, to help me understand how to feel about all this.

"I would love to stand with you, Lady Catherine," I said, pasting a smile on my face.

"Wonderful!"

She beamed and kissed me on the cheek. Her lips were cool on my flushed skin. I didn't have any other option but to go along with it all.

"Are we ready to begin?" the priest asked, positioning himself in front of Lady Catherine and Papa.

"Yes!" she said, opening her missal with a snap.

The priest began the mass, his sonorous voice lending an air of solemnity and finality to the proceedings. This was really happening. Papa was marrying Lady Catherine, a woman he barely knew and I didn't know at all—a woman who was the mother of two girls I greatly disliked. There was no going back after this. Everything was going to change.

I watched Papa throughout the ceremony. He could barely take his eyes off Lady Catherine, eyes that looked at her reverently. I don't think I'd ever seen him smile as much as he smiled at her. For her part, she gazed at him just as much, then cried a bit when the priest announced that they were married. She practically swooned during their first kiss as husband and wife. Papa looked happy. They both looked happy. This sudden marriage was confusing, and I didn't like it, but Lady Catherine appeared pleasant enough, and it was obvious that she made Papa happy. I would accept it, but only because it was what Papa wanted.

CHAPTER NINE

ELODIE FOUND ME HIDING IN the stables amongst the horses, tucked in the corner, reading a book. Out of all the places I'd taken refuge in over the past few weeks, the stables were my favorite. They were small and fairly isolated, perched on a cleared section of lawn next to the château.

The soft whickering and snuffles of the horses made for soothing background noises while reading or trying to calm down, and a few blankets pilfered from the linen cupboard made the stables downright cozy.

I'd started taking refuge in the stables after Lady Catherine began exerting control over the château in ways I didn't agree with. Like sending Claudine away.

I'd entered the sitting room one morning to see Papa and Lady Catherine seated on the sofa, with Claudine standing in front of them. Her back was to me when I walked in, ramrod straight as usual. Her hands were clasped behind her, and I could see how painfully white and bloodless her knuckles were.

"A carriage will pick you up in two days' time," Lady Catherine said, a serene smile on her face. "Please have your things packed by then."

Without a word, Claudine turned and left the sitting room. She didn't even look at me as she passed, but I saw that her lips were pressed tight together and her eyes shone with tears. The expression on her face scared me. I hadn't seen Claudine cry since Maman died.

"Papa, what's going on?"

"Claudine is being sent to manage your father's old château," Lady Catherine said.

"But why? Don't we need her here?"

"We don't, actually. I can manage this estate on my own. Claudine will be more useful at the old château, to oversee its sale. Once it is finalized, she will go on her way."

I didn't know how to respond to what Lady Catherine was telling me. Losing Claudine was unimaginable. It wasn't right to send her away from her home. She was part of the family. And they were selling our *home*? It was too much to bear.

"Papa, this isn't fair! You can't send Claudine away!"

"Cendrillon, it's already done," Papa said, standing in front of newly installed velvet curtains. "There's no use arguing about it."

"But, Papa. You can't—"

"No," he said impatiently, voice raspy as he began to cough between breaths. "Do not disrespect your stepmother. When you're the lady of your own house, you can make the decisions. Until then, don't argue. Catherine is right, and we have no use for a house in the country."

Tears stung my eyes. Papa was never this testy with me, not unless I'd done something really wrong. And I hadn't done anything wrong. Before I could protest, he snatched a handkerchief off the table and clutched it to his mouth as he continued to cough.

"Michel, don't be so hard on the girl. You're upsetting yourself, which is not good for someone who's been feeling so poorly. Drink the tea the physician recommended, mon chéri," Lady Catherine said, sliding a teacup across the table to Papa. "Cendrillon, I understand that you're upset, but this is really for the best."

I didn't answer. There was no point. They weren't listening to me. I ran from the sitting room. I had to find Claudine. Instead, I found Severine, nearly smacking her with the door she'd been pressed up against in an attempt to eavesdrop.

"Watch where you're going!" Severine said, frowning and smoothing the skirts that rumpled when she'd dodged to avoid the door.

"You shouldn't be eavesdropping."

Severine sneered. "I wasn't eavesdropping. I just *happened* to over-hear you throwing a tantrum over the housekeeper being sent away. You and those servants. I truly don't understand your fascination with them."

I went upstairs and all through the house, trying to find Claudine. I didn't find her, but I did make my way to the stables and remained there for a few hours. No one ever looked for me there. Not Lady Catherine. Certainly not Severine. Not even Papa. Only Marius and Elodie. And it was Elodie who walked past the stables and petted a few of the horses before finding me.

"What are you doing in here?" Elodie asked, plopping down on the straw next to me. She was dressed in a servant's uniform with a lace apron and cap. Lady Catherine insisted on it. My mother and Claudine never required it.

"What are *you* doing in here?"

"I'm currently looking for spare bits of fabric in the attic," she said with a tight smile.

"Really? The attic has changed a great deal since I last saw it. When did the horses move in?"

Elodie slapped my arm playfully, and we laughed a bit. It felt nice to laugh. I hadn't had much occasion for it lately.

"If you must know, I told Lady Catherine I was looking for fabric so I could get away for a little while. I've been making a whole host of new dresses for her, Alexandre, and Severine. It's awful. I've been sewing nonstop for ages."

"She's made an awful lot of changes since she moved in, hasn't she?" I said, my shoulders slumping.

"Did you hear she's sending Claudine back to manage the sale of our old château?"

"Yes," I said, tearing up again and then rubbing at my eyes furiously. I couldn't imagine a home without Claudine in it. I'd been ambivalent about Lady Catherine until now, but dismissing Claudine and selling our old house was more than enough to spoil my opinion of her. Not to mention that she was running Elodie ragged.

"Don't cry," Elodie said, but she was starting to tear up too.

Elodie had known Claudine for as long as I had, and that house had been her home too. I grabbed her hand and squeezed it. She squeezed back, and we remained like that for a few moments, quietly trying to compose ourselves.

"Lady Catherine wants me to give my room to Severine," I said, the words tumbling out unbidden. "I don't want to sound like a horrid, pampered brat, and my room really isn't that important, but she's making so many changes, and Papa goes along with each one."

We'd been seated at the dinner table when Lady Catherine brought up the subject of switching rooms.

"Ma choupette," Lady Catherine had said, the dim candlelight barely illuminating the sweet smile on her face. "How would you feel about changing rooms with Severine?"

"What do you mean?" I asked, looking from my father to Severine and Alexandre as I tried to figure out what was happening.

"Your father and I have been talking, and Severine's chambers are quite small. She doesn't have nearly enough room for all her dresses, and some of her furniture would need to be put into storage. Because you don't have as many things as she does, economical girl that you are, we thought the smaller chambers would suit you perfectly."

I turned to look at Papa, hoping that he would intervene and say it wasn't true, that he never told Lady Catherine any such thing. But he just smiled at me as he sipped from his cup of tea and said, "I think it would be an awfully nice gesture, Cendrillon. It's important to make your stepsisters feel comfortable here."

Once again, Papa wasn't going to support me, an occurrence that used to be unheard of but was becoming more and more common. Severine smirked at me from across the table. I felt sick, the lamb on my plate now wholly unappetizing. Everything was coming unmoored around me, and I had nothing to hold to keep me steady.

The horses neighed quietly. At least their lives hadn't changed. Unlike some people's.

"Severine is a piece of work, isn't she?" Elodie said with a roll of her eyes.

"Yes. She's as awful as ever, but not when my father is around. Then she's a perfect angel."

I also couldn't find Lady Françoise, but I wasn't comfortable revealing that to Elodie just yet. I was too worried about her to be able to talk about it. Lady Françoise wasn't staying at her lodgings in the palace, and I got no response after writing to the housekeeper of her château in town. I even asked my tutor, Lady Celia, if she'd heard anything, but she knew only that Lady Françoise hadn't appeared at court in a while.

First Auguste disappeared on me, then Lady Françoise, right when I needed her the most. I suspected it had something to do with my father's wedding, but it felt like a betrayal to Papa to think that.

"I haven't interacted much with Lady Catherine," said Elodie. "She doesn't come to the servants' quarters and never speaks to us unless she needs something."

"But I suppose Alexandre has changed, hasn't she? You two have been spending quite a lot of time together."

Elodie blushed a florid pink and smacked me again.

I scooted away from her, laughing. "Ow! What was that for?"

"We have *not* been spending a lot of time together. She sometimes visits the sewing room while I'm working, that's all. We mostly talk about fabrics and patterns, or what people are wearing at court. She's interested in fashion."

"Of course. Fashion is what Alexandre is interested in," I said with a wink.

Elodie made as if to topple me over, but we were interrupted by Alexandre bursting into the stables, slightly sweaty and a little out of breath.

"Oh! Hello, Cendrillon. I didn't realize you were in here. I was just looking for Elodie. I saw her come in here and—" Alexandre said, gasping between each word.

"Did you run here?" Elodie asked, bemused.

"Well, yes. I saw you come in and I didn't want to lose sight of you, so I did . . . run."

Alexandre and Elodie made a perfect blushing pair. They both looked as if someone had daubed their cheeks in far too much rouge.

"I was hoping—well—that you might . . ." Alexandre was stuttering over her words and looking anywhere but at Elodie. It was quite adorable. My opinion on Alexandre had continued to change over the short time we'd been living together. She was actually quite sweet-natured, like Elodie. We didn't interact much, but she tried to calm Severine during her outbursts and even apologized for her sister's behavior.

"Do you mind coming with me for a walk around the grounds?" Alexandre asked while staring at a particularly fascinating piece of straw on the ground. "I haven't been able to explore properly yet, and I thought you might show me around."

"Me?" I balked.

"No!" Alexandre blurted. "I meant . . ."

I didn't think that Elodie's face could get any more red. I was wrong. For a moment I was afraid that I might have to call for a doctor. When she didn't respond beyond a blank stare, I poked Elodie in the back and nodded toward Alexandre. "Oh! Of course. Please go. You've been working so hard—you deserve a break. I know you don't want to be sitting in the boring old stables with me."

"Will you be all right?" Elodie asked.

"I'll be fine. I'm just a little gloomy today."

Elodie squeezed my hand one last time before climbing to her feet and turning to Alexandre.

In a voice stronger than I expected after all the blushing, she said, "I would love to show you the grounds. Maybe we could start at the pond? There's a lovely path that winds its way from the back of the house, through the trees, to a peaceful little pond that's perfect for picnics."

Alexandre's responding smile was tentative but bright.

Before they left, Elodie ran back to give me a quick hug. "Why don't you try to talk to your father about Severine and Lady Catherine?" she whispered in my ear. "I'm sure he'll listen."

She pulled away, gave me a reassuring smile, and walked out of the stables with Alexandre. Elodie was right. I hadn't made my concerns clear to Papa. I just sat back and let Severine bully me and Lady Catherine send Claudine away without making any real objections. Papa would surely listen if I presented my issues calmly and clearly.

I pulled myself off the floor with some difficulty and made my way back to the château. If I was going to keep sequestering in the stables, I needed to bring a chair in with me. I was far too sore for this to be a feasible solution without having a seat. Hopefully, Papa would help me resolve the issues in our new family so that I wouldn't have to hide in the stables just to get a little peace.

Unfortunately, the first person I encountered when I entered the sitting room looking for Papa was Severine, delicately perched on a chair, with needlework in hand. When she caught sight of me, she frowned. "Is that straw on your skirt?"

I looked down. My skirt was indeed covered in straw. I brushed at it vigorously, sending a flurry of straw onto the Persian rug the king gifted to Papa. That wasn't going to be fun to clean up.

"And why do you smell of horse?" she asked, her nose wrinkled in disgust.

Before I could reply, she continued. "You've clearly been cavorting about the grounds, probably with your little servant friends. They're a terrible influence on you." She pursed her pretty lips in condescension.

Sudden irritation flared in my stomach. "What is *that* supposed to mean?"

Severine smiled sweetly. "It means that, no matter how many etiquette lessons you take, if you keep associating with servants and running about like a child, you'll never become a proper lady of the court. Your poor father, to have such a child. Thankfully, he has me and Alexandre now."

Papa walked into the sitting room, preventing me from saying something I knew I would regret. I bit the inside of my cheek so hard, I tasted blood, but it was better than saying something that would make him angry or think that I was being disingenuous. But I so wanted to tell Severine off for insulting my friends.

"Hello, girls. How are you both this fine morning?"

"I'm wonderful, Papa," said Severine. "How are you?"

I clenched my fists in my skirts to hear her call my father that.

Papa of course loved being called "Papa." He beamed. "I'm well. A little tired, but it's nothing a little fresh air won't fix. I was hoping to take a walk with your mother. Have you seen her?"

"I think she's resting in her room. I can fetch her, if you'd like."

"That would be lovely, Severine, thank you."

"Of course. I'm more than happy to help," she said, practically preening.

Severine bustled out of the room with one last sly wink in my direction. Papa dropped heavily onto the sofa and sank back into the cushions. He really did look tired. His face was sallow and his eyes were bloodshot. Affairs at Versailles must be stressful, and I'm sure the changes to our family weren't making things easier. I had to be gentle with him so as not to cause any more stress.

"And how are you, ma fille? Is that straw on your dress?"

"It is, but that isn't important right now. Papa, can I talk to you? It's urgent."

"Of course. Sit here with me and tell me what's wrong," he said, patting the cushion beside him.

I sat down carefully, unsure how to proceed. If he really was sick, I didn't want to burden him with my problems.

"Are you happy?" I asked him. "I mean, now that Lady Catherine, Severine, and Alexandre have moved in?"

"I haven't been this happy in a long time. Meeting Catherine at my age and persuading her to marry me was a stroke of luck I didn't think I would have again after your mother died. And that she has two daughters to become your sisters makes it even better."

"Good. That's good," I said, unable to disguise my disappointment at his words.

Papa coughed a dry, heaving cough into his elbow a few times.

"What would you like to talk about, Cendrillon? I understand that all the changes must be difficult for you. Tell me how I can help."

"Have you been drinking your tea, Papa?" I asked, concerned about his persistent coughing. "The doctor won't be happy if he finds out you haven't been following his orders."

Papa waved me off. "Yes. Yes. I'm drinking the tea. Catherine won't let me skip even a night. But we're not talking about me. What's wrong?"

"It's about Severine, first of all," I said tentatively, deciding to go with the topic that might offend him the least. Lady Catherine could be saved until I was sure he was receptive.

"Are you two not getting along? She's a lovely girl," said Papa before coughing again. He leaned back farther into the new sofa in our redecorated sitting room.

"I'm sure she is lovely. To you. But not to me. Or to Elodie and Marius. With us, she is worse than unpleasant."

Papa started coughing again, so fiercely his entire body shook. A horrible, gasping wheeze was emanating from his chest.

"Papa, what's wrong?" I asked, fear causing the words to come out as more of a garbled cry than an actual sentence.

I grabbed his arm to steady him, my hands trembling so much, I could barely hold on to him. The coughing wouldn't stop. He couldn't speak. He couldn't lift his head to look at me. All he could do was cough so hard, he began to choke.

My entire body went numb. I didn't know what to do. *What was I supposed to do?*

A particularly strong spasm wracked Papa's body, sending him sliding off the sofa and onto the floor. I slid off with him as I tried to keep him upright, but his weight was too much for me to prevent him from falling.

"Lady Catherine! Severine! Help!" I screamed.

I knelt by Papa's side, tears blurring my vision. Time slowed to a crawl around me. My fingers were sluggish and clumsy as I attempted to untie his cravat, his skin burning hot. Maybe that was the problem. Maybe the cravat was just too tight and everything would be fine again when I untied it, and then Papa would open his eyes and laugh at how ridiculous I was being. But he didn't open his eyes. When I untied the cravat and tossed it to the side, he continued to lie on the floor. Eyes closed. Not moving. Barely breathing. And a strange rash upon his neck.

CHAPTER TEN

IT RAINED ON THE DAY of Papa's funeral. Dark clouds hung heavy in the sky, periodically deluging the assembled mourners. Thunder rumbled in the distance, close enough to be ominous but far enough that we only saw a few streaks of lightning in the sky. The air was warm and sticky with humidity. Everyone was constantly wiping perspiration from their brows and tugging at their soaked clothing.

It was a long, uncomfortable walk in the procession from the church to the cemetery, even when it was only drizzling. Some had parasols, some didn't. Lady Catherine had one umbrella that she, Alexandre, and Severine were all huddled beneath. There was no room for me, but I didn't mind. The cool rain felt nice on my sweaty skin, and ruining my mourning dress didn't bother me in the slightest. It was an awful thing, heavy and scratchy, far too hot. I was drowning in that dress. Elodie and Marius were next to me, equally drenched in their scratchy black clothing.

Bells boomed sonorously in the church tower as Papa's body was laid to rest in the newly built Louvois tomb. Lady Catherine insisted that someone of Papa's status should have a family tomb and somehow persuaded the king to pay for its construction. King Louis XIV was present at the funeral, sequestered from the rest of the attendants with his retinue, including some of Papa's fellow advisors. Even the dauphin was there, but Auguste, disappointingly, did not come.

Lady Françoise wasn't there either. I looked for her. I waited for her. But she didn't come. Why would she not attend Papa's funeral? I could understand that she might have been upset that Papa married Lady Catherine, but so upset that she refused to even come to the funeral? She didn't want to see me, even just to offer her condolences? She never replied to my messages. At first I thought she was upset about the wedding, but now I was getting worried it was something else.

Damp strands of hair stuck to my neck, and water was running into my eyes, mixing with the tears. I squeezed them shut so tightly that they ached. I didn't want to see Papa carried into the tomb, that big iron door closed and locked, leaving him alone in the dark. At the wake, when everyone walked through his bedroom to view the body, I had to hide in my room, unable to look at him like that, his handsome face swollen and blue, skin waxy. It didn't look like my father anymore, and I wanted to remember Papa as he'd been when he was alive, laughing at something silly I said or smiling at Maman.

From the moment Papa collapsed in the sitting room, nothing in my life felt real or permanent anymore. In the week since he died, I had woken every morning begging and pleading with the heavens to bring him back. I would run to his chambers with the senseless, inexplicable hope that he would be alive, that he would hug me and tell me it was all just a bad dream, like he did when I was a child. But the cold, inert body on the bed and the black crepe covering all the window and mirrors, throwing the château into shadow, made it clear that it wasn't a dream, and he wasn't coming back.

It all happened so quickly. Papa was fine, and then he wasn't. After Lady Catherine and I dragged him up to his bedchamber and called for a doctor, he deteriorated rapidly. Pneumonia claimed his lungs, said the doctor, and there was nothing to be done. But he'd been *fine*. He had a cough and was feeling poorly, to be sure, but the doctor had assured us that nothing was seriously wrong. And Papa kept drinking the tea that the doctor prescribed. But he was still dead within two days. The doctor claimed that such an illness could come on suddenly, swiftly wreaking havoc on the body until it was too late.

I'd been distracted. Even Papa noticed it. I wasn't paying attention when I should have been, and now my father was dead, and I was an orphan.

The clang of the iron door closing rang out through the cemetery. I kept my eyes shut. I couldn't look. I wouldn't look. It wasn't real if I didn't look.

Someone grabbed my arm and squeezed. Hard. My eyes flew open, and I found Lady Catherine glaring at me from under her umbrella. "You look ridiculous. Open your eyes. The king is coming," she said in a low voice, inclining her head toward the advancing king.

I jerked my arm out of her grasp and pulled away.

"Let go of me," I said, much louder than I'd intended.

Lady Catherine was too preoccupied with the king to follow as I moved away from the gathered mourners to stand by myself, Elodie and Marius a few feet to my side. My stomach roiled. It was hard to breathe through the tears and the rain. I didn't want anyone to touch me. I didn't want anyone to talk to me. I just wanted to be left alone.

The king walked up to Lady Catherine, who swept into a deep curtsy along with Alexandre and Severine. He grasped her hands and spoke with her for a few minutes. I was too far away to hear what they were saying but not far enough away to avoid hearing Lady Catherine begin to wail. Then she swooned, collapsing against the king. He caught her before she fell to the ground, and gestured for one of his footmen to carry her away, Severine and Alexandre following behind. I turned to run. He would want to talk to me next, and I most definitely did not want to talk to him. But it was already too late. He spotted me and began to walk toward me. There was no escape now.

I'd never seen the king up close before. He was tall and wore a violet justaucorps threaded with silver and a matching waistcoat, the official color of mourning for kings. The violet hat perched on his head dripped water down onto his dark, curly wig, even though a valet held an umbrella over his head. King Louis was older than I'd pictured, the lines around his mouth and eyes evident, but he looked at me kindly with green eyes that looked so very much like Auguste's.

"Please accept my condolences," the king said after my curtsy. "Your father was a good man, one of the best I've ever known. His service was invaluable to me, and he will be missed by all at Versailles. If there is ever anything you need, please ask. It's the least I can do for the daughter of my favorite advisor."

"Thank you, Your Majesty. Your kindnesses to me, as well as my father, are greatly appreciated." It was the first time I was addressing the king directly, and I was glad for all my etiquette lessons.

"I've offered the use of one of my sedan chairs to your stepmother. Would you like one as well?"

"No, thank you, sire. I prefer to walk."

The king nodded. "Lady Celia will miss your presence in her lessons, but please take as long as you need before returning to court. I understand how great the loss you have suffered is."

"You do?" I asked weakly.

The king looked deeply into my eyes, his expression unreadable. My skin felt hot and itchy under his gaze. What was wrong with me? Why couldn't I keep my mouth shut? Did I just challenge the king? I felt a little faint.

"I do, Lady Cendrillon," he said, placing a heavy hand on my shoulder. "I have lost people that I loved. I know that pain, how hard it is to manage, especially for one so young."

The king squeezed my shoulder and smiled before setting off in a flurry of valets and footmen. The rest of the mourners cleared from the cemetery quickly, on their way back to the château for small refreshments. Lady Catherine was being loaded into the sedan chair with Severine in tow, but Alexandre stopped to wait for me.

"Are you coming, Cendrillon? You might not be able to fit in the sedan chair, but we might be able to scrounge up another umbrella," she said.

"No. I'll walk."

"Are you sure? I can walk with you, if you want."

"It's kind of you to offer, but I don't want you to get any wetter. I'll meet you back at the château."

"Okay. Be safe," she said with a small smile before rushing off after her mother and sister.

Alexandre's concern touched me. Thankfully, Severine had been keeping her distance since Papa died, and Lady Catherine remained in her rooms, having her meals delivered to her. But Alexandre offered to bring me food or sit with me if I wanted. Elodie and Marius had barely left my side the past week, so any more company would have been stifling, but it was thoughtful of her to offer. I now asked my two friends to leave me in order that I may have some time to myself to pray.

Once the cemetery was empty of all but me and the dead, I started running. Where I was going, I didn't know. Mud squelched under my boots as I flew down a little path that wound its way out of the cemetery. It took me in the opposite direction of the château, but I didn't care. The only thing waiting for me there was awkward small talk and hollow platitudes from people I didn't know.

The rain began to fall in earnest then, soaking my dress through. I started to shiver violently. Maybe I would catch pneumonia too. The thought only spurred me to run faster into the torrent.

A few days after the funeral, Lady Catherine called me into the sitting room to talk. It was the first time she'd spoken more than a few words to me since Papa died.

As I approached the sitting room door, Marius burst out and slammed the door behind him. He was rubbing at his eyes, and I could see tears on his cheeks. He was only thirteen, and he looked miserable.

"Marius, what's wrong?" I asked, rushing up to him and grabbing his arm. "Tell me what happened."

Marius wouldn't look at me, angling his body so I couldn't see his face. His tears scared me. I'd never seen him cry except at funerals.

"I'm fine," he said, sniffling loudly.

"You're not fine. What's going on?"

When he didn't say anything, I shook his arm gently. "Tell me, Marius. Maybe I can help."

"You can't help." His eyes and nose were both red.

"Why? What's going on?"

I couldn't help but raise my voice at his stubbornness, from fear rather than anger.

In a choked whisper and with tears in his eyes, Marius finally confessed what was wrong. "She's sending me away."

"Who's sending you away?"

Marius nodded at the sitting room door.

"*Lady Catherine* is sending you away?"

Marius nodded and wiped at his nose. "She said I was no longer needed."

I didn't feel uneasy anymore. Now I felt sick and confused. How could Lady Catherine ask him to leave? Where would he go?

"But why?"

Marius shrugged and pulled out of my grasp, running away before I could stop him.

"Marius, wait!"

But he didn't listen. In the distance, I heard the kitchen door slam closed. He was gone. Anger pooled in my stomach as I looked at the sitting room. Without knocking, I threw open the door and stormed inside to see Lady Catherine sitting in Papa's armchair.

"My, what an abrupt entrance," she said, taking a sip from her delicate teacup, the image of a rose with curling vines running the length of the cup. "You look upset. Is something the matter?"

Lady Catherine looked as lovely as always in a simple black gown edged in lace, her silver-blond curls falling loosely around her shoulders. After placing the teacup down gently on the side table, she clasped her hands in her lap and stared at me with those pale blue eyes.

"I just saw Marius. He told me you're sending him away. Is that true?"

"It is."

"Why?" I practically spat the word at her, I was so upset. How could she do this? "First you send Claudine away, and now Marius?" It was all such a mess.

"Your father's elderly little housekeeper had been, in my opinion, doing a poor job of running the château. And that stable boy acts too far above his station. These changes are long overdue."

"And these changes include sending away from their home two loyal servants who have been with us for years."

"Among other things, yes. And it isn't their home. It's mine."

"That's not—" I said, but Lady Catherine raised a hand to cut me off.

"We need to change the way we live, Cendrillon. I don't expect you to understand this now. Maybe when you're older. Your father, may he rest in peace, spent a great deal of money on unnecessary things. Like housing extraneous servants. He didn't have a lick of sense about money and was far too accommodating, letting servants like that housekeeper walk all over him. It is far more prudent to employ them when the need arises rather than paying to house and feed them when they aren't necessary. I'll let the stable boy stay till the end of the week."

"You can't do that. It isn't fair," I said, my voice very small in the wake of such a horrible revelation.

"I'm trying to run an estate, ma belle-fille. To keep it aloft, sometimes that means I can't be fair, only practical."

Lady Catherine picked up her teacup and took another sip. When she was finished, she rested the cup on her lap and smiled at me. "Now, may we please move on from this unpleasant topic and get to the reason I asked you here?"

I glared at her. This conversation didn't even feel real. Nothing in my life felt real now that Papa was gone.

"Good. I wanted to talk to you about the living arrangements. Specifically, yours and Alexandre's." She looked at me, waiting for a response. I managed to nod, and she continued.

"It isn't right that Severine has such a large bedchamber compared with Alexandre's. Sisters should be equal, after all. So, I was thinking, if you didn't mind of course, that Alexandre should have the room you're in now. To make things fair."

"You want Alexandre and me to switch rooms?"

"Oh no. Chérie, no. Alexandre's current room is barely more than a closet. I need somewhere to store my dresses. That room will do."

"But where would *I* go?"

"Like I said, sisters deserve to be treated equally. It wouldn't be fair to stick you in a tiny closet, would it? No. The attic, though, is quite large enough. Perfectly on par with Severine's and Alexandre's rooms."

"The attic?" It was so hot in the summer and would freeze come winter, no place to live, surely. Even Elodie had a cozy nook that was warmed by the nearby kitchen.

I must have looked ridiculous, staring at her blankly, responding with a two-word question. Lady Catherine was smiling like Severine did, wearing the sweetest of expressions while saying the most terrible things.

"Yes, ma chérie. The attic. Won't it be lovely? Such a large space all your own, with so much privacy. You'll have great fun up there, I'm sure. I'll have those little servants of yours help you move your things before they go."

"What about Elodie?"

"The seamstress? Oh, she is very talented. She may stay."

But Claudine and Marius were being sent away. Tears pricked at my eyes, but I willed them away. I didn't want to cry in front of Lady Catherine. She was looking at me like I was a silly child who needed to be condescended to, and crying would only prove her right.

"And now that said servants have been taken care of, I'm sure you'll do your part to take care of this house, won't you? Especially since your father's accounts were not as robust as I had believed. Why, he was barely solvent! The sale of the country estate only paid his debts! Truly all he had was his good name. Thus, we need to conserve," Lady Catherine said, rising from her seat and giving me a few sharp pats on the cheek. "Anyway, what does a woman need a house full of servants for when she has an enterprising stepdaughter to help her? I know your father would be very proud of you for taking on so much responsibility. And of course it is out of the question to have Alexandre and Severine perform any chores. They must keep up at court and school."

Lady Catherine left the sitting room, her rose-scented perfume lingering in the room long after she had gone. The tears began to flow freely now. After Maman had died, Papa was always there to take care of me. And now he was gone, and I was an orphan in a house that didn't even belong to me. It was clear from her words that I had no place here. She had sent Claudine away and now Marius. What if one day she tried to send Elodie away as well?

Without them, I would have no one. I would be entirely alone.

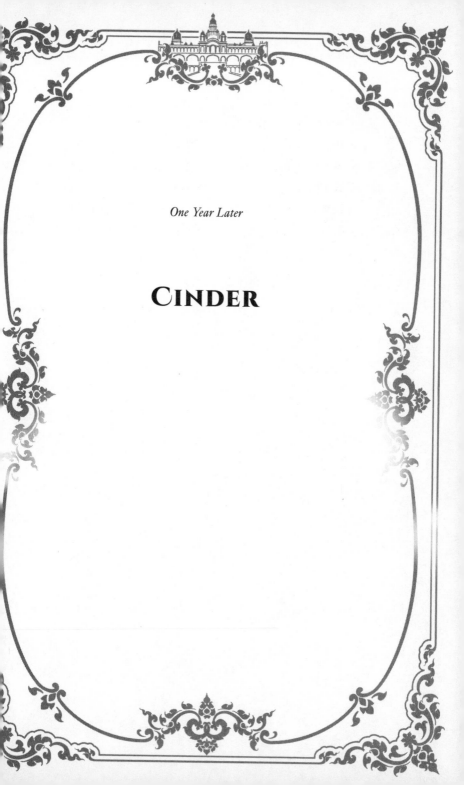

One Year Later

CINDER

Evil is unspectacular and always human,

And shares our bed and eats at our own table.

—*W. H. Auden, "Herman Melville"*

CHAPTER ELEVEN

MY SIXTEENTH BIRTHDAY CAME AND went, and the only person who remembered was me. Elodie had been away for a week, visiting relatives in the country. I was all alone. To be honest, I expected it to be forgotten, but it still stung. On my last birthday, not long before we moved to Versailles, Papa had surprised me with a brand-new dress— a beautiful blue-striped one with red laces running up the bodice, as well as a silver comb studded with pearls, and candied lemon peels from the palace. This year, I hadn't expected anything so extravagant. A simple "happy birthday" would have been enough.

But Lady Catherine, Alexandre, and Severine didn't know it was my birthday. They'd never bothered to ask when it was.

My chest ached when I thought of Papa. I wasn't crying constantly anymore, like I did the first few months after he died, alone in my attic room. But even now, a year later, that bone-deep ache never really eased. Even the memory of my last birthday was tainted by the pain.

I missed him. Desperately. Papa was never coming back, and Lady Françoise had abandoned me. All I had in the name of family was Lady Catherine and my stepsisters. And they weren't much of a family. With them, my life was an unending parade of servitude, trapped in the home that should have been mine with people who didn't care one whit about me. I wasn't going to live my entire life bending to the whims of my stepfamily. That was why I had to get away from them. At any cost.

I'd written to Claudine, who urged me to find some kind of peace with my stepmother, saying that I would only receive my inheritance if Lady Catherine allowed it.

"Cendrillon! It's suppertime. You're late!" Lady Catherine said, yelling up the attic stairs, as if she could tell I was thinking poorly of her.

Maman's old rocking chair creaked underneath me as I got to my feet. My brief respite was over. I grabbed a blue ribbon from my old cracked ribbon box and tied up my hair to get it off my neck. The attic was stiflingly warm and the air stagnant. The one small window overlooking the château's front lawn not nearly big enough to do more than let in the lightest of breezes and the tiniest stream of light. The temperature in the attic was entirely dependent on the weather. In the summer, the blue slates of the roof trapped the heat inside, making the room like an oven. As spring slowly turned to summer, I tried to spend as much time outside as possible. In the winter, the wind's icy fingers crept in through cracks, sending the temperature plummeting. Without a fireplace, I had to rely on a massive pile of blankets as I slept. Comparable with Alexandre's and Severine's room indeed.

I didn't have much in the way of belongings in my attic chambers. Amongst broken bits of furniture and old chests unopened in years that I'd shoved into the corners, I'd pushed my bed underneath the window, next to a small side table with my ribbon box, and a chest for my clothing at the foot of the bed. And of course, my mother's mirror hung on the wall in the spot where the light streamed in most during the day. The rest of my furniture remained in what was now Alexandre's room.

I had also managed to find Maman's rocking chair in the attic, which was a wonderful surprise. It was comforting to have another connection to her in this lonely place.

The château was old, so the attic stairs and floors groaned at the slightest whisper of a footstep. If anyone approached without announcing themselves, I would know. It was a nonsensical worry, to be sure. Lady Catherine and Severine would never set foot in the attic, and Alexandre wouldn't, either, for fear of incurring her mother's anger, but I appreciated the privacy. If there was one decent thing about the attic, it was that I could escape from the constant demands of my stepmother and stepsisters without fear that they would follow. Lady Catherine might call up the stairs, but she would never enter.

During the day, just enough light filtered in through the window to illuminate the staircase so I could see without needing a candle. The steep stairs creaked under my weight as I rushed down, running my hand along the smooth stone wall so I didn't lose my balance. I shouldn't have tried to rest while cooking supper, but I was tired after washing my stepmother's and stepsisters' dresses. I was also upset about my birthday and hoped to have just a few minutes of rest. Now my cassoulet might be burning.

Thankfully, the kitchen smelled divine as I hurried in. There wasn't even a whiff of burned stew, only the rich smell of cooked pork and garlic wafting through the air. Just to be sure, I grabbed a rag and lifted the heavy pot off the hearth and set it down on the table as carefully as I could without dropping it.

The cassoulet had been simmering over the hearth since the night before. I couldn't imagine the disappointment if my hours of work went to waste, or Lady Catherine's anger if she had only bread and cheese for supper. The dining room table was already set. All I needed to do now was serve the food, hopefully without any objections. It was rare that either Lady Catherine or Severine didn't complain about something, but a girl could dream.

With the pot in one hand and a ladle in the other, I made my way into the dining room. My stepfamily was already seated at the table, which was laid with Maman's finest silver dishes and Venetian glass goblets, a gift from her mother at her marriage to Papa. They sparkled in the low light emanating from the crystal chandelier.

"Finally. You're late and we're starving," Severine said with a groan.

I set the pot down on the table next to the trencher laden with the bread I'd baked yesterday. I was quite proud of that bread. It was the first time I'd made one myself instead of buying it from one of the bakeries in town. Baking it might have been born of necessity, as there wasn't enough money to buy bread this week, but that didn't diminish my sense of pride. I'd had to learn so much about cooking and cleaning in the past year, and even minor accomplishments were incredibly gratifying.

"The dish took a long time to cook. I'm sorry for the wait," I said, beginning to ladle the stew into the silver bowls.

Alexandre whispered her thanks with a small smile, but Lady Catherine wrinkled her nose.

"What is this?" she asked, lifting up a spoonful to inspect.

"Cassoulet. It's a new recipe I learned while I was at the market a few weeks ago. It has pork sausage, white beans, and a little bit of duck. It's lovely, isn't it?"

"It isn't exactly high cuisine," Lady Catherine said, dropping the spoon back into her bowl with a plop.

"I didn't have enough money to go to the market again this week," I said, trying very hard not to cry.

"Are you saying that I don't give you enough money to do the shopping? We have more than enough for simple groceries, of all things. If this is the best you can do with what we have, I'll give you *more* money, and you can go back to the market tomorrow," she said, her words clipped and cold. "Now pour the wine, please."

"Yes, Lady Catherine."

I picked up the bottle of wine from the sideboard and uncorked it quickly. It wouldn't do to press her about money anymore today. Our finances—or more appropriately, our lack of finances—had become an incredible touchy subject. Lady Catherine told me the allowance from the king given to the Louvois household was barely enough to keep us fed and housed but not anywhere near enough for the purchase of luxurious dresses and jewelry every month. Or to employ a household staff.

I walked around the table, pouring wine into each glass. As I extended the bottle to Severine's glass, she shifted in her seat, bumping her shoulder into my arm and splashing wine up onto my sleeve and all over the table.

"Cendrillon! You've made a complete mess of things. Why are you always so clumsy?" she said, blinking up at me with wide eyes, not looking put out in the slightest.

I ran to the sideboard to get a rag, drying my hand on my freshly washed apron, which was now stained with red wine. Alexandre stood up to help, but Lady Catherine waved at her to remain seated. "Leave it be. Cendrillon made the mess—she can clean it up."

Alexandre mouthed *I'm sorry* to me as she sat back down. I nodded at her briefly as I returned to the table with the rag.

"I don't want you wandering around with a stained outfit," Lady

Catherine said in between slurps of stew. For such a meticulous lady, she had terrible manners when no one was around. "You'll need to wash it tomorrow. In fact, I just pulled a few of my older dresses out of storage that need to be washed too. You might as well do them at the same time."

"But . . . you told me to go to the market tomorrow. And I just did the washing. Can they wait until next week?"

"I'm sorry that completing your chores and helping your stepmother is such a burden. Your stepmother, the woman who keeps a roof over your head and food in your stomach."

Lady Catherine wasn't looking at me, but her voice was deceptively pleasant and neutral. I knew that tone. She was on the precipice of losing her temper. Any more pushback would result in the both of us tumbling off that cliff.

"It's fine. I'll wash the dresses tomorrow," I said, taking the pot of stew and the wet rag with me as I left the dining room.

"Thank you, ma choupette," Lady Catherine called after me, Severine giggling in the background.

The tension in my shoulders eased when I finally made it back to the kitchen and its blessed solitude, sinking into a chair with a heavy sigh. My stomach rumbled, reminding me that I hadn't eaten since this morning. I hadn't eaten in the dining room since right after Papa died. I wasn't allowed.

The bowls were in the cupboard, but my limbs were achy and my eyes heavy. For a moment, I considered eating right from the pot, but the image of Claudine's disapproving stare as she lectured me about how unladylike it would be popped into my mind. I stood up again with a groan and walked to the cupboard to take a bowl and spoon.

"*Psst!* Cendrillon! Let us in."

The loud whisper was coming from the kitchen door. I turned to see Elodie's face pressed up against the glass, a silly grin on her face.

Laughing, I ran to the kitchen door and unlocked it. Elodie and I hugged in the doorway.

"What are you doing here? You're not supposed to be back for a few more days," I said, my mood instantly brightening.

I wouldn't have been able to survive the past year without Elodie. It wasn't that I wanted her to be trapped in the château with me, but I appreciated her being here. It helped having someone to hold me when I cried, to commiserate with when Lady Catherine or Severine did anything that was particularly humiliating. Elodie was suffering too, making dresses for Lady Catherine until her fingers bled. We needed to leave. Hopefully, soon.

"My cousins are boring. And anyway, we've come to surprise you!"

"We?"

"Yes, we," Marius said, appearing behind Elodie. "It's hot out here. Can you two hug inside the château, please?"

Elodie frowned at him and dragged me back into the kitchen, but I could only snicker at Marius's refreshingly familiar impatience. He looked scrawnier than the last time I saw him, and I worried about him. I knew he worked as a day laborer on a nearby farm and that the foreman of the estate was known for his temper. He wouldn't tell us the worst of it, but we knew the truth about the beatings he'd endured. I wished more than anything that he could be safe with us once more. But he was lucky to be employed anywhere and not just left on the street as an urchin.

"Happy birthday!" Elodie said, pulling a little package from underneath her cloak and holding it out to me. "I wanted to give it to you before I left, but I had to save up the money, and I didn't want to get your hopes up if I couldn't—"

"Elodie! You really shouldn't have. You need to save your money," I told her, touched more than words could say.

"I definitely should have. It's your birthday. How could I not get you anything for your birthday? Open it!"

The package was wrapped in brown paper and tied with a pink ribbon. I set it on the table and unwrapped it slowly, my breath quickening with anticipation. The paper fell away to reveal a strawberry tart, golden and flaky, red jam oozing out of either end. It was the most wonderful thing I'd seen in a long time.

I threw my arms around her. "Thank you so much! You don't know how much it means to me," I said, tears clogging my voice.

Elodie patted my back gently. "You know we would never forget about you."

"I got you something too," said Marius somewhat petulantly.

He poked my back, and I turned to see his outstretched hand holding a beautiful bouquet of pink and white lilies.

"Lilies! My favorite! You remembered."

"Course I remembered. All you used to do was talk about flowers," he said, rolling his eyes. I elbowed him in the ribs. I missed bossing him around more than I could say.

I took the bouquet and lifted it to my nose. The lilies smelled heavenly, fresh and sweet, like they were drenched in the sunlight of warm, never-ending summer days.

"Thank you. They're beautiful," I said, giving him a hug.

He pulled away, blushing, but smiled proudly. "Is that stew?"

Marius promptly lost interest in the gift and walked past me to the kitchen table, leaning over the pot.

"Marius! Don't be rude," Elodie said.

"It's fine. Do you want some?" I asked.

"Of course." He grinned and rubbed his hands eagerly. "It smells good enough to eat!"

"Elodie?"

"Well . . ." she said, uncertain, but she couldn't take her eyes from

90

the pot. "Won't Lady Catherine be upset? You know we're supposed to wait until she's done eating to have our meal."

"Why don't we take the stew, the lilies, and the tart, and have a meal down by the pond. You go on ahead of me. They'll be done with supper soon, and I'll meet you outside after I've finished cleaning up."

"Sounds amazing," Elodie said. "And we have one more piece of birthday news for you. Marius heard about two positions opening up in town in the same household, one for a maid and one for a seamstress. And they might need a stable boy too. The three of us could be together again."

My heart jumped in my chest. "Are you serious?"

Elodie grinned widely and nodded. "Marius can tell you more about it."

She turned to the door only to find that Marius had already scooped up the pot of stew and made his way outside.

"Well, he can tell you more when you're finished in here, but I think this is the one for us!" she said with one final hug before she followed Marius out.

I sat back down at the kitchen table, willing Lady Catherine and the girls to hurry up and finish their supper. The nearest town was small. Positions didn't open up often, so when they did, you had to move quickly. I thought this might finally be the way for me to make my escape from Lady Catherine's grasp. I had stayed, hoping that I would someday receive the inheritance to which I was entitled. But that prospect grew dimmer by the day.

CHAPTER TWELVE

THE NEXT DAY, I SHOULDERED my way through the crowds of people packed into the market, the basket in my hands nearly full and quite heavy. It was warm and sunny with puffy white clouds dotting a brilliant blue sky, and a pleasant breeze made the walk to town enjoyable and helped ease some of the tension of being in a large crowd.

I would have preferred to take the carriage so I didn't have to lug a heavy basket the few miles back to the château, but Lady Catherine wouldn't allow it. A Louvois carriage could never be used for such a base activity as buying groceries, so I had to walk. I didn't really mind. At least the long walk meant I could get away from the château for a few precious hours. I'd started the washing early that morning so I could take my time, maybe walk a few paces slower and enjoy the day.

Lady Catherine only gave me enough money to purchase items she'd specifically requested. She said we had more than enough food in the larder, and I should make do with that and the items I bought today. Anything else would be a waste of money. We didn't really have enough food in the larder, so I would have to stretch everything as far as I possibly could.

My stepmother would rather die than tell me this, but I suspected she'd already spent the allowance she got from the king, presumably on material for the new dresses she'd ordered Elodie to make, and what she'd given me today was all we had left. Next month, when the king sent our three hundred livres, Lady Catherine would conveniently want me to store away as many groceries as possible.

At the butcher's, I bought a few cuts of venison and a whole turkey. From the cheesemonger, I bought a block of hard Cantal and, of course, a round of Brie, Severine's and Alexandre's favorite. Now I just needed fruit, specifically pears, apples, and grapes. Lady Catherine refused to eat cheese without fruit, even though the prices were astronomically high this early in the season. It was difficult to find a fruit seller amongst the seemingly endless rows of stalls.

I stood up on my tiptoes but was still too short to see over the heads of people much taller than I, some clearly displeased that I was standing still when everyone else was moving. After nearly getting knocked over by a grumbling man who bumped me with his shoulder, then whacked in the face by a bushel of sunflowers carried by a woman who didn't even notice me, I decided to just keep moving and hope I came across someone selling the fruit I needed before the sun set.

As I walked, a cacophony of sounds reached my ears. Sellers were hawking their products, loudly calling to anyone passing by. Children were screaming and darting between the legs of adults, who were amused and annoyed in turn. Chatter and laughter rang out all around me, blending into a comforting blur. I liked the anonymity. It was freeing to be not Lord de Louvois's orphan or Lady Catherine's disliked stepdaughter, but simply just another girl visiting the market.

"Fruit! Fresh fruit! Ripe strawberries! Delectable pears! The freshest fruit you'll find outside the king's gardens!"

The disembodied voice was faint and difficult to pinpoint over the din, but I was clearly moving in the right direction now, which was further confirmed when I started to see people with fruit in their baskets or cradled in their arms. I finally found myself in front of a wooden stand with a sign that read FRESH FRUIT scrawled in red paint.

"What can I get for you, mademoiselle?" the fruit seller asked, leaning over the counter and letting his belly rest on it.

"I need apples, pears, and grapes, please."

"Indeed. How much of each do you want?"

"One pound of grapes, nine apples, and nine pears."

The fruit seller turned around and began collecting the fruit from an array of baskets packed tightly into the confines of the stall. I slipped my hand into the secret pocket that Elodie had sewn into the side of my dress and pulled out the little bag of money Lady Catherine gave me, wincing at its lightness.

"Here are the grapes," he said, unceremoniously dumping the clusters on the countertop before turning back around again and crouching down to get at the baskets.

While I waited for him to finish assembling my order, I peered into the shadowy interior of the stall. A particular fruit caught my eye, round and colored, a brilliant, eye-catching orange. An orange. He had *oranges*. For a moment, I was back in the Versailles' Orangerie, exploring the galleries with Marius and Elodie, the thrill of adventure zinging through my blood. But nine apples tumbling across the counter after being dropped by the fruit seller shook me out of my reverie quickly, and I threw out my arms to stop them from rolling right off the counter onto the filthy ground.

"Sorry about that. Here are the pears." He deposited the pears a touch more gently onto the counter. "That'll be five livres."

"*Five?*" I said, trying and failing to keep the shock from my voice. "Really? That seems a tad expensive."

The fruit seller frowned at me and tutted under his breath. "These aren't in season yet. I had to grow them in my own personal greenhouse. Do you know how much money it costs to do that? They're five livres. Take it or leave it."

My cheeks warmed as I played at riffling through the little bag, knowing full well that I didn't have five livres left. Hopefully, I would still be able to bring something home to Lady Catherine.

"How much would"—I poured the remaining money into my hand—"one livre and, uh, twelve sol get me?"

"These," he said, shoving one apple, a small bruised pear, and one bunch of grapes toward me.

"Oh. Well, I suppose—"

"I'll pay for the mademoiselle's order."

I jumped at the intrusion and turned to see a young man standing next to me where none had been just a moment before. He was tall, over a head taller than I, with broad shoulders. He wore a nondescript brown cloak with the hood pulled down low over his face, so I could see nothing of his features. But through the gap in the cloak I caught the flash of golden buttons running down his justaucorps, catching the light and gleaming when he turned to slide a few livres across the counter toward the fruit seller. Golden buttons meant money. But why would a wealthy stranger in disguise be so generous? I pushed the coins back toward him.

"Oh no, Monsieur, I thank you for your offer, but I cannot accept. I'll take whatever my one livre and change will buy me."

I turned back to the fruit seller with what I hoped was a firm expression. There was something unsettling about this man. My trip to the market became taxing surprisingly fast. All I wanted was to get back to the château.

"Please, mademoiselle, I insist," he said, sliding the money back across the counter.

The fruit seller swept the coins into his hands before I could stop him. How irritating. I didn't appreciate this kind of arrogance. If I wanted help paying for my own purchase, I would ask for it. I didn't need anyone to come to my rescue, noble or not.

"There's a few extra here, Monsieur," the seller said.

"Indeed. Would you be so kind as to throw in a few oranges for the lady?"

Oranges? A few? How could he possibly know that I was interested in the oranges? He might have been watching me for longer than I thought, but that still wouldn't suggest that I had any interest in them. Unless he was a mind reader.

"You are very generous and kind, Monsieur, but I *insist* that I cannot accept. It's too much, and I have no way to repay you."

"Repayment isn't necessary. Paying for your fruit is the least I can do," the stranger said with a curious tone of voice.

The way he spoke made it seem like he knew something that I didn't, and I didn't like it. Not one bit. Unease sent goose bumps racing up and down my arms. Something about his voice was awfully familiar.

"The oranges," said the fruit seller, placing three on the counter before pointedly staring at the growing crowd of customers behind us. "Thank you for your business, mademoiselle and Monsieur. Please come again."

"I think that's our cue to leave," the strange young man whispered conspiratorially. "Until we meet again."

He bowed and took his leave, disappearing into the crowd without a backward glance. I stared unabashedly at his retreating figure, as if the back of his cloak might reveal new information to me.

"Please come again," the fruit seller said, much louder this time.

"I'm sorry." I placed the pieces of fruit into my basket as quickly as I could and hurried away from the stall. What an odd day this had turned out to be. I wanted to put the stranger out of my mind, but I just couldn't no matter how hard I tried. It felt like I knew him, or at least had seen him before. But whatever his true identity was, I hoped I never saw him again. Intrigue surrounding an arrogant young man I may or may not have met was something I didn't need.

CHAPTER THIRTEEN

ELODIE AND ALEXANDRE WERE JUST outside the kitchen doorway when I returned from the market, the clicking of my heels on the stone pathway not enough to alert them to my presence. Their heads were pressed closely together, foreheads nearly touching as they smiled and giggled. It was incredibly intimate, and I didn't want to interrupt the moment. I stopped and loitered around the corner of the house, a tad awkwardly, my attention given to a sparrow chirping away in a tree.

It was horribly rude to spy on them, but my legs were sore, making it terribly inconvenient to walk all the way back to the road. Besides, I wanted to be sure that Elodie was happy, that Alexandre was good for her. A little spying in the interest of a friend was justified, right? Elodie complained that I worried too much, but how could I not? She'd done so much to care for me, looking out for her in return was the least I could do.

"Alexandre? Where are you? Your lessons are starting right now. Severine is already in the study," Lady Catherine called from inside the house, her voice growing louder as she approached the kitchen door.

Alexandre pushed Elodie away, hard, then spun around to face her mother, hands clasped primly behind her back.

"I'm coming, Mère. I'll be inside in a moment."

"No, I want you inside *now*. You're already late." Lady Catherine appeared in the doorway and leaned out to speak with Alexandre.

"Is that the seamstress just there behind you? What is she doing outside when she should be working?" Lady Catherine asked, speaking to her daughter and ignoring Elodie entirely.

"She was asking what sort of lace I preferred on my dress and will be back inside shortly."

Alexandre herded her mother into the château and shut the door in Elodie's face. I ran over to Elodie, but she took one look at me, her face turning red, and bolted, circling around me to get to the road.

"Elodie! Wait!"

But she continued to run, faster than I'd ever seen her run before, until she was so far ahead of me I would never be able to catch up. And even if I did manage to catch her, I didn't think she would want to talk to me. When Elodie wanted privacy, she would go to incredible lengths to get it. Maybe tonight, when she calmed down a little, I would see if she was ready to talk.

Anger flared in my belly as I entered the château. I wanted to march right into the study and give my stepsister an earful, but Lady Catherine's presence in the kitchen put an end to that idea.

"It seems that everyone is running late today. What took you so long? You've been gone for hours." Lady Catherine leaned against the kitchen table, arms crossed in front of her chest. She looked perfectly poised and in control, not a pale blond curl out of place or wrinkle to be found on her white satin dress with roses embroidered on the skirt. She scrutinized me as if I had been gallivanting about instead of completing a chore she tasked me with.

Nothing I did was good enough to please her. Severine could throw a tantrum because her mutton wasn't warm enough, and her mother would coo and coddle her, but if I spent the day washing the floors and cleaning the windows, Lady Catherine would complain that I should've done the laundry as well.

"The market was crowded today. I had to push through a mob of people just to walk between stalls."

Lady Catherine sniffed. "Did you get the fruit and cheese? I want Brie and pears for dessert tonight."

I hauled the basket up onto the kitchen table and started to unpack.

"I got the fruit, the cheese, the meat. Absolutely everything you asked for."

Did she detect the sarcasm? I couldn't tell. She didn't seem upset as she walked over to watch me unpack the basket, but the way she looked wasn't always a reliable marker. I knew better than to be sarcastic, especially when she was in a mood. But the mysterious encounter at the market and Alexandre hurting Elodie's feelings had worn away any patience.

I pulled the fruit out first, examining each piece to make sure nothing was bruised. Lady Catherine grabbed my wrist as I picked up one of the oranges, her nails digging into my skin.

"What is that?" she asked. "Is that an orange?"

Her grip on my wrist was tight enough to bruise. My skin was going numb underneath her fingers.

"Yes. Why? What's wrong?"

I tried to pull away, but she only held on tighter. Lady Catherine was not a delicate little flower, no matter how she looked, but I hadn't realized she was this strong. She was starting to scare me.

"Where did you get the money for an orange? No. Wait. Three

oranges?" she said, peering into the basket. "I know I didn't give you enough money to buy our necessities *and* three oranges."

Lady Catherine's icy gaze, accentuated by the pallor of her face, silenced any responses. "Well? Are you hiding money from me, ma chérie? Secreting away precious funds that could be used to care for your family?"

Lady Catherine plucked the orange from my fingers and dropped my wrist. I ran to the other side of the kitchen table. She was blocking the door. I couldn't get out without going past her. Lady Catherine had a temper that was generally contained behind frosty looks and biting words. I'd never seen her like this before.

"I didn't have enough money for the oranges. I didn't pay for them," I blurted out, the words finally escaping only for me to realize that they were the exact wrong words.

Lady Catherine gently placed the orange on the table and clutched the back of a kitchen chair. She leaned on it heavily, like a cane, her knuckles turning white. It was quiet in the kitchen as she looked at me, so quiet that I could faintly hear the tutor speaking on the other side of the château. The air was thick with tension as I watched her in turn. I waited breathlessly for her to move, or speak, or do anything other than stare at me with those pale eyes.

"You didn't pay for them? So you stole them. My stepdaughter is stealing oranges from the market?" she said as she walked slowly around the table toward me.

I watched her approach, my limbs frozen, beyond my control.

"No! Of course not. I would *never* steal. Not ever. A stranger at the market paid for them. I asked him not to, but he insisted and—"

Lady Catherine surged forward and slapped me across the face. I stumbled back into the table, too shocked to even try to run away. There wasn't much time for that anyway, not when she grabbed me again and pulled me toward her.

"Do you think that makes it better, Cendrillon? Instead of my stepdaughter stealing, she's accepting gifts from strange men like a harlot. Is that what you are? Are you a harlot disgracing this family's good name? Your father's good name, might I add," she said, punctuating each word with a jerk of my arm.

Lady Catherine didn't yell, but there was a bitterness to her voice, a venom in every word she spoke that filled my veins with ice. I was trapped by her eyes and her voice more than I was by her hold on my arm.

"What do you think *he* would say, your precious father, if he saw you now, cavorting with men and utterly disrespecting me, after all I've done for you?"

I stayed silent and met her gaze as bravely as I was able, ignoring the stinging in my cheek and the barely contained anger moving behind her eyes.

"Don't expect to leave this house for the foreseeable future," she said, a sneer twisting her face as she dropped my arm and left the kitchen in a huff. "If anyone saw you at the market accepting handouts from men, we'll be *ruined.*"

Lady Catherine's voice faded as she moved away from the kitchen. I waited for a few minutes after I could no longer hear her footsteps before I started putting the rest of the groceries away. My motions were rote, perfected by a year of routine. I hardly had to think about what I was doing. In fact, I tried very hard not to think of anything at all. It wasn't until I saw the oranges resting at the bottom of the basket that all the worries of the day came rushing back.

Scooping the three oranges into my arms, I scurried from the kitchen, up the three flights of stairs to my attic bedchamber. The darkness and quiet of my room were soothing, and the sweet scent of Marius's lilies reminded me of our secret picnic last night. A gentle evening breeze blew through the little window, cooling the air considerably. I plopped down on my bed, the oranges still cradled in my arms, and squeezed my eyes shut. If only I could wish away my argument with Lady Catherine. If only I could wish her, and Severine, and even Alexandre away and put Papa in their place. If only . . .

My cheek ached, a dull throb that radiated down into my jaw. I buried my face in my pillow and took a few deep breaths, letting the breeze wash over me. Lady Catherine had never *hit* me before. I almost couldn't believe it.

There was nothing left for me here. Lady Catherine had control over Papa's money. She wasn't paying me for the work I did around the château, and she was barely paying Elodie a pittance for her labor. If I didn't receive my true inheritance, I had nothing beyond my dresses and Maman's mirror and rocking chair. And these silly pieces of fruit given to me by a stranger who got me into all this mess. I hoped I never saw him again. Worse, I hadn't seen or heard from Lady Françoise in a year. My godmother had abandoned me. She had been the closest thing I had to family besides Papa. My mother's sister had been dead for many years, and Papa was an only child. There was no one else.

As soon as I could sneak away, Elodie and I were going to apply for the seamstress and maid positions that had opened up and make sure Marius was hired as the stable boy as well. I wanted desperately to leave, but even though I was a servant now, I was *born* a lady. All I knew was that we couldn't stay here any longer. With Lady Catherine's temper only getting worse as the days passed, it wasn't safe. I had to figure something out, and fast.

CHAPTER FOURTEEN

"CENDRILLON! YOU'LL NEVER GUESS WHAT happened at court today!"

Alexandre burst into the laundry room while I was scrubbing at one of Lady Catherine's dresses in the big wooden tub in an attempt to get out a large red sauce stain. My fingers were shriveled prunes, while the stain was just as large and red as it had been fifteen minutes ago. I welcomed the distraction.

"What happened?" I asked as I clambered to my feet, my shins sore from all the kneeling.

"You have to come listen," she said, grabbing my hand and immediately dropping it.

"Why are your sleeves all wet?"

I had to fight back the urge to roll my eyes. "I'm doing the washing," I said, gesturing to the giant tub of soapy water that Alexandre was standing next to.

"Oh. Well, just follow me, then. And hurry up!"

Alexandre beamed at me so widely, it looked uncomfortable.

Her eyes were positively sparkling. She even sprinted back out of the room, hauling her skirts up into her arms so high, it was nearly indecent. What could possibly have happened at court to make Alexandre, who sulked through breakfast and refused to eat even one bite of her eggs just this morning, happier than I'd seen her in over a week?

I followed her into the sitting room, where I found Lady Catherine and Severine clasping hands and giggling. Giggling. Lady Catherine's blue eyes were warm for once, and Severine's smile was an actual smile, not a sneer or a pout. I'd never seen them like this before. It was actually a little frightening.

"What's going on?" I asked, making my way tentatively into the room. "Did something interesting happen at court?"

"The most interesting thing to happen at court in ages!" declared Severine.

Alexandre flopped down on the sofa with a sigh. Severine laughed and sat down next to her, their brief feud from a few days ago seemingly over.

"The Grand Dauphin's eighteenth birthday is coming up, and the king is throwing him a series of balls and festivals in celebration," Severine said.

She was talking to me like I was an actual person and not a burden to be gotten rid of. These balls must really be special.

"And why are we excited about these balls?" I asked.

Severine made a dismissive gesture with her hand, as if I was too tiresome to be tolerated. That was much more normal.

"Every highborn maiden in the country is invited to attend. Aristocrats are descending on Versailles. The who's who of the French nobility, all congregating at the palace for the first ball in three days' time. Cendrillon, do you know what that could do for our status, to make such important friends?"

"*Wealthy* and important friends," Lady Catherine said, her gaze hazy and faraway. "No one who is anyone in France would dare miss the dauphin's birthday celebration."

I wasn't really listening to that last bit. My mind caught on what Severine said about every maiden in the country being invited. Might Lady Françoise be there? With her position at court and former relationship to the king, she would have to be. I was still terribly sad that she disappeared when I needed her most, but my feelings didn't change the fact that I still needed help reclaiming the life I was born into. If I asked her to help get me away from Lady Catherine, would she? If I'd been asked that question a year ago, I would have said yes. I wasn't so sure anymore.

If I could find Lady Françoise and she wanted to help, Elodie and I wouldn't have to apply for the servant positions. And if I couldn't find her, or if she no longer cared about me, the positions in town would still be there in three days' time. Marius had assured me that they were still open and that the family hadn't yet been able to find any prospective candidates. I just had to persuade Lady Catherine to let me attend the ball.

"Just think of it! Wearing beautiful dresses, dancing in the Hall of Mirrors, watching fountains in the gardens under the stars, tables as far as the eye can see filled with all manner of delectable treats," Severine said, tossing an arm across her eyes and sinking dramatically against the sofa cushion behind her.

"Hordes of young, handsome, wealthy noblemen," Alexandre teased, poking her sister.

Lady Catherine gave her a sharp look.

"There will be no young nobles for either of you, not while the king is choosing a bride for the dauphin."

"What?" Severine jolted upright and stared at her mother, wide-eyed.

"The dauphin is going to be married?"

"Yes. There are credible rumors that the king will use the birthday celebrations to find a bride for his eldest son. If they're true, I want at least one of you at the top of that list. I won't pass up the chance to make one of my daughters the Grand Dauphine of France."

Severine shrieked and bounced up and down in her seat. Alexandre didn't react outwardly, but I could see her face fall a bit as she listened to her mother speak. I felt a pang of sympathy for her. I couldn't imagine what it was like be in love, then forced to marry someone else. To be fair, I wasn't positive that she and Elodie were in love, but they had been spending an awful lot of time together before the incident yesterday. At the very least, they cared for each other. If so, this would be heartbreaking for Elodie.

"We're going to need new jewelry, new dresses, maybe even new carriages. New everything. The Louvois name will get us far with the king, but it won't take us all the way. You two need to do your part."

"I'd like to come," I said, without fully thinking it through before I spoke.

When three pairs of eyes landed on me, I started to panic. Just a little. "I mean—may I please come to the celebrations, Lady Catherine? It's been so long since I've visited Versailles; I'd very much like to see it again. And all my chores would be done before I went anywhere. You won't have to worry. I'll take care of everything."

In my haste to get them out, the words were mushed together and messy. Did Lady Catherine understand what I said? I couldn't tell by the blank expression on her face. But then she smiled at me. A perfectly pleasant smile.

"Of course you can come, chérie. Every highborn maiden in France was invited, after all. As long as you promise not to let your work around the château slip, I don't have a problem with you attending the celebrations."

I was so sure Lady Catherine was going to say no that I couldn't believe she'd said yes. Every other time I'd asked to go to court with them, she'd refused. I always had too many chores to finish, or there was only enough room for three in the carriage, and neither Alexandre nor Severine could stay behind. There was always an excuse for why I couldn't go.

"But, Maman, I don't *want* her to come," Severine said in a nasally whine.

"Hush, Severine. It isn't fair to exclude your stepsister. Not when she's been working so hard around the house. It will be a wonderful chance for the three of you to bond."

Severine slumped back into the sofa with a heavy sigh. Alexandre was still lost in thought, twirling a strand of blond hair around her finger. I didn't care whether Severine wanted me there or not. If everything went according to plan, I wouldn't have to spend much time with her. If I found Lady Françoise quickly, that is.

"Speaking of chores, have you managed to get that stain out of my dress yet?" Lady Catherine asked.

"I'll get right back to it," I hurried to say at Lady Catherine's raised eyebrow. "Thank you again for letting me come along."

"Of course, ma choupette. I'm sure we'll all have great fun together."

I dipped into a quick curtsy and left the sitting room at what I hoped was a measured pace. What I really wanted to do was run screaming through the house, but I couldn't let on how excited I was to attend the celebrations. This was the first time in months that I'd dared to ask my stepmother for anything. I had to stay quiet, do my chores, act grateful, and not attract any undue attention.

With any luck—something I hadn't had much of lately—Lady Françoise would learn what had become of me, then whisk me away from my awful stepfamily and invite me to live at her estate. Maybe Lady Catherine's acquiescence meant that the tides were starting to turn in my favor.

CHAPTER FIFTEEN

SEVERINE ELBOWED ME IN THE stomach "accidentally" as I stood on a stool attempting to pin a loose curl to the fontange piled atop her head. The offending elbow knocked the wind out of me for a few seconds. I had to clamber down before I fell.

"What did you do that for?" I asked, rubbing my belly.

It wasn't *terribly* painful, but I wasn't going to let Severine off so easily after I'd spent the last three hours helping her and Alexandre prepare for the ball tonight. Elodie had left after receiving a message about Marius, who had been thrown off a horse. I was worried about my friends, but all I could do was attend to my stepsisters.

"You stabbed me with that pin. It was an involuntary reaction," she said, ignoring me completely to preen in the floor-length mirror propped up against the wall next to her toilette.

"Of course. You involuntarily jerked your elbow backward into my stomach. A completely natural reaction." I met Severine's gaze in the mirror. Her glower was no less intense coming through a secondary medium.

"Don't get cheeky with me, Cendrillon. If I told Maman now that I didn't want you coming with us to the ball, she wouldn't let you. So get up here and fix my hair."

I sighed but climbed back up on the stool and got to work making sure that Severine's glossy curls were as perfect as possible. I'd spent so long getting my stepsisters dressed for the ball that I hadn't had time to get ready myself. If I didn't start soon, I wouldn't have enough time to prepare before we needed to leave.

"There. All fixed," I said, pinning the last curl into place and stepping down from the stool. "You look lovely."

"I do, don't I?" Severine replied, smoothing her hands down the length of her skirt and twisting back and forth in front of the mirror.

Severine really did look lovely. Her dress was off the shoulder, the bodice and overskirt a deep crimson satin, with a short train that pooled on the floor behind her. The underskirt was a brilliant gold that perfectly matched the gleaming highlights in her hair. To offset the heavy fabrics, loose sleeves of lace were pinned to the short satin sleeves, and a touch of lace ran along the neckline. Severine's face was lightly powdered and painted, and velvet beauty marks in the shape of stars dotted each cheek. A pearl necklace and pearl earrings rounded out the ensemble.

Alexandre, too, looked radiant, in a style of dress quite similar to her sister's. Perhaps too similar. The only difference in their clothing was that Alexandre's bodice, overskirt, and train were a light pink. Her underskirt was also gold, and her hair was curled and piled atop her head. She even had the same star-shaped beauty marks as Severine. If Lady Catherine wanted her daughters to catch the dauphin's attention, I didn't understand why she wanted them dressed the same.

"Cendrillon, please come help. I can't get my sleeve to stay on," Alexandre said, a note of panic in her voice as she burst into Severine's room.

I turned to see Alexandre holding one lace sleeve in her outstretched hand. I sighed, grabbed a few more pins, and followed her back to her chambers. There was always another problem with these two. At least Alexandre made requests instead of demands. That was something that distinguished her from her sister, even if her clothing didn't.

"Don't get upset. It just needs a few pins and . . . there. All better."

Alexandre's sleeve was now firmly attached to her dress. The lace floated down her upper arm, ending just at her elbow.

I couldn't help but feel a sense of pride in all I'd done to get my stepsisters ready for the ball. I'd laced both girls into their corsets, curled and piled their hair into fontanges, and squeezed them into their dresses. They both looked beautiful. I just had to put the finishing touches on their makeup.

Before she was sent away, Claudine had helped me dress. I'd never done it on my own before, and I had to figure it out myself after she was gone, since Elodie was always working while I dressed. Surveying the work done on Alexandre, I thought I'd come rather far.

"Thank you," Alexandre said with a grateful smile. "I painted my face and powdered my hair already. Do you mind helping me with the rouge? And my lips? My hands are shaking."

I grabbed the little silver pots of rouge and vermilion paint from Alexandre's toilette and sat her down on a chair. It would be easier to work while she wasn't towering over me in her heels.

"Why are you so nervous?" I asked while I daubed a bit of paint on her lips. "You've been to balls before."

"I know. But this is different. Maman wants me to impress the dauphin. What if I *do* impress him and he wants to marry me?"

"Would that be such a bad thing? You would be queen one day."

Alexandre shivered. "I don't want to be queen. Severine wants that. I never have. All those responsibilities, the pressure, the public ceremonies . . . It would be overwhelming."

Alexandre paused while I twisted open the pot of rouge. I smeared a bit on my fingers and began to pat the pigment onto her cheeks. "And, of course, there is Elodie to consider," she said tentatively.

My fingers stilled for just a moment on her cheek. Was Alexandre going to bring up Elodie with me? Both girls avoided the topic of the other whenever I tried to discuss their relationship. The shove I witnessed still upset me, but I was willing to listen to what Alexandre had to say.

"If I was to marry the dauphin, Elodie and I . . . It would be over."

"What would be over?"

Alexandre put her hands on her hips. "Don't pretend you don't know what's going on. You're not stupid. Even if Elodie hasn't said anything specifically, you can see how we are with each other."

"I know that I saw you push Elodie away when your mother called for you."

Alexandre winced and shot me a guilty look. "I didn't realize you saw that."

Sufficiently satisfied with the circle of rouge on her right cheek, I moved on to her left, dabbing it on with perhaps more force than necessary. "I was coming back from the market and saw it all. You know, I think you really hurt her feelings. There's never been a time that Elodie hasn't wanted to talk to me when she was upset. Except for now."

"I didn't mean to hurt her," Alexandre said, her eyes locked on the mirror behind me. "I could hear Maman's footsteps coming toward the door, and I panicked. I care about Elodie more than you know. But Maman would never approve. And if she'd caught us . . ."

I had a fairly clear idea of what Lady Catherine's reaction would have been had she caught Elodie and Alexandre together. Most of my anger abated. Could I really blame Alexandre for being frightened of her mother? Maybe I could before Lady Catherine slapped me, but after watching how fast her rage grew just because a young man paid for my groceries, I didn't want to imagine how furious she would be if she found out that her daughter was in love with a servant. And a girl at that.

"I'm finished," I said, stepping back from Alexandre so she could look in the mirror. "You're gorgeous."

"Really?" she asked, a small smile lighting up her face. "Do you think so?"

"Really. You'll be one of the prettiest girls at the ball. I'm sure of it."

Alexandre pulled me into a quick hug. "Thank you, Cendrillon. I would have been lost without you."

"I never would have guessed."

I dodged out of the way of Alexandre's playful shove. We dissolved into a giggling fit.

"What are you two doing in there?" Severine yelled from her chambers. "Cendrillon was supposed to be helping me, Alexandre, not laughing with you."

"I'm sorry, Severine. I'll be right there," I said as I tried to swallow my laughter.

"Don't bother. I finished the makeup *myself*. Completely useless."

I could hear Severine stomp her way out of her chambers and down the stairs, her shoes thudding loudly on the parquet flooring. As soon as her footsteps faded into the distance, Alexandre and I burst into laughter again.

"Alexandre, we have to go!" Lady Catherine called up the stairs. "Get down here this minute."

Sobering immediately, Alexandre brushed past me and hurried downstairs. I followed right behind. We couldn't be leaving yet. I wasn't ready.

"There you are," Lady Catherine said when we made it to the bottom of the stairs. "Alexandre, your sister is already in the carriage. Get moving. We don't want to be late."

Alexandre frowned at me worriedly but obeyed her mother and rushed out to the carriage. Lady Catherine made as if to follow, but I stepped in front of her, blocking her path.

"Lady Catherine, I haven't had a chance to get dressed. I spent the last few hours helping Alexandre and Severine. You said I could come with you to the ball."

I flinched when Lady Catherine reached for me, but all she did was pat me gently on the cheek. "I know, chérie. I appreciate all your help. But we'll be late if we don't leave immediately. The girls need to be precisely on time if they want to impress the royal family. King Louis prides punctuality."

I clasped my hands behind my back to hide their trembling. My stepmother couldn't leave me behind. I would jump into the carriage in my stained dress and apron if I had to.

"How about I take the girls over now, then send the carriage back for you? It won't matter if *you're* a little late, and then you'll have enough time to get dressed. How does that sound?"

"That sounds wonderful, Lady Catherine. Thank you. I'll be ready by the time the carriage returns."

"Be sure that you are." Lady Catherine swept past me in a swirl of golden satin that perfectly matched Severine's and Alexandre's underskirts. As soon as the door closed behind her, I sprinted up the stairs to the attic. One of my old court dresses, the nicest one I owned, was already laid out on my bed. All I had to do was slip it on and apply minimal makeup. I just needed to be presentable enough to be admitted to the palace. Any extra frills would be a waste of time. Attracting the attention of the vapid dauphin wasn't important. Finding Lady Françoise and asking for her help was all that mattered.

Chapter Sixteen

THE CARRIAGE WASN'T COMING BACK for me, of course. As soon as I finished getting ready, I ran outside and sat on the stone bench just next to the front door to wait, my ears straining for the clopping of horse hooves or the clatter of carriage wheels. I'd hoped that the cool early evening air would soothe my strained nerves. It did, for a little while. But I'd been waiting on that bench for over an hour now, and there was still no carriage. Lady Catherine wasn't going to send it to fetch me. She'd lied.

I shouldn't have been surprised that she lied. On the day she and Papa married, Lady Catherine had said that we were going to be family, and that was a lie too. But I wanted to believe so badly that this time would be different, that she would treat me if not like a daughter, then at least like a human being with feelings.

I stood up slowly, my backside sore from sitting for so long, and went back inside the house. After getting changed in the attic, I returned to the kitchen with a bucket of soapy water and a scrub brush. I wanted to fall into bed, but I couldn't, not when the fireplace was so filthy. Lady Catherine had asked me to clean it the other day, and I was sure to feel the brunt of her rage if I let it go again.

I attacked it with single-minded focus. Sitting back on my heels, I took a deep breath and wiped the sweat from my brow. When I glanced down at my hand, I was met with the sight of a grimy palm covered in soot.

"Perfect," I muttered to myself, using my relatively clean wrist to rub my face only to have it come back black with ashes.

I should have been crying. I wanted to cry, to release the mess of emotions inside me. After the night I'd had, crying would have been an entirely reasonable reaction. My stepfamily being gone made this the perfect time to indulge in a few tears, but I couldn't even muster up the energy. What was the point of mourning my old life? My lot wasn't going to miraculously change because I wished it would. My stepmother's behavior made that clear. The hope of finding Lady Françoise at the ball and escaping from the château was a flickering ember I'd cradled in my palms, burning hot but utterly unstable. I'd trusted Lady Catherine to keep her word, but instead she'd dumped ice water on the ember, snuffing it out completely. Now all I was left with was an empty château and a cold, soot-caked fireplace. Crying was pointless. It changed nothing.

The heavy brass door knocker thudded against the front door once, twice, three times. I groaned and clambered to my feet. Who could be knocking at this hour? It wasn't the coachman, surely. My stepmother was nothing if not punctual. If she was going to send the carriage back for me, it would have been here already. No, it had to be someone else. Could I just ignore them and pretend no one was home? But knocks rang out again and again and again, beating out a steady rhythm on the oak door. With my luck, it would be another debt collector come to demand money we didn't have. I was not in the mood to argue and negotiate for just a few more months' leniency. It was getting harder and harder to convince them that Lady Catherine was actually going to pay what she owed.

I strode to the front door with purpose. Any sign of weakness would cause the debt collectors to pounce. With what I hoped was a neutral yet firm expression on my face, I threw open the door to face the unwelcome visitor.

A coachman in fine livery stood on the threshold, a surprised look on his face at the force with which I opened the door. Or perhaps he was surprised at my dreadful appearance. This wasn't one of Lady Catherine's coachmen; his uniform was completely unfamiliar to me. A small yet luxurious carriage done up in blue with golden scrollwork waited in the courtyard. There was a crest on the door, but I couldn't make out any identifying details in the dim light.

"What do you want?" I asked sharply.

The coachman roused himself from his stupor and straightened. "Madame wishes to speak with a Lady Cendrillon de Louvois. Is she in residence?"

Me. Some mysterious lady wished to speak with me. I could hardly believe it. No one had called on me in over a year.

"Who is this lady of yours?" I asked, with more bluster than I felt.

Before he could answer, the window of the carriage clattered open.

"Adam, what's taking so long?" said the woman in the carriage. "Are you having trouble finding her? Do you need my help?"

My gasp was so loud, the coachman looked at me strangely again. I knew that voice. No. It wasn't possible. Not after all this time.

Pushing past the coachman, I sprinted down the stone steps into the courtyard, stopping a few feet from the carriage. I held my breath as the carriage door opened. My entire body was trembling, as if I had a fever. I must have looked mad, standing in the courtyard, shaking and covered in filth, my hands clenched so tightly my nails nearly drew blood. If it wasn't her, I really would go mad. My hopes could only be dashed so many times.

A woman wearing an emerald-green dress, her chestnut-brown curls falling to her shoulders, stepped down from the carriage. It was her. It was my marraine, Lady Françoise.

She scanned the courtyard, her gaze dancing from the dark woods surrounding the château to Adam, the coachman, until she finally spotted me standing just inside the pool of light emanating from the torches positioned on either side of the bottom of the staircase. The shock in her hazel eyes must surely have mirrored mine.

I let go of the breath I'd been holding. The sight of her only made my shaking worse. I couldn't believe what I was seeing.

"Cendrillon," she said, barely more than a whisper, but I heard her clearly in the quiet of the courtyard.

She reached out for me and smiled, like she'd done so many times before, and for the moment, all the anger I'd held for her fell away. I ran to her and threw myself into her arms, nearly knocking her over with the force of my hug. Her embrace was warm and gentle and very, very real. I wasn't dreaming. Lady Françoise was finally here, after so long. She was smaller than I remembered. Or maybe I was taller. I buried my face in the crook of her neck and started sobbing. I guess I could cry after all, big, heaving sobs that would have been embarrassing any other time. But not now.

"Ma douce, what's the matter? Oh, don't cry. Please, don't cry," she said, but I could hear tears in her voice as well. "Ma douce, douce fille."

Lady Françoise held me tightly for what felt like hours but could only have been a few moments. I could've stayed there forever, but she pulled back slightly and tilted my face toward hers. She gasped when she got a look at my face.

"What *happened*? You are so thin." Lady Françoise pulled me over to the glow of the château's torchlight and cupped my face in her hands. "Why are you covered in cinder and ashes?"

It was a little unnerving how intently she looked at me, her kind hazel eyes, so familiar it hurt, roving over my disheveled appearance. I'm sure I got soot on her lovely green dress. But she didn't seem angry, although she looked tired and wan.

"It's nothing. Lady Catherine and my stepsisters are at the ball, and I was cleaning the fireplace while they're gone. I'm sorry if I got your dress dirty."

"I don't care about my dress. I care about why you're home by yourself cleaning the fireplace while your stepmother and stepsisters are at the ball. Didn't you want to go too?"

"I did. Yes. I actually hoped . . ." I trailed off, unable to admit that I was hoping to find her at the ball. It sounded pathetic when I thought about it, and I was sure I seemed pathetic enough already. "I wanted to go. And Lady Catherine said I *could* go, and then she and my stepsisters went ahead so they wouldn't be late. She was supposed to send the carriage back for me, but she never did."

Lady Françoise stared at me, agog. "She left you behind. On purpose?!"

There was an anger burning in Lady Françoise's eyes that I'd never seen before. Even though I knew the sharpness of her words wasn't directed at me, her tone still scared me a little. I nodded my head. She huffed in displeasure, her frown only deepening.

"Is this behavior common for your stepmother?"

I hesitated before answering, sudden doubt making me taciturn. Could I trust Lady Françoise with the truth? After all, she'd abandoned me, not for one night but for an entire year. But it felt so wonderful to be around her again, and she did seem to care about me, if her anger at Lady Catherine's behavior was anything to go by. My marraine was all I had. Who else could I even hope to trust?

"This behavior is . . . common. That and worse," I said tentatively.

"I see. You can tell me about the 'and worse' while we ride."

"What do you—"

Before I could finish my question, Lady Françoise grabbed my hand and ushered me into the carriage. I put up no resistance, thoroughly confused. Everything was happening so quickly.

"Adam, we're leaving," she said, climbing into the carriage and sliding into the seat next to me.

"Where are we going?"

"To my estate. We need to get you ready."

"Ready for what?"

"For the ball. I will see you dancing in the Hall of Mirrors, no matter what your evil stepmother says."

CHAPTER SEVENTEEN

IN THE DARKENED INTERIOR OF the carriage, Lady Françoise wrapped me up in an impossibly soft blanket to soothe my trembling while I told her what had happened over the past year. I couldn't stop the tears from flowing as I talked about Papa's funeral; the dismissal of Marius and Claudine from the château; and my new status as a servant to my stepfamily. The pain in her eyes was evident when I talked about Papa, as was the simmering anger when I told her that Lady Catherine slapped me after my trip to the market.

"That young man you met would be very unhappy to know his actions caused you such pain," Lady Françoise said, her arm wrapped around my shoulders. "He only wanted to be kind to you."

"You *know* him?"

"A little. I saw him at court, and he told me about your meeting at the market. He's the reason I even knew where to find you."

I'd hoped to put the mysterious stranger out of my mind forever, but here he was, reemerging at the most unexpected time. And he knew Lady Françoise. But how did he know me, and why would he mention me to Lady Françoise?

"Who is he, then? He seemed familiar when we met, but I couldn't place him."

Lady Françoise looked away, suddenly finding the empty fields abutting the little country road supremely interesting. A twinge of doubt hit me. I couldn't stand when people kept secrets. Papa kept it a secret that he was marrying Lady Catherine, and look how that turned out. I didn't want whatever was going on between Lady Françoise and the stranger to be equally detrimental to me.

"Marraine? Who is he?"

She turned back to me and said, with an apologetic smile, "I'm sorry, Cendrillon, but it isn't my place to say. He hoped you would be at the ball tonight so he could meet you properly and talk things through."

"But that's impossible! I would like to go to the ball, of course, but look at me. I'm filthy! And I have absolutely nothing to wear. If I showed up to Versailles looking like this, they would toss me out on the street!"

To my surprise, I did still want to attend the ball, even though I no longer needed to search for my godmother. Now I wanted to go solely to defy my stepmother. I was tired of being subservient to her whims. I was Lady Cendrillon de Louvois, the daughter of Marquis de Louvois, who had been one of the king's closest advisors. It was my right to attend the ball, whether she wanted me to or not.

"That's why we're going to my estate, ma petite. I have so many lovely dresses you can wear, and with how much you've grown over the past year, you're nearly my size. If something doesn't fit, I'm sure one of my maids could alter it quickly."

I pulled away from Lady Françoise and leaned my head back on the plush purple velvet cushion behind me. Closing my eyes, I took a few deep breaths to calm my spinning head. I'd been with Lady Françoise for no more than an hour, but it felt like everything I thought I knew was being turned upside down.

"Why did you leave me?" I asked abruptly, the question burning a hole inside my throat until I finally released it into the warm air of the carriage.

I sat up so I could look at her properly while I asked the questions I'd been wishing to know the answers to for so long. My voice was soft, yet firm. Bitter, even. I wanted her to hear the bitterness, to know that she'd hurt me.

"Papa died, and you didn't come to his funeral. You *knew* that I was an orphan. That I was alone. And you didn't come to see me. You didn't even write me a letter. I thought you didn't care about me anymore. I'm still not sure."

I started crying as I spoke. The tears were warm and sticky on my cheeks, and my nose was starting to run, but I had nothing to wipe it with. I was afraid Lady Françoise would be unmoved, but my chest ached when I saw the answering tears in her eyes. She reached over and grasped my hands tightly.

"Of course I care about you, Cendrillon. I've loved you like my own since the moment your mother first handed you to me when you were a newborn babe wrapped in swaddling clothes. It hurts that you think I don't care about you. But that's my fault."

"Why didn't you come to Papa's funeral?" I asked, harshness still seeping into my voice even though some of my anger was starting to dim.

"I'm sure you realized that I cared about your father as more than a friend. Am I correct?"

I nodded slowly. "I thought you and Papa were going to get married. And I saw the way he looked at you. He never looked at anyone else like that."

"That's sweet of you to say," she said, her smile sad. "I also thought that he loved me. I certainly loved him, and I was going to tell him the night of the ball, but I suddenly felt ill and had to go home. The next thing I knew, he was marrying Lady Catherine. I was devastated. Please don't take this as an attack against your father, because it's not, but his marriage to Lady Catherine Monvoisin broke my heart. And then he died, and everything became so much worse. I wanted to go to his funeral, but *she* was going to be there. It was too painful for me to grieve Michel and see Catherine. To have to speak with her. It was cowardly on my part. I regret it to this day."

I scooted closer to her on the bench and squeezed her hands tighter. I couldn't blame Lady Françoise for not going to Papa's funeral. It hurt that she wasn't there, and I was so angry about it for so long, but I understood why she couldn't. If I were in her shoes, I don't know what I would have done.

"I don't blame you for not coming to Papa's funeral," I told her.

She opened her mouth to object, but I ignored it and forged ahead. "I don't understand why you never came to see *me*."

Lady Françoise's voice was firm and her eyes pleading. "I could not be more sorry. After Michel's passing I took some . . . time away from court, to visit family in England. I haven't been well. I just got back last month and only found out that you were still living near Versailles after speaking with our friend from the market." She looked a bit fragile, almost brittle, and I worried for her, especially since I had just found her again.

"Where else would I have been?" I said, looking out the carriage window.

"I heard that you were sent to stay with your aunt. I wrote you letters at her address. I'm surprised she didn't send them on. If I'd known you were alone with Lady Catherine, and certainly if I'd known how horribly she treated you, I would have insisted that you come live with me."

My heart jumped at the thought of living with Lady Françoise, but what she said about my aunt didn't make any sense.

"My aunt? Maman's sister? She died six years ago. Papa was the only family I had left."

Lady Françoise looked as if she might faint at this news. "Oh, ma chérie! I had no idea. At court, everyone said you'd been sent to live with your aunt. I never thought to check whether it was true or not. Who would have started that kind of rumor?"

I had a guess. Could Lady Catherine have started the rumor so that Lady Françoise didn't go looking for me? So she could use me as free labor without anyone's bothersome concern for my well-being getting in her way? I wouldn't put it past her.

"But I did send you a letter before I left for England, and that one went to the château. Didn't you get it?"

"No. I never got any letter."

Lady Françoise gasped. She wiped her brow. "How strange. I wasn't sure of your aunt's address, having heard nothing, so I sent it to the château instead. I had hoped that Lady Catherine would send it on."

As soon as the words left her mouth, I knew. If Lady Françoise said that she sent me a letter, then she sent me a letter. It was lost either accidentally or on purpose, and I was fairly certain it was on purpose.

I hugged Lady Françoise tightly. I'd been so angry at her for so long, but that was all over now. She'd loved Papa and was grieving for him too. It was clear to me that Lady Catherine had destroyed the letter.

"I'm just glad you're here now," I said, breathing in the comfortingly familiar scent of her jasmine perfume.

"I won't leave you again. I promise," said Lady Françoise, her arms tightening around me. "We're family. We'll look out for each other."

For the first time since Papa died, I was filled with hope for a future that I'd only been dreading.

CHAPTER EIGHTEEN

"I WOULD VERY MUCH PREFER not to wear my hair in a fontange," I said, dancing away from one of Lady Françoise's maids, my hands covering the top of my head protectively.

"Why not, my lady? It would look so lovely on you, and it's quite in fashion," she said, a pile of wires and lace cradled in her arms like a baby.

"That is kind of you to say, but truly, I would prefer almost any other hairstyle."

Just looking at the materials brought back memories of Severine screaming in my ear because I'd accidentally pulled her hair or pricked her with a pin while trying to wrangle the towering ornament into place atop her head. I shuddered at the thought.

"Fine," the lady's maid said with a sigh, dropping the wires and lace onto a blue velvet footstool. "Will you at least allow us to style your hair a little?"

"Yes, of course. I mean it when I say any other hairstyle. Just not a fontange. Thank you," I said awkwardly.

I felt out of place in Lady Françoise's boudoir. It was all so luxurious, with marble walls, blue velvet furnishings, and gold accents. Her toilette table was covered in gold, silver, and crystal bottles that looked as if they would shatter at the slightest touch, while a large mirror covered almost the entire length of one wall. A chandelier dripping with crystals hung from the ceiling. The candlelight that reflected through the crystals was dappled and gentle, as if we were standing in a shady glen in the forest and not a lavishly ornate boudoir.

After I took a lovely bath that was drawn for me, filled with the most heavenly oils, Lady Françoise sent three of her lady's maids to help me prepare. Now I was sitting in my underthings and a silk robe, waiting for the seamstress to finish the alterations on one of Lady Françoise's dresses while the maids completed the rest of my toilette. Their enthusiasm was intimidating. The maid with the fontange materials looked so upset at my refusal that I almost wanted to apologize and relent. Almost.

"Don't pout, Marianne," the second maid said, coming up behind me, grabbing my shoulders, and forcefully leading me back to my seat at the vanity. "We can put her hair up in a chignon. You love those."

"Would that be suitable, mademoiselle? I can pull the top half of your hair into a chignon and leave the bottom half in curls around your shoulders? It's an older style, but quite pretty."

"That sounds perfect. I'm sure you'll do a wonderful job."

Marianne beamed at me again and got to work on my hair, while the other two maids started applying makeup. The steps were familiar. I'd done them all a thousand times with Severine and Alexandre, but it was another matter entirely to be the person who was waited upon.

"Yvette, which color of rouge do you think would look best on her? The lighter pink or the deep red?" the third maid, Doreen, asked.

Doreen held up the two pots for Yvette's inspection. She peered at each one closely, then at me, then back at the pots, and then at me again. This went on far longer than I thought strictly necessary before Yvette made her decision.

"The pink one. Yes, definitely the pink. The red will be too garish."

Doreen nodded and began to smooth the rouge onto my cheeks while Yvette crouched down in front of me with a little brush to apply the vermilion to my lips.

"Look what I found," Marianne said excitedly as she returned from her foray into Lady Françoise's jewelry box. "This string of sapphires will look gorgeous against her hair. And it matches the dress perfectly."

Yvette and Doreen oohed over it, then Marianne wrapped it around the chignon and pinned it in place.

I was jittery with nerves about finally getting to attend—instead of just sneaking into—a ball at Versailles. This was one of the things I'd dreamed about before even moving here. I was also nervous because Lady Catherine and my stepsisters were going to be there. What would happen if I ran into one of them? I wasn't going to hide from them anymore, but I didn't want to confront them either. I was also excited for the chance to see Auguste again—I'd written to him, too, but never heard back. Now I realize his reply may have been intercepted. But he was sure to be at the palace tonight.

"My lady, which perfume would you like to wear?" Yvette asked, holding out two delicate silver flasks engraved with flowers.

"Lady Françoise has set out two for you: rose water and orange flower water. Which would you prefer?"

"Orange flower water," I said immediately, standing in my silk slip.

Yvette began to daub the orange flower water on my wrists, neck, and décolletage. It was a delightful scent, subtly sweet and fresh.

"Beauty patches?" Doreen asked, proffering a box with little black satin patches arrayed on white linen.

I pointed to the crescent moons, nearly laughing at the irony of the patches that appealed to me being of a piece with my stepsisters' star patches.

"The dress is ready!" Lady Françoise's seamstress, Charlotte, said, bursting into the boudoir with a mound of fabric slung over a shoulder, Lady Françoise following at her heels.

"I don't think I've ever worked so fast in my entire life. That was stressful. But it's over, and now you need to try it on," Charlotte said, her words rushing together in her excitement.

Before I could even utter a reply, Charlotte, the maids, and Lady Françoise crowded around. I stepped into the puddle of material and petticoats, and the maids helped me pull it up and navigate my arms into the sleeves. I wouldn't have been able to get into such an elaborate dress by myself. When all my limbs were in the right places, Charlotte laced up the dress in the back. The bodice was snug but not constricting, the sleeves tapered to the correct length, and I had plenty of room to move my legs in the skirt.

"You did an amazing job, Charlotte! It fits *wonderfully*," I said, grinning at her.

The seamstress smiled back at me, blushing slightly. "Take a look in the mirror, mademoiselle. You haven't even seen yourself in it yet."

Lady Françoise took my arm and spun me around to face the massive mirror on the opposite wall.

"What do you think?"

My breath caught when I saw myself in the mirror. The dress was stunningly beautiful, so beautiful that I could hardly take my eyes off it. The bodice and overskirt were a rich sapphire-indigo satin, as was the short train attached to the dress at the shoulders, that draped to the floor behind me. I'd never seen a more vivid blue. The dye must have been unimaginably expensive.

The boned bodice was encrusted with gemstones that caught the light and sparkled brilliantly with the slightest movement. The neckline was modest but allowed a hint of my bosom to show. I would not go so far as wear it below the nipples, as some saucy courtiers did, with only a sheer neckerchief covering them that a favored gentleman would then tear off at the party as a game. A full skirt made of gathered tiers of fabric tumbled gracefully to the floor, dotted here and there with gemstones to continue the transfixing shimmer. And the underskirt, a pristine white, was embroidered in gold thread with twisting vines and flowers. As I stared in the mirror, Yvette quickly attached the lace at the sleeves and neckline.

"I have two more gifts for you," Lady Françoise said as she walked up behind me and wrapped a delicate pearl necklace around my throat.

"Oh no, Marraine, please, you've done so much for me already. You don't have to—"

"But I *want* to. Besides, this necklace is special. My mother gave it to me before I attended my first ball. I want you to have it."

"Thank you," I whispered. Tears stung my eyes, but I forced them back. I couldn't cry now. It would ruin my makeup.

"And these are for you as well," she said, handing me a pair of brocade slippers.

The slippers were covered in blue velvet that, to my surprise, perfectly matched the color of the dress. I held on to Lady Françoise's shoulder while I slipped them on. They were surprisingly comfortable, even with the pointed toe and high heel. Embroidered on the velvet were large golden flowers, with glass crystals scattered between them.

From head to toe, I sparkled when I moved. It was mesmerizing.

"You've become such a beautiful young woman," said Lady Françoise. "Are you ready to head to the ball and dazzle everyone you meet?"

I rolled my eyes and laughed, but I couldn't deny that I did look older. More mature. I'd never felt like I would belong at Versailles, especially not after Papa died. But in that dress and those shoes, I was poised and elegant. And maybe even a little beautiful. I could imagine myself amongst the nobles of Versailles. As long as I didn't open my mouth and say something foolish, I might even be convincing to a real courtier, or Alexandre at the least.

"I'm ready," I said.

Glancing in the mirror once more before we left, I gave myself a firm nod of encouragement. I could be that strong woman I saw reflected back at me. A woman like Lady Françoise, who endured disrespect from no one. A woman who was in charge of her own fate.

GLASS

Beauty begins the moment you decide to be yourself.

—*Coco Chanel*

CHAPTER NINETEEN

"SHALL WE GO INTO THE ball now?" Lady Françoise asked, her hand resting on my shoulder. "If you want, I'll stay with you the entire time. I promise." Her voice was scratchy and weak, and I worried for her health once more, but when I mentioned it, she dismissed it with a wave of her fan. "Oh, I'm all right, I have the heart of a bull," she said, laughing, and I felt assuaged.

Lady Françoise and I were huddled in a corner of the Salon of War, watching the crowds of lavishly dressed nobles wander in and out of the doorway leading into the Hall of Mirrors, where the ball was being held. My confidence had remained strong during the carriage ride to the palace, but as soon as we entered the state apartments and joined the massive procession of people making their way through the palace, I started to panic at the very real possibility that my stepmother would notice me and have me thrown out of the party.

I'd thought the ball Elodie, Marius, and I snuck into had been crowded, but this was so much worse. The heat from all the bodies pressed together and the overpowering smell of perfume and musk nearly smothered me. When we finally made it to the Salon of War, I had to drag Lady Françoise out of the procession and into the corner so I could breathe without so many people close by, and attempt to calm my racing heartbeat. I don't know what I thought the ball was going to be like. People from all over France were attending. Of course the crowds would be enormous.

"Cendrillon, you do not have to worry," said Lady Françoise as she rubbed my back soothingly. "I know there are a lot of people here, but it won't feel so crowded once we get inside the Hall of Mirrors. It's such a large gallery, you'll hardly even notice."

She was right. I was being foolish. After everything I went through tonight to get here, was I really going to throw it all away because of a fear of running into Lady Catherine? That would be ridiculous. So what if I ran into her? There was nothing she could do to me here, in front of all these people. And as soon as we picked up Elodie after the ball, I would never have to set foot in that château again. I took one last deep breath of relatively fresh air and turned to Lady Françoise with what I hoped was a reassuring smile on my face.

"Let's go in. If we wait any longer, I'll lose my nerve entirely. I'm ready now."

The skeptical look on Lady Françoise's face made me assume that my smile wasn't particularly reassuring, but she still took my arm and led me out of our corner. We slipped back into the procession behind two giggling girls not much older than me, their arms linked and heads pressed together, so consumed with their conversation that they barely looked up at their surroundings.

"You're going to have so much fun tonight," Lady Françoise whispered as we approached the archway leading into the Hall of Mirrors. "I still remember my first ball. It was a magical night."

I nodded distractedly, too absorbed with making sure my sweaty palms didn't leave stains on my godmother's lovely dress. That would be disastrous. I crossed my fingers behind my fan as we made our way through the archway into the Hall of Mirrors.

The gallery was dazzlingly beautiful. It ran the length of the central block of the palace, stretching so far ahead of me, I had to squint to see the other side. I stood still in the entranceway, enchanted by the splendor. It was crowded, to be sure. Courtiers were standing shoulder to shoulder in tight clusters, talking and laughing so loudly, it was hard to hear the music over their chatter, but the length of the hall and the impressive height of the soaring ceilings made it feel larger than it really was. So consumed was I with gawping like a child that I didn't notice I was blocking the people behind me from coming in.

"Let's go this way," said Lady Françoise, taking my arm again and pulling us farther into the hall.

To our right, massive windows that reached nearly to the ceiling ran along the entire length of the gallery, and within each window embrasure were tiered seats packed with even more courtiers. Some sat with glasses in hand, chatting with their neighbors, while others turned to look out through the windows at the gardens beyond. It was dark enough that they couldn't have been able to see much. Some people even stood on the seating, their backs pressed against the windows or those sitting behind them, gazing at the crowds with much the same look of awe on their faces as I assumed was on mine.

Directly across from each window, ensconced in their very own arches, were the massive mirrors that gave the hall its name. Each mirror, made up of many smaller panels, stretched up nearly to the ceiling, pairing perfectly with the windows on the opposite wall. On either side of the mirrors and windows were mottled-red-marble pilasters topped with gilded capitals. If I looked hard enough, I could just make out what was carved into the capitals: a sun atop a fleur-de-lis, between two Gallic roosters. All three were symbols that represented France. Really, everything about the Hall of Mirrors represented the glory and power of France and its king.

The king himself sat on his throne on a dais at the other end of the gallery, raised high enough that he could comfortably survey the entirety of the hall and all his assembled subjects. Arrayed behind him on the dais were men whom I assumed were his advisors, or perhaps favored courtiers. I strained to see if I could find Auguste anywhere.

I grabbed Lady Françoise's hand and pulled her with me as I wove through the crowd. It wasn't as difficult as I'd feared; many of the men even bowed to me, while the women looked appreciatively at my dress. All the nobles seemed to be in a wonderful mood. Maybe it was excitement at the prospect of a royal marriage. Maybe it was the flowing wine. Either way, we made quick work of getting to the other side of the hall.

The mirror I chose to examine was very near the dancers. While both ends of the narrow Hall of Mirrors were occupied with mingling courtiers, the very center of the gallery was reserved for dancing. I could see them in the mirror behind my own reflection, face flushed and eyes wide, a rainbow's assortment of colors twirling in the background. The dancers moved so quickly that their forms blended in the mirror to become an indistinguishable blur in the dim lighting. I couldn't tear my eyes away from the sight.

"What do you think?" Lady Françoise asked, standing by my side to gaze into the mirror with me.

"It's wonderful! So much grander than I imagined. I just wish Papa could be here with us."

Grief for Papa always slunk back in, no matter how hard I tried to push it away. He *should* have been here with us, twirling Lady Françoise around the dance floor or competing with me to see who could eat the most candied orange slices.

"I know. I wish he were as well." Lady Françoise's words were barely more than a whisper. Sadness was etched deeply on her face. I shouldn't have said anything. This wasn't supposed to be a sad night. We both deserved to have a little fun.

"One of my stepsisters, Alexandre, raves constantly about how beautiful the Hall of Mirrors is," I said brightly, as if I'd never brought up Papa. "But I never thought it would—"

"Françoise!" called an older woman in a precariously placed fontange and a cream-colored dress embroidered with cherry blossoms. She practically shoved me to the side in her excitement to talk to my godmother.

"Adalene! You just *pushed* my goddaughter." Lady Françoise glanced at me apologetically. I shrugged my shoulders and smiled. It didn't bother me. I was more concerned with whether or not Lady Adalene's bobbling fontange would topple right off her head. Considering the way she was vibrating in place with excitement, setting the fontange to swaying, it seemed a real possibility.

"You're late! You missed the king's announcement," Lady Adalene said, ignoring me entirely.

"What did he say that was so important you had to dispense with all social graces to come and tell me about it?"

If Lady Adalene picked up on the sarcasm, she didn't react, her smile remaining firmly in place as she soldiered on with her gossip. "The rumors about Prince Louis finding a wife at the celebrations were correct! The king announced that the dauphin will be picking twenty-five girls *tonight* to court. By the end of the season, one girl will be chosen to become his bride! Isn't it exciting?"

Lady Françoise opened her mouth to speak, but Lady Adalene cut her off. "I need you to come speak with my daughter. You remember Margot, don't you? She's grown up to be such a lovely girl. I'm sure she'll be one of the girls chosen tonight."

"Why do you need me to speak to Margot?"

Lady Adalene leaned forward and whispered loudly, "You know the king better than most, what he likes, what he disapproves of. He will surely be helping his son choose from amongst the girls. I'm aware that it's been a number of years since your liaison, and that Madame de Maintenon knows the king best now, but I don't know her. I know you."

"What are you saying, Adalene?"

The other woman didn't seem to notice Lady Françoise's face fall when she brought up her former relationship with the king, but I did. Should I intervene? Would the indomitable woman even listen to me, or would she simply brush me off again like a pesky insect?

"I want you to help prepare my Margot for a possible future relationship with the dauphin. Tell her what it's like to be so intimately acquainted with royalty. I've only ever spoken a handful of words to the king, and that was years ago. I wouldn't even know where to start. But you *do*."

"I really don't think that would be appropriate," Lady Françoise said, but Lady Adalene grabbed her hands and started pulling her back into the crowd of courtiers.

"We'll only take a few minutes of your time. Please, Françoise. I won't take no for an answer."

I wanted to laugh at the look of surprise on Lady Françoise's face. I'd never seen her so flustered before.

"I suppose it will do me good to sit down—I am a bit tired. Would you like to come with us?" Lady Françoise asked.

"I'll be fine," I said.

Lady Adalene led her away. "Enjoy yourself while I'm gone. Maybe find a nice young gentleman to dance with," she teased.

I smiled and waved her off. There would be no nice young gentlemen for me tonight. I wanted to enjoy the atmosphere and watch the proceedings, not participate.

Within seconds, Lady Françoise disappeared into the throng, and I was all alone in the midst of the ball.

Placed along each mirror were three little silver stools where people could sit. Many were already occupied, but I managed to swoop in and take one that opened up after a very intoxicated noble-man awoke from his nap and stumbled off into the crowd.

It was quite the chore to sit down in a dress with such large skirts. I had to position myself so the skirts remained under me without riding up or subsuming the stool entirely, making for an embarrassing scenario when I needed to stand, and also making sure that the deli-cate satin didn't wrinkle too badly.

I had a wonderful view of the dancing from my stool, one that was relatively unobstructed by roving courtiers. The current dance was a rigaudon, which brought back certain memories of Auguste, who didn't seem to be *anywhere*. He was also the king's son, after all, and royalty tended to appear at balls. No. I wasn't going to muse on things that would make me melancholy. I was going to focus on the dancing in front of me. It was exciting to watch. I enjoyed listening to the dancers' shoes clacking reassuringly against the parquet floor. If I could have spent the rest of the night sitting and watching the dancing, I would have been satisfied.

The dim lighting in the hall was making me feel a little sleepy, even amongst all the noise of the revelry. One effect of the many mir-rors was that the light from the crystal chandeliers and candelabras reflected in the mirrors to create a warm golden glow. That glow felt heavy and tangible on my skin, as if I could take it in my hands and wrap it around me like a cape.

Outside, where night pressed against the windowpanes, I was an orphan girl living with a stepmother who hated me. Inside the Hall of Mirrors, I was a mysterious noblewoman in a shimmering sapphire dress who belonged with these glamorous people. It was all so much like a dream, a magical, pleasant dream from which I didn't want to wake.

My eyes lazily drifted up to the ceiling, which was painted in a similar style to the ceilings of the state apartments, deep, rich colors bringing to life angels floating through the heavens and men in fine armor.

"Are you admiring the paintings? They are impressive, aren't they?"

I nearly fell off my stool. The voice, startlingly close to my ear, pulled me roughly from my daze like a child dragged from the warmth of their bed in the early morning. I turned to see a boy where there had been none a moment ago, sitting on the stool next to me. He had dark brown hair, blue eyes, and a crooked smile on his face as he looked at me far too intently for my liking.

"Charles Le Brun, one of the greatest painters in France, created them. They depict some of the many successes of my father's reign."

"Your father?" I said slowly, the boy's smile growing as he saw the realization of who he was cross my face.

I stood up as gracefully as I could while still making sure that my skirts were in the right place, spun around and dipped into a low curtsy in front of none other than the Grand Dauphin of France, Louis.

"Monseigneur le Dauphin, I apologize for not recognizing you sooner. I am . . . new to court."

The prince stood up. He was tall and broad-shouldered, so tall that I had to crane my neck to look up at him. So, this was the awful boy from the Orangerie, all grown up. He was certainly handsome in his burgundy justaucorps with gold braiding and buttons, paired with matching breeches, dark stockings, and a lacy cravat with a black satin ribbon at the throat. There was a mischievous twinkle in his eyes that made them hard to look away from. It was difficult to believe that this was the same spoiled child who made fun of me for being friends with Elodie and Marius and needed his brother to stop him from throwing a tantrum after I told him off. He cut quite the regal, poised figure now. Hopefully, his manners had improved along with his looks.

"It's perfectly all right. I assumed you were a newcomer. I surely would have remembered seeing a girl like you," the prince said with another dazzling smile.

I blushed and averted my eyes. Compliments made me supremely uncomfortable, especially when they came from the dauphin of France I'd insulted a year ago. But it was obvious that he didn't remember me. If he did, I can't imagine his reaction would have been quite so pleasant.

"What is your name, mademoiselle?" he asked as he bowed at the waist.

"Cinder," I blurted out in a panic.

My fireplace-cleaning adventure from earlier in the evening was the only thing on my mind in the moment. It was silly, but I didn't dare use my real name. While I didn't think the dauphin would recognize me, I didn't want it getting back to Lady Catherine that I was here just yet. It would be better to keep my identity secret for a little while longer so I could enjoy the ball in peace.

"Cinder? What an unusual name."

"It's what my father used to call me."

"Would the lady care to reveal her given name?"

I bit my lip and looked away from his searching gaze, off into the crowd of courtiers. Where was Lady Françoise? She promised she would be back soon. Hadn't it already been at least fifteen minutes?

"Ah, a girl of mystery. How intriguing," the prince said contemplatively.

That wasn't good. I didn't want to seem intriguing to a pampered prince. I wanted to enjoy the ball. Alone.

"I'm really not so mysterious."

Before I could finish my sentence, the dauphin grabbed my hand and started pulling me toward the dance floor.

"What are you doing?"

"Will you honor me with a dance, Lady Cinder?" he asked with great confidence.

"Oh! I'm not sure I deserve such an honor." I tried to pull away, but he held my hand tightly.

"Nonsense. All the lovely young ladies at the ball should have the honor of dancing with me," he said, dropping my hand to walk up to the musicians sequestered in an antechamber just off the main hall.

It would be so impolite to refuse, and the dauphin took my hand again and started pulling me forward.

The dauphin clapped his hands and called, "Begin the music!"

The musicians struck up a tune for a lively gavotte. I sighed in relief. The gavotte was a dance that required four participants, made up of two couples. We formed a square with another couple, each couple facing the other, and with a series of little hops that were much less strenuous to perform than those in the rigaudon, began switching places in the square. Each dancer inhabited every corner of the square before finally returning to their original spot. It was a short dance, thankfully, and one that I quite enjoyed.

I might have enjoyed it even more if the dauphin hadn't held me so close, as if I were property that he already owned. When it came time for us to switch positions, twirling gracefully around each other in the middle of the square, his hand brushed mine, lingering for just a moment before we parted. There was no reason at all for a couple to touch during a gavotte. If I were any of the highborn maidens, I would have been thrilled, but even a year later, I found his arrogance off-putting. My stomach felt queasy, as if I had eaten something bad.

Beyond my father, I hadn't had much experience with men. There was Auguste, of course, but I didn't think our youthful flirtation counted as experience. I truly hoped I would see him tonight. I wasn't upset about his deception. Not anymore. Such a silly lie seemed inconsequential after everything I'd been through.

Louis's hand brushed mine again. After finishing the steps, I glanced back to see him gazing at me. There was no mistaking his attention. Sweet revenge after the way he had initially dismissed me when we first met.

Lady Adalene had mentioned that he was going to be choosing twenty-five women to court during the upcoming season tonight, but naturally, he would choose the daughters of foreign dignitaries or high-ranking nobles. I was the daughter of a high-ranking noble, but he didn't know that yet.

An enthusiastic round of applause greeted the end of the dance. Of course, most of that was for the dauphin, but at least some of it had to be for me. At least, I imagined it was. I'd done well for being so rusty. I hadn't tripped on my train, and I'd executed the steps as accurately as possible. Pride flared in my chest. It felt nice to be recognized for doing something well.

I curtsied to my dance partners while the dauphin bowed. I tried to follow the other couple off the dance floor, but Prince Louis slid in front of me, blocking my path.

He took my hands in his with a flourish and said, "I must take my leave, Lady Cinder. I enjoyed dancing with you immensely. Thank you for doing me the honor. I hope to see you again very soon."

The dauphin grinned at me, bowed, and left the dance floor, heading in the direction of the king's dais. A wave of nobles parted for him as he walked by, creating a clear path through the Hall.

I hope to see you again very soon.

I wasn't sure if I wanted to see him again. My face was warm, and I could feel perspiration beading at my hairline and temples. What I did want was to reclaim my stool and catch my breath.

Spinning around to make my way back to the mirrors, I smacked right into the chest of someone else blocking my path off the dance floor.

"I'm sorry, Monsieur. I didn't see you there."

"It's no trouble at all. I was in your—"

I knew that voice. It was the man from the market. I looked up to see a face I knew very well, a face I treasured dearly, staring back at me with a surprised look of his own.

CHAPTER TWENTY

"AUGUSTE?" I GASPED, MY VOICE little more than a whisper. "It was you at the market!"

"It was me," he said, a blush coloring his cheeks.

"But you're so tall!" And so much more handsome than I remembered.

He smiled. "It's good to see you again."

I stepped backward, bumping into a couple performing the first steps of the next dance. They glared at me as I jumped out of their way only to end up in the path of yet another pair of dancers. I looked around the dance floor and realized that it had filled considerably. Everyone was partnered to dance the allemande, one of the most popular court dances, especially for young lovers. It was one of the few dances where you could hold your partner's hand throughout. Auguste and I were stuck right in the middle of the pack of dancers.

Auguste held his hand out to me. "Would you care to dance? Courtiers can become quite put out when their dancing is interrupted, and I don't think we're getting out of here any other way. We can talk after."

I put my hand in his. The minute our fingers touched, an electric shock coursed through me. I felt my heart speed up. So different from when I was dancing with his brother.

I launched into the dance with him immediately, taking one short step right, then left, before turning underneath his arm. As Auguste started the turn beneath mine, I gazed at him, amazed that he was really here, that his presence wasn't some cruel joke being played on me by Lady Catherine or the dauphin. I completed my second and third turns and watched him do his. His height and broad shoulders were different from yet highly reminiscent of those from a certain prince I'd just been dancing with. But those eyes—a clear sea green that that held just a hint of shyness. Those eyes I remembered.

We danced side by side for a moment, our hands clasped, one arm stretched above our heads, the other behind each other's back. He held me close and firm, and it took my breath away a little.

"Why didn't you tell me who you were at the market?" I asked, raising my voice to be heard over the chatter of the crowd and the clapping of heels on the floor.

We pulled apart, and I spun again.

"I'd hoped that you would realize who I was when I asked the merchant to include the oranges with your order. I'm not too proud to admit that it stung when you didn't," he said, our hands clasped again as we swayed back and forth across from each other.

"You wore a cloak that covered your entire face. For all I knew, you were just a presumptuous stranger," I said as we danced back to back before turning into the final spin.

"I know. It was silly of me."

The final spin brought me up against his chest, our faces close together. We stood, unmoving, unspeaking, until applause rang out around us and our fellow dancers began to bow and curtsy. Startled, I stepped back to gain some much-needed distance. I truly couldn't breathe in this corset; it was much, much too tight, that had to be why I was feeling so overwhelmed. Auguste had grown in the intervening year, but he wasn't so changed as to have been unrecognizable. He was still the friend I remembered.

"I'm so happy to see you!" I cried, throwing my arms around him in an overwhelming burst of joy.

I pulled back just as quickly, suddenly aware of the impropriety of such a public display of affection. No one seemed to be paying me any attention anymore now that Prince Louis was gone, but we couldn't be too careful.

He grinned, and for a moment, he looked like the boy who made fun of etiquette lessons with me.

"Is there somewhere we can talk?" I whispered.

My preferred stool was taken, unfortunately, as were all the others, but I spotted a relatively unoccupied window embrasure closer to the entrance of the Salon of War. Perhaps most of the other courtiers considered it too far away from the dancing and the king's dais, which was a boon for us. It was quieter there. More secluded. The only other occupants were a young couple sequestered in the shadows on the very top level of the tiered seating, wrapped in each other's arms. I blushed to see them. But they didn't even notice Auguste and I approach and sit down.

The massive window was partially open, allowing for a gentle night breeze to waft in and cool the warm air. As soon as I got myself properly settled, I turned to face Auguste, who glanced away when he saw me looking. He'd behaved this way when we were first introduced in Lady Celia's lessons, all shy and nervous, even as he was friendly and chatty. It was very sweet and very endearing. At least that hadn't changed.

All that confidence from the market seemed to have evaporated. Maybe that was why I hadn't recognized him. I wasn't used to Auguste being so forward. But of course I would never tell him that.

"I'm sorry I didn't recognize you before," I said, nudging him with my shoulder gently to get him to look at me. "I was distressed that day. And flustered."

Auguste laughed and nudged me back. "It's all right. Really. I was mostly joking when I said you hurt my feelings."

"Mostly?" I teased.

"Well, it did sting a *little*, but I don't hold it against you. And I'm sure my evasions didn't help matters," he said with a sheepish grin.

"No. They really didn't. I couldn't wait to get away from you," I said, smiling.

Auguste winced and clasped a hand to his heart dramatically. "Your words wound me, mademoiselle!"

I couldn't help but laugh, even as I rolled my eyes. Everything felt so natural between us, like the past year hadn't happened. We could have been on our way back from one of Lady Celia's lessons, joking around like we always did. It was nice to slip back into my former, lighter self with Auguste and pretend nothing had changed.

"You shouldn't have worried about upsetting me; I would have been overjoyed to see you. We could have had this conversation ages ago."

"You're right. But I didn't want to put the burden of having to interact with a long-lost friend on you when you seemed so busy. I hoped the oranges might help you remember, and that we would be able to meet again soon." At my skeptical look, he continued. "It was a harebrained idea. I see that now. To be honest, as soon as I left the market, I realized I was being ridiculous. That's partly why I mentioned seeing you to Lady Françoise. I hoped she knew where you lived so I could apologize."

Auguste's slightly crooked smile was soft and genuine. I couldn't help but believe him, but I wasn't ready to let *everything* go just yet. "You neglected to tell me who you really were a year ago," I said. "It was an accident that I found out at all!"

Auguste winced again, this time seriously. I kept my expression carefully neutral so I didn't start laughing. It would be nice to see him squirm a little.

"You found out? How?"

"Do you remember the ball that the king threw a year ago? The one I told you my father wouldn't let me attend? I snuck in and saw you there with your brother and the king."

"I wanted to tell you," Auguste blurted, his face turning a bit red. "I thought about telling you so many times, but I never mustered up the courage."

"Why not? I wouldn't have been upset. I didn't care when you told me . . . well, when you told me that you were illegitimate."

I watched Auguste's shoulders rise and fall as he drew in a deep breath before answering me. "It's different when you're the king's illegitimate son, when your mother was his mistress."

"Does that matter more?"

Auguste laughed, but there was no humor in it. "It matters. People treat you differently when you're a prince. They want things from you. Favors, titles, patronage. Anything, really. And they hang on your every word, and flatter you, and throw parties in your honor in the hopes that you'll give it to them. Especially when you're heir to the throne.

"But when you're the king's bastard and *not* the king's heir—kept away from court for most of your life—they still treat you differently. But in this case, more like you're useless, because you can't do anything for them, not even intervene with the king on their behalf. They might hang around if they think you have influence with the

155

dauphin, but when they find out you don't, off they go again. You aren't even useful as a marriage prospect, because illegitimate children can't marry someone of noble birth without first being legitimized by the king. And my father hasn't done that for me, although he always promises that he will one day. So, no, I'm not a prince, Cendrillon. I might be the king's son, but I'm nobody."

The overwhelming sadness in Auguste's eyes hit me like a physical blow. I knew I was right to distrust court life. It might be beautiful and decadent to look at, but there was so much hidden underneath that I didn't understand. I reached out and took his hand.

He looked up at me and smiled weakly. "I was afraid that you would treat me differently, too, if you found out who I really was. I finally met someone who just wanted to be my friend, and I didn't want that to change. I'm sorry."

"You don't have to apologize," I said as I squeezed his hand gently. "I understand why you did it. Court politics seem so . . . so ridiculous and cruel."

Auguste beamed at me then, leaving me breathless. He'd grown much more striking than his brother. They might both take after their father, with dark hair and strong jawlines, but Auguste had the finer, more beautiful face, mostly due to the kindness in his expression.

"You don't know how much I've missed you," he said, breaking eye contact to glance back at the couple sitting behind us.

I took the opportunity to catch my breath. My cheeks had begun to burn as if I had a fever. What was wrong with me? I needed to get ahold of myself. It was just Auguste, my old friend. That one time when we almost kissed . . . just a childhood folly. Nothing more. I was going to make things strange between us if I didn't get my misbehaving thoughts under control.

"I had to endure my lessons without the reward of seeing you afterward," he continued. "They were dreadfully dull without you."

"I would have liked see you," I said, "but I needed some time away from court after my father died."

"I never got the chance to tell you how deeply sorry I was to hear of your father's passing," Auguste said. "I wanted to go the funeral, but I was told your father's wife wanted a small service. Also, I think she found it distasteful to imagine the king's bastard there. Some people at court believe that I should not be so public as I am."

"Oh!" I said. "I'm so sorry. I would have wanted to see you." Yet another comfort my stepmother had taken away from me. The messages I sent—it was clear he never received them either.

He scooted closer to me on the bench and tightened his hold on my hand, startling me. I hadn't even realized we were still holding hands. It wasn't entirely proper, but I couldn't bring myself to pull away.

"He was a good man. Every time we met, he always had a kind word for me. That's not something I can say about all my father's advisors. And he would talk about his beloved daughter to anyone who would listen."

I smiled. That sounded like Papa.

"Where have you been for the past year? Lady Françoise seemed surprised when I told her I saw you in the market."

I hesitated for a moment before answering, "I've been living in my father's château with my stepmother and stepsisters. I'm sure you remember them. Alexandre and Severine, the girls from the Orangerie."

"*Those* are your stepsisters?" Auguste asked in surprise, almost falling off the stool. "And I thought having Louis for a sibling was bad luck." When I didn't reply, he hurried to say, "I don't mean to be indelicate, Cendrillon, or offend you, but I know what they're like."

I fidgeted in my seat. I didn't want to tell Auguste the depressing details about what happened to me over the past year, but I didn't want to lie either. Eventually, I would tell him everything. But not now. Not here. Not while I was having so much fun.

"They're not so bad once you get to know them. Well, Alexandre isn't, anyway. And Severine . . . Well, I can endure Severine."

I silently begged Auguste to drop the subject. It was my fault, really. I shouldn't have brought up my stepfamily. It was only going to lead to questions I didn't want to answer.

"How do you find your stepmother? I can't even imagine having to adjust to living with a new family on top of your father passing away."

I extricated my hand from Auguste's grasp. My palms were starting to sweat. He was far too observant and would notice that I was getting nervous. Not to mention I was aware that my hands were rough from cleaning, not as smooth as Auguste's. I was afraid he would notice.

"It has been difficult, to put it plainly. I didn't have much time to get to know my stepmother before the wedding, but we've had ample time since to get acquainted."

That was terrible. It sounded as if I was talking about a distant cousin coming for a visit, not a woman whom I lived with and was meant to love.

"I haven't met Lady Catherine personally, but I've heard other nobles speak of her. She seems to be quite a determined person."

Ambitious, he meant. He was being careful, even if I couldn't help but wish he'd change the subject. Every word he spoke was carefully and deliberately chosen so he could prod for information without upsetting me. It was obvious that he knew Lady Catherine was desperate to get ahead at any cost, and had been worried when he found out she was my stepmother. I didn't dare speak ill of her in case she found out about it somehow, but it couldn't hurt to acknowledge his tact, especially when it was coming from a place of concern.

"She *is* very determined," I said slowly. "And very proud. Very dedicated to her family. Lady Catherine can come across as uncompromising in her ambitions, but she just wants to ensure that her children have everything they might possibly need." I let my eyes wander across the increasingly raucous celebration, hoping that skewed close enough to the truth to satisfy Auguste's curiosity.

It was true that Lady Catherine was dedicated to her family—she simply didn't consider *me* to be part of that family. And even if pushing her daughters up the social ladder was really for *her* benefit, they would still benefit from it regardless.

"Perhaps we could talk about this another time, Auguste," I said, feeling my mood dipping with just the barest mention of Lady Catherine. She ruined everything she touched. I wouldn't let her ruin the ball too.

"Will you be visiting court more often now?" Auguste asked mildly, his voice cutting through my knotted thoughts.

Thank goodness he was changing the subject.

"Oh. I don't think so. This ball is just a special occasion for me."

"May I call on you at your château? I don't want for us to lose touch again."

I glanced over to see Auguste's gaze on me, warm and insistent. The thought of not seeing him again was something I didn't even want to contemplate. I would have to talk to Lady Françoise and see what she said. I didn't want to invite people to her home when I wasn't even properly living there yet, but I was sure that she wouldn't really mind.

"I would like that," I said cautiously. "Maybe we can—"

A persistent thudding rang out through the hall, thunderous and commanding. The music stopped abruptly, and the loud chatter quieted to a low murmur. I poked my head out of the embrasure to see a valet pounding a cane against the floor of the dais. When the assembled nobles were sufficiently silent, the valet stepped aside and bowed to the king, who got up from his throne and walked to the front of the dais, Prince Louis by his side.

"As we come to the end of this night of celebration, it is time to announce the names of the young women who my son will court this season. I am honored that so many of my kingdom's fairest maidens attended the ball tonight, but only twenty-five of you could be chosen."

"I have to go," Auguste said. He stood up and clambered down from the tiered seating, nearly tripping in his hurry to get to the floor. "I'm supposed to be up on the dais while the announcement is made. My father will be furious if I'm not there."

Auguste left before I even had time to utter a single word. Just as I was about to lose sight of him in the crowd, he turned around and came back to me, walking as briskly as possible without running.

"Please don't go anywhere. I'll find you after the announcements are over. We'll figure out a way to see each other," he said with a reassuring nod, before setting off into the throng again.

I remained sitting on the bench, flustered yet thrilled by the strange turn of events I'd stumbled into.

Chapter Twenty-One

I remained sitting on my bench in the window embrasure as the selection began. The proceedings weren't interesting enough for me to desire a better view, and anyway, I could hear everything that was going on perfectly from my comfortable, private seat. There was nothing to look at beyond the king reading a list of names and the dauphin's reaction.

It was probably safer to stay out of sight anyway. Lady Catherine was sure to be at the foot of the dais with Alexandre and Severine. I wasn't going to risk her spotting me for something as frivolous as names being read aloud. Besides, Auguste might not be able to find me later if I moved, and I wanted him to find me.

"The first young lady to be chosen is Lady Anna de Medici of Tuscany," the king said, his strong voice carrying clearly through the hall. "We are honored to host you at Versailles this season, my lady."

The king moved on right away, announcing the names of Princesse Henrietta of England and Duchesse Maria Anna Victoria of Bavaria in quick succession. I wasn't surprised that the girls were foreign princesses and nobility. Even if the ultimate choice of bride was up to Prince Louis, the match still needed to have some kind of political advantage. And the foreign nobility would need to be housed in the palace, unlike the local French ladies, who could remain in their homes if chosen.

The king carried on announcing the names on the list, paired with platitudes about how honored he was to have some so-and-so maiden court his son or how special it was for her to grace Versailles with her presence. I didn't recognize most of the girls, but the murmurs and gasps that moved through the crowd every time a name was called meant that the courtiers did. They were far more invested in the proceedings than I was. I was looking forward for the announcements ending so Auguste could find me again.

I rested my cheek against the cool marble of the wall and tried to tune out the whispering of the couple behind me, who were still entwined in each other's arms. The scent of hot candle wax from a nearby candelabra mixed with the sweetness of the orange flower water I wore. It reminded me of the times my mother would tuck me into bed when I was a child, leaning over to kiss me on the forehead, her perfume wafting over me while a solitary candle burned on my nightstand. My eyelids were heavy, far too heavy to hold open for much longer.

"The next two young ladies are sisters, so I'm sure they won't mind if I announce them together," the king said. "Lady Severine de Louvois and Lady Alexandre de Louvois. I'm honored to have two daughters of one of my most favored advisors—may he rest in peace—court my son."

I jolted upright, fully awake in an instant. The king did not just announce both Severine and Alexandre, did he? A shriek erupted from the crowd that sounded remarkably like Severine. Lady Catherine was probably overjoyed, which could be a good thing or a bad thing.

The power might go to her head, making her even more insufferable, but she might be so consumed with ensuring that one of her daughters wins the dauphin's heart that she won't care at all whether I moved in with Lady Françoise.

So lost was I in thoughts of Lady Catherine's potential distraction that I nearly missed the king calling my stepsisters Louvois. When I processed what he actually said, my mood soured immediately. Their family name was Monvoisin. When did they start using Papa's name? It had to be Lady Catherine's doing. Would Alexandre and Severine have even been chosen if they weren't known as the daughters of the Marquis de Louvois? The king might be giving them a chance because of his affection for Papa.

The thought made me inordinately angry. If Lady Catherine had approached me just then, I don't think I would have been able to stop myself from slapping her.

It was just a name. It shouldn't have upset me. Papa wouldn't have cared. But I cared. That was *my* name. I was Lady Cendrillon de Louvois. Lady Catherine used my name to advance her daughters' social standing while the true Louvois daughter languished at home, scrubbing the fireplace.

I didn't want to be the obedient stepdaughter anymore, the girl who kept her mouth shut and ran the house while getting nothing but abuse in return.

"The final name on our list is an unusual one," I heard the king say through the angry haze clouding my mind. "All we have to go by is the young lady's pet name. If only my son hadn't been so smitten, he might have asked for her family name."

The crowd chuckled loudly at the king's fond ribbing of the dauphin.

"The final name on the list is Lady Cinder. Lady Cinder, will you make yourself known to the court? A hearty congratulations are in order for our twenty-five lovely maidens. I can assure you that my son and I both eagerly await commencement of the courtship events."

The king kept talking, but I couldn't hear him over the rushing of blood in my ears. A cold sweat broke out on my skin as I sat frozen in place. My limbs felt so heavy and sluggish, I didn't think I could move them even if I wanted to.

I had only danced with Prince Louis once, and we barely talked for more than ten, *maybe* fifteen minutes. Just because I had a pretty dress and nice manners didn't mean I was important, or that I would make a good queen. It didn't make any sense. Why would the king allow the dauphin to put my name on the list?

But more important—did I even *want* to marry the dauphin? He was handsome and much more charming than when last we met, and he could offer me a life of luxury and security. He was the heir to France! The king's word was law, and if I was his queen, my word would become law too.

I couldn't stop the thoughts racing through my head. Marrying the dauphin would mean that Lady Catherine would no longer have power over me. But I didn't need to marry the dauphin to escape my fate; I had Lady Françoise now.

When Alexandre had spoken to me of her concerns over the prospect of being queen, the incredible duty and responsibility that came with the crown, I'd agreed with her. If I married the dauphin, what Auguste said about the courtiers with beseeching eyes and demanding hands would be my life. I saw how the capriciousness of the court had hurt Auguste. Would I even be able to assert myself amongst people like that, with people like Lady Catherine?

And if Louis chose me, what about Auguste? How would he feel about this turn of events if he knew I was Lady Cinder?

It was ridiculous to worry about what Auguste thought. We were only friends. But it was best to avoid the drama entirely and live a peaceful life with Lady Françoise. I couldn't consider coming back to the palace until I fully recovered and got my bearings. But I had no interest in courting—much less marrying—the spoiled dauphin.

"The clock nears midnight, and the first day of the dauphin's birthday celebration draws to a close." The king's voice cut cleanly through the excited chatter that had risen up after the reading of the list. "Before we depart to get some much-needed rest in preparation for the events to come, I would like the twenty-five maidens to come to the dais so that they can be introduced to the court. And to me. I'm sure we would all like to meet you before courtship proceedings begin in earnest tomorrow."

Panic—sharp and icy—stabbed my stomach. The mass of courtiers undulated as girls began to emerge and climb the dais to speak with the king and the dauphin.

I couldn't do it. Alexandre and Severine would be there. Lady Catherine would see me. Maybe if my marraine were with me I would know what to do, but I was too confused about how I wanted to proceed to even think about enduring a confrontation with my stepmother. I decided I would not present myself. It would be better if the king and the dauphin forgot all about me.

Where *was* Lady Françoise? It was nearly midnight. If we didn't leave right away, we would never make it back to the château before Lady Catherine and my stepsisters.

I cast my eyes across the Hall of Mirrors, desperate to catch a flash of emerald green, but there was nothing. I had to find my own way out. Lady Françoise would understand if I didn't wait for her.

The courtiers were pushing forward to crowd around the dais, leaving this end of the hall increasingly empty. A particularly large group of nobles hurried toward the dais, leaving a wide-open path from my bench to the archway leading to the Salon of War. An opportunity like this couldn't go to waste.

I stood up and jumped from my seat to the parquet floor below. Pain radiated from my ankles up through my legs when I made impact with the floor, but I ignored it. Gathering my voluminous skirts into my arms, I dashed from the Hall of Mirrors as fast as my slippers could take me.

CHAPTER TWENTY-TWO

MY CHEST WAS TIGHT AND aching as I burst through a door chosen at random onto the Water Parterre at the back of the palace. The fresh air was invigorating, but it did nothing to help my ragged breathing. My slippers clacked loudly against the stone of the terrace.

Torches lined the branching paths of the gardens, casting a dim orange glow that was just bright enough to ensure that I could see where I was going. Lady Françoise's coachman was waiting with the carriage in the large open space in front of the Great Lawn, where a few other carriages also milled about. We had taken secluded country roads to get to Versailles, roads that allowed us to avoid the main courtyards and arrive in the gardens instead. I was grateful for that decision now. It was so much easier to remain undetected in the dark, quiet gardens than in courtyards that were crawling with guards, servants, and nobles alike.

It was when I reached the long staircase leading down to the Latona Fountain that I heard a voice calling after me.

"Mademoiselle! Mademoiselle, please come back!"

The voice was unfamiliar to me, but it was close, so close that I stopped at the top of the stairs to turn around and look. I couldn't keep running without knowing whether or not I was going to be taken at any minute. One of the king's valets was leaning out a window in the Hall of Mirrors, frantically waving his arms at me. How did they realize I was gone so quickly?

But it didn't matter. I couldn't stop running, not when I was so close to getting away.

I hurried down the steps as fast as I was able in my heels, which wasn't nearly as fast as I would have liked. The stairs were wide, and the torches that ran along either edge didn't illuminate them entirely, leaving the center steeped in shadows. I ran as fast as I could, and all the while, the valet's cries of "Mademoiselle" rang out into the night, spurring me to move faster.

Just past the halfway point, the toe of my right slipper caught on the stairs, sending me flying forward. I stumbled down a few steps and fell to my knees but managed to catch myself before I fell to the bottom. My hands and knees smarted as I pushed myself up and sat for a moment on the step. The stone was cold against my stockinged foot as I got to my feet on trembling legs. What happened to my slipper? Climbing back up the staircase, I found it resting perfectly on a step, as if I had positioned it there intentionally.

"Mademoiselle!" the valet called, appearing at the top of the steps.

Frantically, I grabbed the slipper and pulled. It wouldn't budge. I yanked it again and again, but it barely shifted. It was just my luck that I would step on the only crack in the entirety of the otherwise perfectly maintained staircase and get my slipper stuck.

I glanced up to see the valet making his way down the steps. He wasn't running, but if I remained to yank at the shoe, he would catch me. Huffing in frustration, I pulled off my other slipper, tucked it under an arm, and continued running, leaving my trapped slipper behind.

I managed to make it down the stairs, across the Latona Parterre, and down the last flight of stairs before the Great Lawn without slipping once. My pace increased considerably without the hindrance of my heels, so much so that I outpaced the valet with ease. Maybe I should have stayed and tried to pull the slipper out one more time. I hated to leave such a beautiful gift behind.

Only a few carriages were left in front of the Great Lawn, their coachmen huddled together in a small group around a nearby torch. It wasn't hard to spot the dark blue carriage with the golden crest on the door. I ran toward it, hoping I could hide there until Lady Françoise arrived.

As I approached the door, someone poked their head out of the window and stared at me. It was Lady Françoise's coachman, who immediately hopped out of the carriage with a guilty look on his face and regarded me nervously.

"Mademoiselle, are you all right? You seem . . . distressed."

"I'm fine. Where is Lady Françoise?" I asked, the words staggered as I gasped for air and clutched at my cramping side. "We need to leave. Right away."

The coachman's eyes were fixed on my bare foot. "I have word that Lady Françoise has become indisposed and left the ball. I was sent to escort you back to your home whenever you like. Lady Françoise wants you to know that she apologizes and promises to come for you tomorrow. Would you like to leave now?"

"Yes, please," I said, hoisting myself up onto the plush seats of the carriage and collapsing backward with a sigh.

The coachman closed the door, and we set off, the carriage rumbling across the stones in the courtyard. My mind was a whirl of confused emotions and thoughts, and my body was in no better shape. It wasn't just my legs that ached. My knees and palms were bloodied and sore from my fall, and it felt like someone was stabbing me in the side with a hot poker. I lay back and took in great, heaving gasps of air, every breath grating against my parched throat.

I hoped that Lady Françoise was all right, because I'd expected her to wait for me. Still, she hadn't looked well. This was a very odd turn of events. Everything about this night was impossibly strange. I was supposed to be going home with her, not returning to the château. This change wasn't an ideal situation, but it would be fine just as long as Lady Françoise came for me tomorrow like she promised.

My urgent need leave to the ball as quickly as possible had paid off, and the château was blissfully empty when I arrived. I had just enough time to dash up to the attic, change out of my dress, and wipe off all the makeup. It seemed a shame to shove such a beautiful dress into the bottom of my trunk, but I couldn't risk Lady Catherine finding it in case she actually climbed up the stairs to the attic.

Ideally, it wouldn't be there long. When Lady Françoise came for me, I would carry it out of the château in my arms, and my stepmother would know that I had gone to the ball despite her attempts to keep me away.

After hiding the dress, I lay down on my bed to get a few precious moments of rest. I would have to pretend that I wasn't exhausted when my stepfamily returned. But I couldn't rest, no matter how hard I tried. It didn't feel right to just lie down when so much had changed.

My lumpy mattress was just as uncomfortable as it had been this morning. The wooden beams above my head were still dusty. The seams of the old woolen dress I was wearing were fraying. There was still only the slightest of breezes blowing through my little window, one that did absolutely nothing to cool the attic down. The banging of the front door against the wall downstairs and Severine's shrieks of "Cendrillon! I need you!" were achingly familiar.

Everything was the same as it always had been in the château.

Except me. I realized I was still wearing the other slipper, and I sat up to remove it. It glittered in the slim shaft of moonlight, like a rare and precious jewel.

Chapter Twenty-Three

"**Well, I for one want** to know who this *mystery* girl is," Severine said with disgust, as if the very thought of said girl was repulsive to her. "Lady Cinder? What kind of name is *that*?"

I smothered a smile as I walked around the breakfast table, pouring hot chocolate into the cups of Lady Catherine, Severine, and Alexandre. Hot chocolate was a luxury we couldn't afford often—a luxury I wasn't allowed—but Severine had insisted on the treat as a reward for her wonderful performance at the ball the night before. Lady Catherine had readily agreed.

I'd been forced to stay up into the wee hours of the morning helping my stepfamily get undressed and ready for bed. Lady Catherine gushed the entire time about how proud she was of her beautiful daughters and what a success it was to have them both competing to become the next dauphine. She was behaving as if one of them had already won, planning for her move to the palace as the dauphin's mother-in-law. Severine had been equally smug, gloating all night about how besotted the prince was with her, how he'd practically fallen at her feet after their dance. There was just one blemish marring Severine's perfect imaginings of her marriage to Prince Louis.

"What are you smiling at?" Severine asked, shooting me a glare. "This is no laughing matter. That girl ruined our first proper introduction to the court, and she wasn't even there. She'd left!"

"I'm not smiling. It's *terrible*," I said, hurrying to the sideboard to deposit the carafe.

As I turned away to collect the bowl of fruit and the cheese I'd brought out for them, I let myself smile for just a moment.

"There's no use upsetting yourself about it, dear," Lady Catherine said. "As you said, the girl wasn't even there."

"Exactly! The dauphin was furious. He had twenty-four other ladies he was meant to personally introduce to the court, but all he could do was focus on the girl who wasn't there. He didn't spend any time with us at all!"

I took the fruit and the cheese board to the table and set it down carefully. Would anyone notice that the amount and selection of cheese was sparse? I'd done it on purpose so I could spend more time in the dining room. As soon as I was done serving, Lady Catherine would send me back to the kitchen, and I wouldn't be able to hear what else happened at the palace.

Lady Catherine picked up a slice of cheese and took a look at the rest. "There's hardly anything here, Cendrillon. How are three people supposed to eat this for breakfast?"

"I'm sorry, Madame. I'll add more."

I picked up the tray and hurried back to the sideboard as Lady Catherine waved me off without another glance in my direction. Success! Normally, my negligence would have made her far angrier. She seemed completely distracted by Severine's recounting of the events at the palace. Could I get away with slicing the cheese slowly so as to listen a bit longer? I hoped so. I picked up the knife and a block of the stinky Maroilles my stepmother prefers and got to work.

"If the girl doesn't reappear for the events, she'll be taken out of consideration," said Lady Catherine. "Problem solved."

"I don't think the dauphin will allow that to happen," Alexandre said, piping up for the first time in the conversation. "Didn't you hear him demanding she be found at any cost? He threatened to tear the kingdom apart if she wasn't. He must be quite taken with her."

"See? Ridiculous!" Severine spat.

I heard porcelain rattling roughly as Severine slammed her cup onto the saucer. The dauphin of France really *demanded* that I be found?

Escaping with Lady Françoise was still a superior option to competing with other girls—including Alexandre and Severine—to marry a spoiled princeling who made threats when I didn't show up to his little event.

As if I would be successful at winning the dauphin's heart anyway. No. My marraine would be arriving any minute now. I'd found time earlier in the morning to tell Elodie all about the magical and confusing events of the previous evening. She had good and bad news of her own. The good news was that Marius was okay, sore but nothing broken. The bad news was that the servant positions at the same household were no longer available. Elodie also told me there was a rumor around town that Lady Catherine's servants were to be avoided at all costs. Lady Catherine had started the rumor herself, essentially guaranteeing that no one would hire us. But Lady Françoise was about to rescue us, and I told her to start packing her things.

"I wonder who she is," Alexandre said, a little dreamily. "I didn't see her, but Diane saw her and the dauphin dancing and told me all about it. She said the girl wore a shimmering dress of the deepest blue, and had golden-brown hair studded with sapphires that tumbled down her back in lustrous waves. She danced with the utmost grace."

Severine snorted and muttered something under her breath that I couldn't make out.

"Oh, hush. Don't you want to hear? You didn't see the girl either," said Alexandre.

I hoped that Severine would shut her mouth just as much as Alexandre did. It was immodest, but I wanted to hear what people were saying about me.

When her sister remained silent, Alexandre continued. "The girl is quite beautiful and mysterious. Apparently, she gave the dauphin a false name and fled from the Hall of Mirrors before she could be called to the dais. All that was left of her was a brocade slipper encrusted with glass crystals. No one knows who she really is! Isn't it exciting?"

I smiled at the delight in Alexandre's voice. It was almost unbearably strange to hear myself talked about in this way. Briefly, when I looked in my godmother's mirror, I'd imagined myself as a grand, mysterious noblewoman, but that was just pretend. To know that courtiers actually thought of me like that . . . it was terrifying. And exhilarating.

"No, it isn't exciting!" Severine exclaimed. "Why are you fawning over this girl? She could be anyone. Even . . . *a peasant*."

Everything would be ruined if I started laughing at Severine's horror of the girl being a peasant in disguise. She even whispered *peasant*, as if it were a dirty word. Would my stepsister be more offended if the mystery girl was me or a peasant? It was hard to say.

"And the dauphin is completely consumed with finding her, taking attention away from *us*. Mère?"

"Severine is right," Lady Catherine said, her words slow and contemplative. "If the girl is found, I don't want you associating with her, Alexandre. Don't romanticize this. She is a threat to you and your sister, and you are far too naïve and trusting to realize it."

"Yes, Maman," Alexandre said quietly, the enthusiasm stripped from her voice.

Every time Alexandre tried to exert even a small amount of autonomy, her mother reeled her right back in. In the long run, her having more courage would benefit Elodie as well. Nothing could turn out well between them while Alexandre was so firmly under her mother's thumb.

The door knocker thumped loudly against the front door. I jumped, and the knife slipped out of my hand and clattered onto the sideboard. The knocker thumped again and again, just as insistently as it had last night.

The knock was Lady Françoise's. It had to be.

"Answer the door, Cendrillon, and tell whoever it is to call again tomorrow. I'm in no mood for visitors."

I wiped my hands on my apron and walked out of the dining room. As soon as I was out of their line of sight, I sprinted to the front door and threw it open. Standing in the doorway was a tall, rail-thin man peering down at me through a small pair of spectacles. The man had a stark, stern appearance, dressed as he was in an unadorned gray justaucorps that perfectly matched the gray of his hair. Most curious of all was the carriage in the courtyard that bore the seal of the king. That couldn't mean anything good. Where was Lady Françoise?

"Are the Ladies Catherine Monvoisin de Louvois and Cendrillon de Louvois at home?" he asked. "I have urgent matters to discuss with them. I am Lord Bernard and I have come from the palace."

I froze in the doorway at the sound of my name. I think I knew what this man was here for. This wasn't supposed to be happening. No one was supposed to know who I was. How did they find out? And where was Lady Françoise?

But I had to remember my manners. I curtsied to the visitor. He was a representative of the king, and one always bowed to the king.

"Lady Catherine is in the dining room. Please follow me," I said, leading Lord Bernard down the hallway.

I wrung my hands on my dress and tried to calm myself. Lady Catherine wouldn't do anything to me while Lord Bernard was here. All I had to do was weather her rage long enough for Lady Françoise to get here. She promised me that she would come. She promised.

"Lady Catherine, there is someone here to see you," I said as I opened the door to the dining room.

"I said no visitors, you stupid child. Don't you ever... Oh! Lord Bernard," Lady Catherine said, her tone changing instantly from one of disdain to the paramount of sweetness. "I didn't realize you were our visitor. Please, sit down. I can have refreshments brought to you."

"No, no, Madame. I cannot stay long. I'm just here to inform you of your daughter's admittance into the competition. It was brought to the dauphin's attention that you and she might not have been made aware, explaining her absence from the palace yesterday."

"I do know that my daughters are being courted by the dauphin. They were both at the palace last night. I don't understand."

I winced and shrunk back as Lord Bernard said, "Your step-daughter, Madame. Lady Cendrillon de Louvois. She has been chosen by the dauphin as well. It seems that the king was right to assume that you were both absent when her name was called. In any event, her presence is required at the next courtship event. If I could just speak with the young lady, I will then take my leave."

Lady Catherine carefully placed her hands on her lap and smiled at Lord Bernard.

"That's impossible. Cendrillon was not at the ball, so she could not have been chosen by the dauphin."

"Madame?" Lord Bernard sighed and began tapping his foot impatiently. Lady Catherine wouldn't even look at me. It was like I wasn't in the room. I couldn't decide whether the disregard was intentional or whether she actually forgot I was there.

"You must be confused, Monsieur," she said sweetly.

"The king of France is never confused, Madame," he said in a tone that brooked no argument. "If I may speak to the lady in question, I am sure we can clear up your confusion."

Lady Catherine glanced at me. "The lady in question is right in front of you and can answer anytime. I, for one, would very much like for her to clear things up."

Lord Bernard turned to me and raised his eyebrows. Then he did the most extraordinary thing. Even though I was wearing a shabby work dress and apron stained with ashes, he bowed respectfully. "Lady Cendrillon de Louvois, I am pleased to make your acquaintance."

I curtsied again. "And I yours, Lord Bernard."

My stomach roiled as I waited to see Lady Catherine's reaction. Severine and Alexandre were silent, their eyes bouncing back and forth between the three of us.

"I beg your pardon, mademoiselle," said Lord Bernard, bowing once more. Then he turned to Lady Catherine and pulled a letter from his justaucorps. "This is a letter from the king. It explains everything," he said, handing the letter to her.

It took her only a moment to read the letter. When she finished, she set it down on the table and slowly rose from her chair. But she didn't address Lord Bernard. Instead, she looked at me and smiled. It was a beautiful smile, one that lit up her entire face. It sent a chill running down my spine.

"I didn't realize the dauphin's mysterious missing maiden was living under my own roof. How exciting! You should have found us at the ball. We would have been most pleased to see you," she said. "Lord Bernard, do you mind giving us a moment?"

"Certainly, Madame," he said. "I shall repair to the front room."

When Lord Bernard had left us alone, Lady Catherine turned to me, and her glare could turn sailors into stone. "You!" she seethed. "You were there!"

I cringed, readying myself for the blow that was sure to come.

"Wait. Wait!" Severine said, holding her hands up in the air like a queen commanding her court. "Are you saying that Cendrillon is the mystery girl? That Lady Cinder is *Cendrillon*? You must be joking."

Alexandre tried to shush her, leaning over to whisper in her ear, but Severine brushed her off as her volume increased with each word. "That's impossible. The dauphin would never be interested in someone like her. She was here last night anyway. There's no way she could have made it to Versailles on her own. This is all a lie. The brat is making it up! She has to be. Mère—"

"Shut up, Severine. I am trying to think!" her mother said.

I'd never heard Lady Catherine speak so sharply to her golden child. Even Severine was surprised. She slumped back in her seat with a pout and crossed her arms. Alexandre tried to whisper something again, but Severine turned her face away.

"How did you get to the ball, Cendrillon?" Lady Catherine asked, sitting down once more and fixing her pale blue eyes on me.

"When the carriage didn't come back for me, I did not think I would be able to attend. But then Papa's friend Lady Françoise came calling. When she realized that I had been left behind, she was kind enough to escort me herself."

"I see," said Lady Catherine, coolly assessing the situation. She leaned back on the velvet chair and adjusted her skirts.

There was a knock on the dining room door, and Lord Bernard appeared. "I do apologize, Madame, but I still need to speak to Lady Cendrillon."

"By all means," she said.

"The topic of Lady Françoise de la Valliere is the other order of business that I have to address with you, mademoiselle," Lord Bernard said, clasping his hands together and taking a few steps toward me. His face was gentle and pitying. Why? My hands began to tremble. What did he have to pity me about?

"Lady Françoise?" I asked, starting to panic. "What of her?"

"I am unaccustomed to being the bearer of bad news, but the king wished for me to tell you. Lady Françoise passed away last night. Please allow me to offer both my own condolences as well as those of the king. He understands that you two were quite close."

I stared at Lord Bernard. The words coming out of his mouth made no sense. They were wrong. Wrong and untrue. My marraine couldn't be dead. I'd just seen her last night. She was coming to rescue me. Today. Because this couldn't be happening. Not again.

"Oh, the poor dear. What did she die of?" Lady Catherine asked, and to her credit she managed to keep the glee out of her voice.

"Consumption, Madame. It was a long illness; one she'd been battling for a little over a year. She met with physicians in England to no avail. Unfortunately, she collapsed after the ball last night, the illness finally taking hold. There was nothing to be done."

Their voices were muffled, as if bits of cloth were stuffed in my ears. My body was numb. I couldn't even tell if I was still standing, or if I'd fallen to the floor in a jumble of limp limbs. There was no one left to look after me. Maman was gone. Papa was gone. And now Lady Françoise was gone, just when I'd finally found her. I was never going to see her again. Why wasn't I crying? I should have been crying. Everyone who ever loved or cared about me was dead.

"I am very sorry, mademoiselle," Lord Bernard said to me. "The funeral will be held in a week. The king understands that you will miss some of the courtship activities, and they have rescheduled the opening so you may attend." With that, he gave us his leave.

"Come here," said Lady Catherine, enveloping me in an embrace.

But her kindness was all a façade. "You're not going to participate in the competition. Did you hear me, Cendrillon? You are *not* going to participate in the competition," she whispered.

I pulled away. I was wrong. There was still someone who loved me living right under this roof.

Me.

I would take care of myself now that I was all I had left. And I could feel something pooling deep in my gut: resolve.

"No," I said out loud, raising my ash-covered face to the light. I was dressed in rags and smelled like the kitchen, but I was still a lady.

"Excuse me?"

"I will compete."

The smile dropped from my stepmother's face.

"In case you've forgotten, you're living in my house. I feed you, I clothe you, I give you a space to sleep. My word is law in this château," my stepmother sneered.

"Does the word of the king not trump yours, even in this château? He has *ordered* me to participate, and I will participate." The sound of my voice scared me, flat and emotionless. "You cannot keep me here. I'll walk to the palace if I have to. If you try to lock me up, someone will come looking for me. Perhaps then the king will have your head for interfering in the business of the court."

I left the dining room without waiting for Lady Catherine's reply. My mind was made up.

My eyes began to burn and blur as I made me way to my little attic room. I had to clutch at the walls for support the entire way up so I didn't tumble back down the stairs. As soon as I made it to the room, I collapsed on my bed and lay still. Even the lack of movement didn't calm the nausea beating away at my insides.

"Cendrillon," came Elodie's voice from the doorway. "I overheard the conversation in the dining room. I am so, so sorry."

We were grieving for my godmother, but we were also grieving for ourselves.

The bed dipped as Elodie lay down next to me and wrapped her arms around me. Her embrace was warm and safe. Only then, my face buried in my pillow, did I let the tears come, great, heaving sobs that wracked my entire body.

Today, I would cry and grieve for Lady Françoise, for everything that could have been. Tomorrow, I would enter the competition and win the heart of the dauphin. That was the only way now to get myself and Elodie away from this horrid château. I knew deep in my heart that it was what Lady Françoise would have wanted for me, to be free from Lady Catherine.

CHAPTER TWENTY-FOUR

THERE WERE VERY FEW OF us at Lady Françoise's funeral. Once, she had been the popular favorite of the king, but even the king did not attend. It was a rainy, soggy day that matched my mood. I said a prayer for my godmother and laid flowers on her grave. The next day I returned to Versailles to take part in the competition as I'd promised myself I would.

The Hall of Mirrors felt different in the daylight.

On the night of the ball, entering the gallery had felt like journeying into another world. Now that it was morning, it felt very much a part of the palace. The mirrors reflected back images of the gardens and pools through the windows, doubling and redoubling the magic of Versailles.

The room was airy and fresh, the windows thrown open to let in the warm midmorning breeze. Everything from the parquet floors to the crystal chandeliers gleamed in the sunlight. I wandered through the gallery slowly, taking it all in and trying to decide if I preferred the Hall of Mirrors in the night or the day.

Taking in the sights wasn't the only reason I wandered slowly. The twenty-four other girls chosen by the dauphin were waiting at the other end of the hall, huddled together near the still-erected dais. I wanted to avoid joining them as long as possible.

It was the day of the first true courtship event, and my nerves were a wreck. I didn't really want to be there, and Lady Celia's lessons had been so long ago; what if I'd forgotten all my social training and made a complete fool of myself? It was a real possibility.

The lack of sleep over the past few days wasn't helping. I'd spent that first night after Lady Françoise's passing in Elodie's arms, sobbing, only to wake up to a carriage bearing Lady Françoise's crest filled with trunks containing heaps of her fine dresses. Just before she died, she willed her clothing and one of her carriages to me. But her estate went to her sole male heir, a distant nephew, as was the law. For the next week, Elodie and I had been altering the dresses so that they fit me perfectly. The only reason I had any chance of success in the competition was because of Lady Françoise. Somehow, she knew that I'd been chosen, and she knew that I would need resources that Lady Catherine wouldn't give me. My marraine was taking care of me one last time. I only wished that I'd been able to tell her how much I loved her.

I ran my fingers across the string of pearls around my neck. I'd never been able to return them, and now I was never taking them off. They were a reminder that I needed to stay strong and keep fighting. Once the competition was over, I could mourn her properly. But for now, I needed to focus and push my grief aside. This is what Lady Françoise wanted for me. If I won the competition, I would be the dauphine of France. And when I left the château to move into the palace, I would take Elodie with me, and Marius and Claudine as well. I *had* to win.

I had to put aside my growing feelings for Auguste, and I should count myself lucky that we never had the chance to truly reconnect, as it would have only made today more painful. There was nothing between us, and nothing could ever happen between us now.

I approached the dais slowly, the young ladies clustered into small groups of threes and fours, with a few pairs scattered about as well. A girl with red hair broke away from one of the larger groups and hurried toward me, waving excitedly the entire time.

"Cendrillon," the girl called when she reached me. "I'm very happy to see you! It's been a whole year, hasn't it?"

"Right," I said slowly, trying very hard not to flinch as the girl grabbed both my hands and swung them excitedly between us. She was pretty and bubbly, with bright green eyes and a light dusting of freckles across her nose and cheeks. Her smile was warm and welcoming, and it instantly put me at ease. It was silly, but I liked her immediately.

"Don't say you've forgotten me," she said with a laugh. "I'm Diane. Remember?"

"Diane. Yes, of course I remember! From Lady Celia's lessons. I'm sorry I didn't recognize you right away."

Diane and I never interacted much during or after our lessons. She had her own friends and I had Auguste, but she was never rude or dismissive like some of the others. She'd made sure to be kind, and I hadn't remembered her.

"I'm sure you've had more important things to think about than old classmates." Diane lowered her voice and leaned closer to me. "I was so sorry to hear of your father's passing. I would have told you sooner, but you never came back to lessons. I can't imagine how hard it's been for you."

She had no idea how hard it had been. No one did. But I smiled and tried to look well rested and well cared for, just another girl at the competition. Not a scullery maid in disguise.

"How wonderful that you're here with us now," Diane finished.

"Thank you. I appreciate the condolences. It has been difficult, but . . . I'm ready to start fresh."

"I'm so glad! Let me introduce you to the other girls. We were all dying to know who the mysterious maiden was, and when Alexandre told us that it was you, appearing at Versailles so long after you'd left us, we were all even *more* desperate to talk with you!"

She smiled and started leading me toward the dais, practically skipping across the floor. I had to jog so I didn't trip and fall flat on my face. I'd done enough tripping to last me a good long while; my palms were still scraped from my tumble on the stairs above the Latona Parterre.

"Mathilde, Paulette, meet Cendrillon de Louvois. Or should I say, 'Lady Cinder.' Cendrillon, these are my dear friends."

Mathilde and Paulette were overly dressed in garishly colored gowns. They glanced at each other in surprise. "*You're* the maiden from the ball," Mathilde said loudly. "The one who ran away from the dauphin."

The Hall of Mirrors had been relatively quiet. Most of the ladies were speaking softly, if not outright whispering, as if they didn't want to break the sanctity of the room. Or maybe they just didn't want anyone to hear what they were saying. But Mathilde's voice echoed off the high ceilings, amplifying her words tenfold, and heads turned in our direction. I winced.

Diane said, "Perhaps we should lower our voices a bit? Cendrillon has just returned to court, and we don't want her to feel uncomfortable."

Mathilde cast her eyes downward and mumbled an apology under her breath.

While I didn't want to stand out more, everyone thinking that I was rude or standoffish wouldn't help me make friends. "No, it's all right," I rushed to say. "No one has made me uncomfortable. I promise."

Mathilde lifted her eyes and smiled at me. "You've been the talk of court for days. I honestly wasn't sure whether we'd see you."

"Some people even thought that you might be a witch," Paulette blurted out, looking at me expectantly, as if I would pull out my book of spells and admit to being a witch right here in the Hall of Mirrors.

"Paulette, hush! You're being ridiculous!" said Diane.

She stepped in front of her friend and started whispering, but Paulette poked her head around Diane's shoulder and continued. "An enchantress, specifically."

Diane groaned and buried her face in her hands. I had to try very hard not to laugh at the eager look on Paulette's face. "Does Versailles have a witch problem?" I asked.

Glancing around the room a few times, Paulette said in a whisper, "There are rumors that some of the contestants are hiring witches to cast love spells or use potions on the dauphin. The queen tried to ensnare the king that way last year, but it didn't work. So now they're trying to capture the heir to the throne in the same way."

"And what does that have to do with me?" I asked, backing away a bit so I leaned against the wall between the ballroom's many mirrors.

"People thought you may have cast a love spell and succeeded, and that's why the guards had to capture you. They said the dauphin wanted you found because he wanted you punished."

I clapped a hand over my mouth to hold back my giggle, but it didn't muffle the sound well enough. Paulette's face fell slightly.

"I don't know any love spells, and I don't want to *ensnare* the dauphin. I left the ball early because I had stayed out too late. If my stepmother found out, she would have been furious. It was all perfectly mundane."

"Oh," Paulette said quietly. She and Mathilde looked as if I'd just kicked their favorite horse.

Diane took my hand and pulled me away without another word to her friends. "I'm sorry about that," she said. "I didn't know they were going to say all those inane things."

"It's all right. Your friends seem very nice."

"They're just a little excitable on occasion. Don't pay attention to rumors."

When I'd left the château that morning, I never imagined all this was coming.

Witches, love, spells, and lovelorn maidens. What had I gotten myself into?

☙❦❧

Diane had been exaggerating when she said that all the ladies were desperate to speak with me. Some of them were curious, like Mathilde and Paulette, and asked slightly inappropriate questions about where I'd been for the past year or whether I had a secret relationship with the dauphin. Most were very sweet, complimenting me on the dress I'd worn to the ball and my dancing. I knew from Severine's gossiping that they might say very different things behind my back. Diane was a wonderful guide, though, introducing me to the many different participants and moving me along when questions got too personal or unfriendly.

She had a skill for remembering names and backstories that was beyond me. Unless someone particularly stood out, her name slipped from my mind.

The dauphin was on an outing with Princesse Henrietta of

England, so I couldn't meet her, but Diane briefly introduced me to Lady Anna de Medici of Tuscany. Anna was less than enthused by my presence and said only a few short words to me before turning back to her entourage of ladies-in-waiting.

We were on our way to meet the Bavarian duchesse when we ran into the person I'd hoped to avoid, as far-fetched as that plan might have been.

"Cendrillon, I wasn't sure that I would see you here," Severine said, approaching me with Alexandre and another girl at her heels: Veronique. I remembered her from Lady Celia's lessons. She was never as kind as Diane was. It was unsurprising that she was associating with Severine.

"Yes. You and Alexandre left so early in the morning, I wasn't able to take the carriage with you. Luckily, Lady Françoise was kind enough to bequeath her carriage, so I was able to make it to the palace with plenty of time to spare."

"Sorry about that," Alexandre said sweetly, but she recoiled and fell silent when Severine glared at her. They were still dressed alike, in ice-blue gowns to match their eyes and silver hair.

"Be that as it may, I didn't expect you to come," said Severine.

"Why not?" I asked, curling my lip a little.

I knew that I should have kept my mouth shut and walked away, but I couldn't stand the smug look on Severine's face. In the moment, I wasn't even considering the retribution from Lady Catherine for talking back to her.

"It was horribly rude of you to run away from the dauphin. After committing such a grave offense, I can't imagine why you thought you would ever have a chance with him."

My cheeks flushed when I saw the discomfort on Diane's face. Severine didn't care that she was insulting me in front of someone else. In fact, she relished it.

"I won't argue with you," I said, keeping my voice carefully neutral. "I'm here because the king invited me."

I put extra emphasis on *the king*. I thought mentioning the king would be sure to get a rise out of Severine, and it did. She snorted and looked as if she wanted to strangle me right there.

"As you made very clear to your mother, the dauphin spent the entirety of last week consumed with finding me. You said he didn't pay attention to any of the other maidens, including you. That must mean I have *some* chance with him, don't you agree?"

The potential retribution was worth it just to see the abject rage on my stepsister's face. She took a step toward me—to do what, I didn't know—when a flutter of activity erupted at the archway to the Salon of Peace.

It was the dauphin, looking as handsome as ever in a justaucorps of deep red silk. Many of the ladies rushed toward him as he entered with whom I could only assume was Princesse Henrietta. He bowed to her as she curtsied; then she retreated into the assembled crowd while he let his eyes wander across the hall.

He didn't let his eyes linger on any one person for too long. Until his gaze landed on me, that is. When he spotted me, his eyes lit up, and he started to make his way toward me. Severine was going to be furious.

CHAPTER TWENTY-FIVE

"I THINK WE'RE LOST," I said as I stared down the length of an-other long, empty corridor in the Labyrinth.

"We're not lost," said Louis, his voice growing ever fainter as he walked off to scout the path ahead. "I've been running through the Labyrinth since I was a child. I can't get lost in here; it was designed for me."

"All right. Where's the exit?"

I hoped my question wasn't rude, but Prince Louis insisted it would be fun to spend our outing exploring Versailles's famous Labyrinth. He also insisted that he knew the way through and would show me all the beautiful fountains designed after Aesop's Fables.

We'd been wandering alone for at least half an hour, and while we did encounter a few fountains that lived up to the fanfare, we were, in my opinion, hopelessly lost. The dauphin had a different opinion on the matter. "I think . . . probably . . . this way! Follow me!"

He took off running down the path and quickly disappeared, leaving me alone in the maze. I sighed heavily. The world of courtships and romance was completely foreign to me, the vagaries of acceptable and unacceptable behavior while trying to win the heart of a royal utter mysteries. Maybe I could ask Diane for tips. I didn't want to be discourteous—even I knew that wasn't the way to endear myself to the dauphin. But it was hard to keep my annoyance in check when said dauphin abandoned me in the maze to find my own way through.

The hedges were high, soaring up into the air so even the tallest of people couldn't see over. While some sections of the maze had paths wide enough to accommodate large groups, this particular path was quite narrow. The hedges pressed in close, allowing only two people to walk abreast of each other. Even though it was a bright, sunny day, because of the height of the hedges, the path itself was chilly and cast in shadow.

"Please wait for me!" I called, but there was no response.

It was laughable, but I felt trapped in this quiet, lonely place. This path wasn't as charming or cheerful as the others, which were dappled with sunlight and filled with birdsong. If I didn't start moving soon, it felt like I was going to be lost forever amongst the statues and hedges.

"Monseigneur le Dauphin," I called again, hoping that he would reappear and guide us to the exit.

Alas, he did *not* reappear.

I rested my hand on the right wall of hedges to ground myself, the dark green leaves soft and silky against my fingers, and set off down the path. It would have been preferable to run, but this dress wasn't designed for running—a pretty thing, white with blue stripes and red laces running down the front of the bodice—but the train tangled around my legs. I was afraid I would trip and not be able to get up again if I attempted to run. So I walked briskly down the path, wondering why I ever agreed to go in the first place. The night before, I had convinced myself that winning his hand was the only way out of my predicament. But could I really do that? While he was attractive, I wasn't attracted to him. Could I actually marry someone I didn't love?

When I reached the end of the path, I had two options: turn right or turn left. Both options looked the same, but the right path curved a few feet down into a patch of sunlight, while the left kept on going into the shadows.

"Monseigneur?" I said loudly.

Once again, there was no response. I took the right path. If I found the exit before the dauphin did, I was going to leave. I would tell a valet that he was still in the maze, but I wasn't going to wait around hoping he would reappear.

Turning right was a good decision. As soon as I rounded the curve, the path opened up into a lovely little tree-lined enclosure with an adorable fountain at its center. Sitting on the ground in front of the fountain was the dauphin. He was so captivated by the fountain that he didn't notice me approach. It was odd. He told me that he had played in the Labyrinth hundreds of times before. What was so special about this fountain?

"You forgot me, Monseigneur," I said as I walked up behind him.

The dauphin jumped and blinked up at me owlishly. "Lady Cendrillon, I didn't forget you. I thought you were right behind me." I don't think the dauphin had ever noticed where anyone was in relation to him, always sure they would be there when he called. He's the grand dauphin of France after all.

"You took off running and were gone before I could catch up. These," I said, tugging on my skirts with a small smile, "make running a tad difficult."

Prince Louis blushed and looked away. "This is my favorite fountain, and I haven't had a chance to visit for a long while. I should have waited for you. My apologies."

I smiled and said, "All is forgiven. I found my way. I might not have been so forgiving if I'd gotten hopelessly lost and needed to be rescued."

"I'm thankful that didn't happen," he said with a laugh. "But rest assured, I would have come to your rescue."

"I'm glad to hear it."

"Please, sit with me. With all the wandering I've made you do, you deserve to rest for a while."

"I can't traipse through the palace with a filthy dress," I said with a pointed look at the ground. "I would be the laughingstock of Versailles."

Alarmingly, the dauphin began to unbutton his justaucorps.

"What are you doing?" I asked, panic in my voice.

"Providing you with a place to sit."

He pulled off the justaucorps with a dramatic flourish, spreading it out on the ground next to him.

"Your seat, mademoiselle."

"But then *you'll* be traipsing through the palace with filthy clothing."

He chortled and pulled on the lace of his sleeves. "I'm the dauphin. The courtiers will judge me behind my back, to be sure, but they won't say anything about it to my face."

I couldn't help but laugh. The justaucorps covered a large swath of the ground. If I positioned myself just right and was careful with my skirts, it would be possible to avoid getting any unsightly stains on Lady Françoise's dress.

Holding on to the dauphin's hand for assistance, I lowered myself slowly and tucked the skirts around my legs. There was even room to spare.

"That's not so bad, is it?" he asked, giving me his sideways grin.

"No. It isn't so bad."

We sat in companionable silence for a few minutes, listening to the gentle wind rustle through the trees and to the cheerful burbling of the fountain. It was much more pleasant here in this little enclosure than on the paths. The fountain, which depicted the fable of the Fox and the Crane, brightened the space quite a bit. The basin was bordered with colorful rocks and shells of all different sorts, many of which I'd never seen before.

Atop a mound of rock and shell stood a red fox. Water arced from its mouth high up into the air and fell back into the basin. Opposite the fox was a crane, painted gray and black. It perched on one reed-thin leg, its neck curved down so it could sip from an elevated section of the basin. The colors were so vivid and the figures so lifelike that it felt like I was watching a real nature scene play out in front of me.

"I think I prefer the fountains in the maze to the ones in the main section of the gardens," I said. "The main fountains are beautiful, but these feel a little more personal."

"They were always my favorite too. Did you know they were designed with me in mind?"

"You mentioned it earlier. I didn't know what you meant."

I shouldn't have been surprised that the fountains were designed for him. He was the heir to the throne after all. But it was striking how different our lives were. Even with Papa's close relationship with the king, we hadn't lived so ostentatiously.

"Charles Perrault worked with my father's first minister of state. He suggested that my father have statues representing Aesop's Fables built and placed throughout the maze to further my education. My tutor was impressed with Lord Perrault's ideas. I hear he still collects little stories for children.

"I spent many hours playing and exploring in here as a child.

My tutor would take me through the maze and have me read the plaques on each fountain and tell me the fables. It's how I started learning to read."

Prince Louis had a soft smile on his face as he recounted these memories. He looked gentler than I'd ever seen him. There was a childlike wonder in his eyes as he talked, and not like the child I'd met a year ago. Like someone kinder.

"Monseigneur, why did you choose me to court?" I asked abruptly.

The words escaped my lips before I even realized that I was speaking. I hoped he was too lost in remembrances to hear me, but those hopes were dashed when he turned to me with a curious expression on his face.

"It's just . . . we hardly know each other," I continued.

"I hardly know any of the other twenty-four ladies either. The entire point of these events *is* to get to know each of you so I can decide who would make the best bride."

"But you didn't know who I was—I could have been someone the king would never approve of you marrying."

"It's true that I didn't know who you were when we *danced*. I approached you because I found you beautiful and wanted to talk with you."

My cheeks were warm as I turned away to stare at the delicate figure of the crane. Anywhere but at the dauphin was preferable. Words like that often accompanied a seduction, or so I'd heard, but he didn't sound like he was trying to woo me. He sounded quite matter-of-fact, and he didn't even seem to notice my embarrassment.

"It was only after the dance that I realized who you were. The girl from the Orangerie."

I whipped my head back around so fast, my neck cracked. "What did you say?"

The dauphin broke into peals of laughter so forceful, his whole body shook. I could only stare at him. His laughter didn't suggest anger at my long-ago slight, but my expression must have suggested indignation on my part, because he sobered quickly. "I'm sorry. I shouldn't laugh. But the look on your face . . ."

"How did you recognize me? I wasn't even sure you could make out what I looked like."

My annoyance had loosened my lips to a startling degree. This was the dauphin that I was talking to. But again, he didn't seem angry, only contrite.

"When I recognized you, I remembered how awfully I'd behaved, and I was ashamed. I'd like to think that I've changed."

Prince Louis looked at me beseechingly. I sighed. "You seem to have changed a great deal. I don't think the boy I met a year ago would have apologized for anything, much less for something as silly as running ahead of me in a maze."

His answering smile was dazzling in its brilliance. "That's nice to hear. There was no excuse for my rudeness. But, in my defense, you and your friends *were* trespassing in my father's Orangerie."

"That's true. We shouldn't have done that. But if *I* may offer a defense, I was new to court and its protocols."

"It's ancient history now. It doesn't matter. What does matter is why I chose you as the twenty-fifth maiden."

He paused. If he was trying to achieve a dramatic effect, it worked. I leaned forward, caught on his every word.

"This," he said, spreading his arms out wide, "is my apology. I decided to make it up to you by giving you the chance to become the future dauphine."

I had to smile. As apologies went, this was certainly a unique one.

"I know this must seem overwhelming, but the solution presented itself to me at the ball. The way you were dressed made your nobility clear. And you were accompanied by Madame de la Valliere. But when I learned you were the daughter of the Marquis de Louvois, I knew it was fate. Everything couldn't have worked out more perfectly."

"I don't know what to say. I am most . . . humbled."

I meant most everything I said, except for that last part. I appreciated that he wanted to apologize for his past behavior, and to my surprise, I was enjoying the outing after all. Monseigneur was amusing to be around. He'd turned a stodgy walk through a hedge maze into an adventure, and he'd given me a chance to escape from Lady Catherine, for which I would always be grateful. I wanted to win this competition for my own personal benefit, but I'd never considered that a true attachment with the dauphin might also arise from this endeavor.

It was almost as if Louis read my mind when he said, "I can't promise that I'll choose you in the end. That wouldn't be fair to the other ladies. But I can give you this chance. To see where things go between us. How we fit together. Or don't. Though I certainly like how things are going so far."

My stomach turned again as I glanced away from the intensity in his gaze. I could hardly believe that his apology entailed offering me the chance to wed him.

That wasn't the entirety of it, of course. A crown was in the mix as well. The thought of that was difficult to wrap my head around. Was there an astonishing amount of arrogance wrapped up in the dauphin's apology? Indeed there was, but it wasn't the kind of arrogance that had made me dislike him so much a year ago. There was an earnestness, an honesty, that hadn't been there before, and I appreciated that he was willing to reveal it to me. I couldn't deny that I came away from this feeling a little softer toward Prince Louis.

We soon parted ways, Prince Louis successfully guiding us to Labyrinth's exit. He had an outing planned with Severine right after.

I chose to be vague when he asked me questions about what she was like now, having not interacted with her again beyond that first day. He was taking her to the Menagerie; he would find out what she was like soon enough.

To avoid encountering them, I decided to wander across the parterres for a little while. All the girls had to be back at the palace by late afternoon for an announcement about the next courtship event, but I wanted to take a look around.

When I was sure that enough time had passed, I made my way back to the palace. It was in the Salon of War, just as I was about to pass through the archway into the Hall of Mirrors, that I smacked right into someone coming through from the other side.

"I'm so sorry," I said, then looked up to see that I'd bumped into Auguste. "Oh, it's you." My heart caught a little at seeing him again. "This is the second time we've literally run into each other here. I wonder if it's becoming a tradition."

What I'd said wasn't particularly funny, but I expected Auguste to smile at least a little. But he just frowned and stepped around me without a word. Without thinking, I grabbed on to his arm to stop him from leaving. "Auguste, is something wrong?"

"Nothing, nothing, nothing's wrong," he said, but he wouldn't look me in the eyes.

"Tell me, please," I begged. "You look troubled." I had tried not to think about Auguste since my name was called for the courtship competition, but I had to face it now.

Auguste finally turned around to look at me. His eyes were bleak. I tried to reach for him again, but he pulled away from me.

"Why are you so upset?"

"I'm not," he said. "Truly, I'm just having a bad day."

I knew he was lying. "Please, we're friends, aren't we?" I wanted to believe we were still friends. "May I help?"

He laughed a hollow laugh. "No, sadly, you may not." Then he looked at me once more, with so much feeling, that something inside me ached.

"Is it about the competition for your brother's hand?" I asked, unsure still of what had come over him. "To see that the court is obsessed with his choice of bride?"

Auguste shook his head vehemently. "No, I don't care about the court. I only care about..." Then he pulled away from me once more.

"Auguste!" I called, but he was already gone, disappearing into the state apartments without a backward glance.

I stood frozen in the salon, my heart breaking.

"Cendrillon, you're back!"

Diane was waving at me from a window embrasure in the Hall of Mirrors. I waved and entered the gallery, but my heart was in my throat, and I felt as if I had hurt my dearest friend.

CHAPTER TWENTY-SIX

"That's so romantic," Diane said dreamily after I finished telling her an edited version of my outing with the dauphin. "I wish he had taken me on a secluded stroll through the Labyrinth. All we did was walk around the Grand Canal. There were people everywhere. We didn't get even a moment alone."

"If it makes you feel any better, it wasn't *that* romantic. I was hopelessly lost for most of it and just wandered aimlessly on my own, because he left me behind. He didn't even notice I wasn't following him. The fountains were pretty, though."

Diane gave me a skeptical look.

"I'm being honest! I can see why it's so popular with the court, but it just wasn't for me."

"As if the Labyrinth was the most important part of your walk together. Are you really telling me that you didn't have a good time? The dauphin was so excited when he saw you earlier. That has to mean something, right?"

"Maybe." I sighed and poked a stray lock of hair back into my bouffant.

"Honestly, Cendrillon, if I didn't know better, I would think that you didn't even want to marry the dauphin."

"Oh! That's . . ." I was about to say that's not true, but *that* wasn't true. I was still thinking of how upset Auguste had looked when I bumped into him and had almost forgotten about my walk with the dauphin.

Before I could finish my sentence, Prince Louis and Severine emerged from the Salon of Peace. Severine headed straight for Alexandre while he climbed up on the dais.

"Aren't they back a little soon?" Diane asked. "They were supposed to be going to the Menagerie. Looking at all the animals takes at least an hour. Has it even been forty minutes?"

"I don't think so. Something must have happened. Look at Severine. She seems upset."

Severine seemed quite a bit more than upset. Her face was ashen, and there was a bit of dirt smeared on her cheek. She was gesticulating wildly while Alexandre just stood there with her shoulders slumped.

We overheard a few words like *dirt* and *stupid monkey*. It would be horribly rude to laugh at Severine's obviously failed outing with the dauphin in front of Diane, so I kept my face perfectly composed and promised to giggle about it later with Elodie.

"Mesdemoiselles, can I have your attention, please?" the dauphin said, his voice booming through the Hall of Mirrors. "I have news both pleasant and unfortunate to share with you. First, the pleasant news. I would like to announce the next courtship event. I'm looking forward to this one."

The dauphin paused for dramatic affect. He really did love doing

202

that. I wondered how long it took for his mannerisms to feel annoying instead of charming.

"A select few of you will accompany me on a royal hunt!"

Gasps of excitement filled the air. The royal hunt was a significant event at Versailles. The king allowed only his most favored courtiers to join him on his own hunts. Papa had been on one once, but he never really liked horseback riding and declined the king's future offers. The girls the dauphin chose to accompany him would have to be his most favored.

The anticipation was nearly tangible, and Louis knew it. He looked so smug up there on the dais, basking in the attention and desire. I liked him a little less than I had earlier in the Labyrinth. With arms spread wide, he said, "The maidens who will be joining me on the hunt are Lady Anna de Medici, Princesse Henrietta, Duchesse Maria Anna Victoria, Lady Diane, and Lady Cendrillon."

Diane squealed and grabbed my arm. Even though our outing had gone well, the announcement came as a surprise. I couldn't believe that he picked me over so many more impressive girls here.

"The hunt will be held in a week's time. More details are forthcoming."

He paused again, this time to paste a solemn expression onto his face.

"Now we must move on to the unfortunate news. Five of you will be removed from the courtship proceedings today. If I could keep all of you here with me, I would. But it simply isn't possible. The ladies who are leaving will of course always be welcome at Versailles, but they will no longer be participating in courtship events."

Ignoring the dismayed murmurs, the dauphin named the girls who were going to be leaving. Four of them I didn't know. The only one I recognized was Veronique, who looked like she was about to weep, while Severine looked relieved that whatever disaster had be-fallen her and the dauphin during their trip to the Menagerie hadn't resulted in her dismissal.

The dauphin jumped down from the dais and waited while a few of the girls crowded around to talk with him, all five of the removed girls among them. I could see the eyes of the rest fixed on me and Diane, who was chatting about what she would wear on the hunt and whether Princesse Henrietta ever hunted at home in England. She seemed oblivious to the jealousy being sent our way.

One of the sets of watching, jealous eyes were Severine's. She wasn't even trying to hide her hatred of me at this point.

"This is going to be so amazing! And you! I never imagined that he would choose me. You, definitely, but not me."

"How could he not choose you, Diane? You're probably the sweetest person here."

Diane rolled her eyes. "I am not. Promise that you'll stay with me during the hunt as much as possible. I don't have much experience with horses."

"I promise."

I squeezed her hand and smiled to hide my worry. Things were moving faster than I had anticipated, and it was frightening. I wanted to win the competition. I did. For my own sake and Elodie's. And it truly seemed that, if I were to win, I would at least be somewhat compatible with the dauphin. But every time I tried to focus on Prince Louis and the competition, Auguste lurked around the edges of my mind, pushing out everything else until all I could think about was him.

CHAPTER TWENTY-SEVEN

THE CHÂTEAU WAS DISTURBINGLY QUIET when I returned from the palace. After what I assumed to be Severine's disastrous outing and the dauphin choosing me to join him on the royal hunt, I expected Severine to be hiding around the corner, waiting to pounce on me for getting so much attention. But she was nowhere to be seen. I slipped off my heels and crept down the hallway as quickly and quietly as possible.

"Severine told me you had an absolutely wonderful time at the palace today, Cendrillon."

I jumped and turned to see Lady Catherine standing in the doorway to the sitting room, her eyes fixed on me. Severine only had a head start of about fifteen minutes, but that was enough time for her to relay the day's events to her mother.

"I wouldn't say that it was a wonderful time. Perhaps a perfectly average time would be a better descriptor. The dauphin had to meet with so many ladies that he couldn't spend much time with any one particular person," I said quickly as I began backing down the hallway. Plus, it wasn't wonderful. Something was wrong with Auguste.

Lady Catherine smiled and walked closer even as I backed away, looming over me. "Severine told me that the dauphin invited you to join him for a royal hunt."

"I wasn't the only girl that he—"

"No. But you were one of the few who were chosen. I would consider that to be a wonderful occurrence. You're being modest, Cendrillon. It doesn't suit you."

The inside of my cheek stung where I bit it trying to smother any potential retort. I was already on dangerous footing with Lady Catherine. Any backtalk, no matter how justified, would only make it worse.

"Is that Cendrillon?" Severine asked, her voice emanating from the sitting room.

"Yes, ma jolie fille. She finally got back from the palace."

Severine sounded weak and distressed, as if she were suffering from some kind of mysterious malaise. She had been fine when leaving the palace. I suspected that she was playacting to gain sympathy from her mother. And why wouldn't she? It always worked.

"I don't want to see her," Severine called out.

I heard Alexandre in the sitting room, saying quietly, "Severine, you're being mean."

"No! She's the one being mean! She's ruining everything! I do not want her in my presence!"

Lady Catherine was nodding her head in agreement and eyeing me contemplatively.

"Your stepsister is very distressed, Cendrillon," she said. "It wouldn't be appropriate to strain her nerves further. Perhaps you should spend the rest of the night in your room. There's no need to come down for supper. I'm sure you had plenty to eat at the palace."

"But—"

"No objections. Please think of Severine, and do what is best for her health."

The small smile on my stepmother's face belied the "seriousness" of her words. So this was what my life was going to look like from now on at the château. Punishment anytime I succeeded over Severine. That depressing prospect only strengthened my resolve to win... and escape from this place.

My stomach rumbled as I turned my back on Lady Catherine and quickly ascended the stairs. I hadn't had anything to eat at the palace and was very hungry. Maybe I would be able to sneak downstairs after everyone went to bed and get some food from the kitchen. As soon as I opened the door to the attic and started climbing the steps, the familiar chill began to seep into my skin. But after the heat and the stress of the day, I welcomed the soothing darkness.

"Cendrillon! How did everything go today?"

I shrieked and clutched at my chest, whirling around to see Elodie standing in the shadows just beside the door, a hand covering her mouth as she failed to stifle her giggles.

"Elodie! What are you doing just standing there in the dark? I nearly jumped out of my skin."

Laughing, Elodie grabbed my hand and led me over to one of the only places to sit in the attic, my little bed. As we plopped down on the bed, Elodie said, "You forgot that I was hiding up here finishing the alterations on Lady Françoise's dresses, didn't you?"

I winced. "Maybe a little. I've had a long day, though, and a distinctly unpleasant encounter with Lady Catherine just now. Severine is upset because the dauphin invited me to go on the royal hunt with him, so now I'm banned from leaving the attic for the rest of the night."

My stomach rumbled again as if to emphasize my point. Elodie blinked at me. "Apparently, we have a lot to talk about. But I have a solution to one of those things."

Elodie reached down under the bed and pulled out a plate arrayed with enough slices of bread and cheese for us to share.

I threw my arms around Elodie's shoulders and squeezed. Elodie laughed again and pulled back, gesturing to the dresses piled up on Maman's rocking chair.

"I finished nearly all the alterations. I think there might be one or two dresses left, but you should have enough to carry you through the competition."

When Elodie returned to the bed, I grasped her hands tightly. "You're amazing," I said. "Truly. I would be lost without you."

"I brought you bread and cheese and mended your dresses," she said skeptically, but I could see a faint blush coloring her cheeks. "I don't know if I would call that amazing. And you wouldn't be lost without me, clearly. Not if the dauphin is already inviting you on a royal hunt. You're taking care of yourself just fine."

"I wouldn't have been able to get through the last year without your support, Elodie. After losing Papa, I don't know what would have happened if you and Marius hadn't been there for me. And after Lady Françoise's passing . . . well, you are the only thing keeping me together. That's why I'm going to do everything in my power to get you out of here. I hope Lady Catherine didn't treat you too terribly today."

"I hardly saw her. I spent the entire day in the sewing room, working on the dresses. If I can manage to keep this pace up, I should be finished in no time. But, Cendrillon," Elodie said worriedly, "I hope you're not just competing in the competition for my sake. I want you to do this only if *you* want to marry the dauphin. I can take care of myself. Lady Catherine isn't going to hurt me. I'd still be able to find work somewhere even though she's tried to damage my reputation.

It would be awful if you were trapped in a marriage you didn't want because of your worry for me."

"I'm not just doing it for you," I said with what I hoped was a reassuring smile on my face. "Prince Louis has changed since we first met him. He's kind, funny, and courteous. The perfect gentleman. He would be a good husband. Freeing you, and myself, from Lady Catherine's clutches is just a bonus. And if I marry him, he can force her to give me my inheritance." I was so convincing, I almost convinced myself.

I pulled a piece of bread off the plate and held it out to Elodie. "Why don't we start eating, and then we'll go through the dresses and make sure they fit."

Elodie still looked a little uncertain, but she took the bread from me and began piling it up with slices of cheese. I'd gotten much better at lying since living with Lady Catherine. I didn't like it, but I didn't want Elodie to worry about me.

I couldn't risk Lady Catherine or Severine hurting Elodie— especially if they found out about her and Alexandre. I was doing what was best for us both. And marrying Prince Louis wasn't a death sentence. Everything I said about him was true. He *had* changed. I'd just neglected to mention that there was another royal brother who was also taking up a not-insignificant place in my thoughts.

CHAPTER TWENTY-EIGHT

FAR AHEAD I COULD HEAR the Grand Veneur's squire blast his horn three times, sharply: the stag had been spotted. Through the trees I could see flashes of the hunters' colorful coats, red and blue among the greenery. I wished I could join them, that I could feel the pounding of the horse's hooves beneath me, the wind rushing in my hair, follow the baying of the hounds. Instead I was jolting along in a small creaky carriage with Diane and Anna de Medici, who was (as it turned out) the dullest person I'd ever met, despite her famous family. The ladies were not permitted to hunt. Just to observe. To witness the dauphin's prowess and coo over his kills.

As I watched my rivals primp and preen over lace and bows, curls and lace fans, it occurred to me that it was possible to hunt without horse and saddle and hounds and weapons. To hunt a different kind of prey altogether.

Next to me in the carriage, Diane was trying to chat with Anna about the competition, about mutual friends, about her home in

Tuscany, and even about the weather, but to each question Anna only said, "No," or "I couldn't say," and flicked her fan over her face impatiently.

Perhaps she wished she'd been assigned to ride in the other carriage, with Princesse Henrietta and Duchesse Maria Anna Victoria, who were leaning together and whispering. Gossip among the girls in the competition had it that Princesse Henrietta was the dauphin's current favorite, and it had seemed, before he rode off that morning to begin the hunt, that he did spend more time speaking to her than the rest of us. "Mesdemoiselles," he'd said, his arm resting on the side of the carriage nearest Princesse Henrietta, "I promise not to leave you to your own devices for *too* long." He'd given the princesse a long glance, and then followed the sound of the horns into the trees.

I watched the English princesse and the Hapsburg duchesse with interest and wondered if the quality of their gossip was better than ours or if Anna was simply an ambitious social climber who had no interest in girls from less exalted families. It was no surprise to me that the higher nobility preferred to stick close to their own kind, though I wished more than once to have the opportunity to learn from the princesse and the duchesse about their families, their countries—to know whether things were better there than in France, or even different. Different enough for people like me.

I'd barely made it out the house that morning. Perhaps as revenge for Severine not having been invited to the hunt, Lady Catherine had woken me and demanded I perform several chores before leaving: First, I had to help Elodie carry several heavy pieces of furniture up the stairs, including a heavy chest and an enormous clock; then I had to dig up potatoes for supper, enough for nearly a week's worth of evening meals; and *then* she had me scrub the entire staircase top to bottom because (she said) I had soiled it by perspiring too much when

I helped Elodie carry the furniture. She stood over me the whole time to make certain I didn't rush the job either. I suspected she was trying to make me late to the hunt so I'd be left behind, or else so tired I could barely keep my eyes open, much less hold a tantalizing conversation with the dauphin.

In the first case, it hadn't worked. I had arrived with two minutes to spare, even if I was still tucking pins into my hair when the carriage stopped. In the second case, though, I began to fear her scheme would eventually find success. As the sun mounted the sky toward midmorning and the air grew hotter, I began to feel my eyelids droop. The stimulating conversation of Lady Anna didn't help matters in the least.

"I hope there will be lemonade with luncheon," she was murmuring, mostly to herself. Luncheon was hours away, a picnic that had been prepared for the entire hunting party in a cool grove near a pond. She turned to Diane. "Do you think there will be lemonade?"

Diane, who by then had given up trying to make friends with Anna, managed to eke out, "I couldn't say," without a hint of sarcasm, bless her.

It was tremendously hot. I could feel my petticoats sticking to my calves and a trickle of perspiration down the middle of my back. Somewhere close by I could hear a bee drone, probably drawn by the purple irises Anna had tucked in her hair. Imagine that: actual fleur-de-lis. She might as well have written, "I'm yours for the taking, Louis," across her forehead.

Between the heat and the morning's hard work, I was exhausted. My knees still hurt from scrubbing, and my hands were chapped and red. I kept them hidden under my fan, but I couldn't help but be envious of how the princesse and the duchesse, and certainly Anna and Diane, likely slept all night in a comfortable bed, had their breakfast brought to them on a tray by servants, and been given a chance to bathe and dress at leisure. They didn't have to scrub Severine's underthings or clean garden dirt from under their fingernails before trying to impress the dauphin.

The air was warm and drowsy and the hunters far away, and Anna said, "I couldn't say," one more time to one of Diane's polite queries. Surely no one would notice if I closed my eyes for just a moment.

From far off, I could hear someone calling my name. *Cendrillon,* it said. *Cendrillon.* It was Lady Catherine with more chores for me: to sweep the larder, to feed the pigs. It was Severine with a cruel taunt: look at Cinder, covered in ashes. It was Auguste in the Hall of Mirrors, his face so deathly and dejected that I was terribly worried for him.

"Cendrillon!" Diane poked me in the ribs.

"What?" I sat up and opened my eyes.

The carriage had stopped. We were surrounded by more than a dozen hunters on horseback, a pack of ten or fifteen restless hounds, several squires, a valet—and the dauphin, who sat on his horse with a crooked but expectant smile, as if he'd just asked me a question. When I noticed a dozen riders around the carriage looking at me, I snapped my fan, sat up straight, and gave Diane a questioning look. Clearly I'd missed something.

"The dauphin asked you a question," hissed Anna, as if she were the one who'd been affronted.

"I beg your pardon," I said, giving the dauphin a nod.

Louis just gave me another crooked smile and asked, "I wondered if this outing bores you, Lady Cendrillon?"

I was aware of at least two dozen pairs of eyes on me. "Not at all, Monseigneur," I said. "It's only that I didn't sleep well last night. I do apologize."

Anna whispered something under her breath that sounded like "Who does she think she is?" and beamed at the dauphin. She probably believed Louis was so affronted that I would be one of the next girls eliminated.

For a terrible long second, I believed she might be right, and I was frightened. No rescue from Lady Catherine. No life beyond drudgery and humiliation. I would be trapped in that house for eternity, with no escape. No inheritance. Someone else would be dauphine—Princesse Henrietta, perhaps. Or, horrors, even Severine.

But before this thought could coalesce into ice around my heart, Louis wheeled on Anna. "Did you have something to say?" he inquired in his haughtiest tone. "A criticism of Lady Cendrillon? It's hardly a crime for a young lady to close her eyes for a moment. Especially one who did not sleep well the night before."

"I beg your pardon, Monseigneur. I did not mean anything by it—" Anna started, but Louis had already dropped down from the saddle to take my hand and help me from the carriage.

It was then that Louis did something truly remarkable. "Would a ride refresh you?" he asked.

"A ride?"

The entire party was completely silent. This was a breach of etiquette on the dauphin's part. I wasn't dressed for riding, and no horse had been provided for me. I would have to ride with Louis on his horse. It seemed almost impossible, the two of us. And astride, for that matter, not even sidesaddle.

I could feel them all watching me. And yet no one would tell me no, not today. Not when the dauphin himself was asking.

"I'd be glad to," I said, and allowed him to swing me up in front of him in the saddle.

Anna was halfway out of her seat to object, and Diane's mouth had dropped open—but before either of them could speak a word, Louis tightened his arms around me, touched his spurs to his horse's flanks—and we were off.

The squires and hounds, the carriages and other ladies all fell away. There was only the feel of the horse thundering through the trees, the calls of the birds, and Louis's arms tight around me, holding me to him.

It seemed an age that we raced ahead of the others, but it must have been only a few minutes until the picnic came into view and Louis slowed the horse to a canter, then a walk. I was sorry to see it end, my wild ride on horseback with the dauphin of France.

And yet it was possible that this would be the first time, not the only. If he chose me to be his queen.

"Well, then," Louis murmured against my ear. "What do you think?"

When I caught my breath again, I said, "That was incredible. I've never ridden astride before. It was so fast!"

"You enjoyed it?" He bent to give me a sly smile.

"I did. Very much." It was wonderful to ride so freely with the wind in my hair.

"Then we shall have to do it again sometime. With your permission, of course."

"Thank you. I . . . would like that."

He swung me down to my feet, then led his horse by the reins to a groom waiting under a nearby tree. The animal was flecked with white foam from the heat and exertion. I barely felt more composed, and yet I didn't care if my hair was mussed or my dress wrinkled. For a moment, I forgot Lady Catherine, Severine, my place in the world. For a moment I was the dauphine, and I loved it.

I looked back the way we'd come. The carriages and squires weren't visible yet, but I could hear them approaching. Soon it would be dull polite conversation about lemonade or the weather, and the horrified eyes of my rivals judging me for my impulsive decision to go with Louis. And yet, given the chance, I'd do it again.

"Don't worry about them," Louis said, and I was disarmed that he'd seemed to have read my mind. "They're just jealous."

We only had a moment alone. I might never get the chance again. "Since we're on the subject, why *didn't* you invite one of them?" I asked. "None of the others were rude enough to fall asleep on our outing."

"Because," said Louis, "I knew you would be the only one who'd say yes."

CHAPTER TWENTY-NINE

THE ROYAL STABLES WERE SITUATED in the Place d'Armes, opposite the palace. After the luncheon was over and the hunt ended for the day—as dull and spiritless as I'd feared after the thrill of my ride with Louis—the carriages returned us there and deposited Anna, Diane, and myself.

Anna and Diane had carriages waiting to return them home. My own carriage was nowhere to be found. Not wanting to be seen walking home, I slipped inside the Small Stables for a moment until the rest of the party cleared out.

The musky smell of horse and hay hit me like a wave as soon as I walked in the door. Elodie thought I was a fool, but I loved that smell. I'd spent so much time hiding in the stables from Lady Catherine and Severine that they were safe spaces for me, and that feeling extended to most any stables I encountered. These were no different, even if they were much larger than any I had been to before.

Row upon row of wooden stalls lay before me underneath the high-arched ceilings of cream-colored stone, occupied by the widest variety of horses I'd ever seen, from golden palominos to gorgeous white Arabian stallions. The king only kept the best animals, and it showed. A few stable hands and young squires hurried up and down the stalls, but they paid me no mind. It was nice to wander through the stables while they were so empty. Normally, the Royal Stables would be a hotbed of energy and packed to the brim with people, but the royal hunts were such a huge endeavor that the services of most everyone who worked in the stables were required.

I wandered down a row of stalls at the far end of the stables. At this point I didn't think I was going to find the coachman, so I decided I might as well take the chance to explore without constantly feeling like I was getting in someone's way. And the soft whickering of the horses, the rustle of hay, and the clicking of my shoes on the cobblestone floor were comforting and familiar.

The peace was disturbed by a few harsh curses accompanied by a tall, dark-haired figure tumbling backward out of one of the stalls and landing flat on his back.

I rushed toward him. That looked terribly painful.

"Are you . . . ?" I started to ask, the rest of the words catching in my throat when I realized who the figure was.

Auguste. He was lying on his side, facing away from me, but I recognized the deep voice that was swearing up a storm as he clutched at his knee. His eyes widened when he saw me. "Cendrillon? What are you doing here? Shouldn't you be on the hunt?"

"The hunt is over. Are you all right?"

"Yes. It's nothing," he said, shaking it off and standing up. His hair was mussed and his cheeks were red.

"You always say it's nothing."

He shrugged. He didn't look as wounded as he did the other day, but he was definitely aloof. "If the hunt is over, do you need a way home?" he asked. "I can call a carriage and—"

"No, thank you. I'll wait for my carriage. If you haven't seen the coachman, I'll look elsewhere," I said shortly.

"You can't just go wandering all over the palace looking for a coachman. He could be anywhere. Etienne," Auguste called.

A little boy no more than ten years old poked his head around the corner. "Yes, Monsieur?"

"Have you seen a dark blue carriage recently?" Auguste asked, standing tall in his coat and breeches.

"Yes, Monsieur. Early this morning. That lady there climbed out," the boy said, nodding to me. "But it drove away."

"Find it for me, will you? Ask the coachman to come back to the Small Stables. His mistress is waiting."

Auguste fished around in his pocket and pulled out a few gold coins. He tossed them to the boy, who caught them with ease. "There will be a little something extra in it for you if the carriage returns quickly."

The boy nodded and took off running. Auguste waited to speak until the sound of Etienne's shoes no longer clomped against the cobblestones.

"Getting rid of me as fast as you can, are you?" I said, with just a hint of sadness.

He looked shocked. "What do you mean?"

Now it was my turn to be mysterious. "Nothing," I said. I was starting to feel ridiculous for worrying about him so much.

"Why don't you sit down while we wait?" Auguste said. "You look hot."

"I'm fine."

"You're awfully flushed."

I felt myself blush even hotter. Auguste took hold of my arm and steered me toward a stool pushed up against one of the stalls, and his hand on my arm generated even more heat inside me. I had never felt this way around Louis, not today, not even when he had his arm around me, and I suspected I would never feel this way about him. But I didn't want to think about that too much. "Of course I look flushed. It's hotter than Hades and I'm wearing eighteen layers of clothing."

His mouth quirked. "So, how was the hunt? Did my brother get his stag?"

"He did. Two of them, in fact. Enough that all the ladies were swooning over him through the luncheon."

"*All* the ladies?"

"Well, perhaps not all."

Auguste looked astonished. Even though I was irritated that he was so moody, I couldn't help but find him charming, and he was, with his furrowed brows and the confused pout of his lips. "Not one of his many admirers, then," he said. "You must be the only one."

When he smiled, I forgot all about Louis's arm tightening around my waist and his breath in my ear. Auguste was standing a few feet away, but the heat he sparked in me was palpable. I would have to stop looking at him; that was the only solution. I tried to look elsewhere.

"Louis has admirers aplenty," I said tartly. "I doubt he'll miss me."

"I would miss you," said Auguste, "if I were him." He wasn't looking at me when he said it, but he was looking at me now.

I could feel my entire body trembling as I met his eyes. "Why were you so upset the other day?"

"Don't you know?" he asked lightly.

"Am I supposed to be a mind reader?"

He laughed.

"So it is the competition, isn't it?" I asked.

He shrugged.

"I'm sorry," I whispered.

"I'm sorry too," he said.

I wasn't sure what we were talking about anymore. A silence stretched between us of all the things we somehow could not say to each other.

"May I ask you something?" he asked after a silence.

"Anything."

"Do you want to win?" he asked.

Did I want to win? What kind of a question was that? I *had* to win. I had to get out of my stepmother's clutches, and I couldn't fail Elodie and Marius. I debated silently over whether or not I should tell Auguste the entire truth about Lady Catherine. Even if he'd been acting a little strange, I decided that we were friends after all, and I could confide in him.

"I need to tell you something. My stepmother is . . . unkind to me. She is the reason I had to stay away from court for so long."

"Unkind? How?" His brow furrowed.

"Lady Catherine doesn't allow me to leave the château very often, beyond going to the market. But she can't dare mistreat me as long as I agree to court your brother. I couldn't say no."

His eyes flashed. "She mistreats you?" The anger in his voice was sharp.

"It's all right; I can handle it," I told him. I didn't want him to worry, and I was telling the truth: I could handle it.

He sighed and raked his fingers through his hair, mussing the dark brown locks completely. I moved to the left and motioned for him to sit on the stool. He raised his eyebrows and sat down. There was just enough room for both of us to fit, though our shoulders were pressed close together.

"I know you can handle anything. You were always full of spirit. I'm sorry about your stepmother. And I haven't even had the chance to give my condolences for Lady Françoise."

"Thank you. I appreciate that very much."

We sat in a companionable silence for a few minutes before he asked quietly, "You didn't answer my question."

"You didn't answer mine," I pointed out. "Why were you so upset the other day? And what were you doing in the stall that made you fall over and curse so vulgarly?" I asked, my voice high and tight, betraying my nerves.

"I was . . . ah . . . reading," he said haltingly.

"Reading? I didn't realize reading was so difficult for you that it sends you into convulsions."

"Oh, yes. Very funny. I may be dense in some respects, but I'm not that dense." He laughed.

Miscalculating his strength compared with my size, Auguste bumped me with his shoulder and nearly knocked me off the stool. I would've fallen face-first into the dirt if he hadn't caught me and dragged me back up just in time.

We burst into a fit of laughter that lasted so long, my sides started to ache and my eyes watered. The stables were a smeary blur of browns and creams. The only thing that was clear was Auguste. One of my arms and legs was flush against his, but I had no desire to move away. Auguste didn't move either.

"So what made you fall?" I asked.

"I'd been sitting on the floor, reading, and when I tried to get up, I stubbed my toe on a horseshoe someone left on the floor and tripped."

"Is that all? A stubbed toe?"

"It hurt! That horseshoe was made of steel."

I smirked and said, "Maybe you should have been more careful. It *is* a horse stall. I would expect there to be horseshoes in a horse stall. Why were you reading there, anyway?"

He sighed. "When I'm feeling bad, I like to hide in the stables to calm down. I've been doing it since I was a child. It's a place where no one would find me if I didn't want to be found. It's held up pretty well. Until you, that is."

Auguste must have noticed the surprise on my face. "What? What is it? Too strange for you? I know it's a little odd."

"No! I mean, it is strange, but not to me. I do it too. Hide in the stables when I'm upset, that is. I don't know why I'm telling you this. I guess I'm just excited to find out that I'm not the only person who likes to hide in the smelly stables on piles of hay," I said. "It wasn't nothing. And you're still upset, which is why you had to come here today."

"Yes," he finally admitted.

"What were you upset about?"

"Do you really not know?" he asked huskily.

I noted suddenly how terribly close we were to each other, the warmth of his thigh pressed against mine and the few inches of space that separated us. And when he turned down to look at me, his face was so close to mine that if either of us leaned forward . . .

"I might have a guess?" I whispered.

He chuckled softly, sending shivers through my body.

His lashes are so long, I thought, closing my eyes as I felt them brush my cheek as he leaned closer. The press of his lips against mine was soft and warm. This was not like the time we almost kissed—so quick that it was over before it started. This was different. My whole body trembled as he wrapped his arms around my waist and pulled me up against him. I wrapped my arms around his neck, relishing how soft his hair felt. The kiss was sweet and unhurried, a careful exploration, growing stronger and more urgent until we were both breathless.

When we parted, I opened my eyes and found his were still closed. I touched his lashes with the tip of my finger. They were as light as butterfly wings.

His arms were still around me when a clatter from somewhere close by in the stables startled us, and I noticed that I was sitting on his lap. We pulled apart and jumped to our feet. As reality came crashing back in, I realized that we'd been kissing in full view of anyone who walked by the stables.

"Is someone there?" Auguste asked, his voice echoing through the seemingly empty hall as he took a few steps forward. "Hello?"

"I'm back, Monsieur," said a little voice, high-pitched and excited.

Etienne appeared from around the corner, a bounce to his step, with Lady Françoise's coachman in tow.

"I found him! I found him! Do I get my reward now?"

Auguste glanced back at me and began riffling through his pockets again. "Of course, give me just a moment."

I pressed my fingers to my lips. They were swollen and tender to the touch. My dress was slightly askew, and I had no idea what the state of my hair was. Would the coachman be able to tell what Auguste and I had been doing? Did they see anything? That clatter had been awfully close by.

"I'm sorry I wasn't waiting for you like I promised, Lady Cendrillon," the coachman said. "One of the king's men asked me to move. I couldn't refuse. Are you ready to leave?"

"Yes, I'm . . . I'm ready. I'll see you soon, Auguste."

Walking past Auguste, I started to follow the coachman out of the stables.

"Cendrillon, wait!"

I stopped to get one final glimpse of Auguste. He appeared the same as always, except for his eyes. There was a heat in them as he looked at me that I'd never seen before.

"Goodbye," I whispered, turning away. But when it was clear we were alone in the corridor, Auguste pulled me to him once more.

"We should say goodbye properly," he said, and kissed me, his hand grazing my cheek.

It was sweeter the second time, and I kissed him all over his face, his jaw, his neck, and buried my face in his shirt, just breathing in the smell of him, intoxicated by the heat of his body. I cleaved to him, and it was almost physically painful when we parted.

"Goodbye, then," I said.

"For now," he said, squeezing my hand.

This time, I all but fled from the Small Stables, my heart pounding painfully against my rib cage. We shouldn't have given in to temptation. If anyone found out what we'd done, the scandal would be horrendous. I was courting his brother, the dauphin of France. Just hours earlier we had ridden together, and now here I was, kissing Auguste.

But I couldn't muster up any shame. I felt light, giddy, and happier than I'd been in a year. My dear friend felt the same way about me as I did him. I still wasn't sure what would happen now that our relationship had changed—and it had changed irrevocably—but I was excited to find out.

MAGIC

The pleasure of love is in loving.

—*François, Duc de La Rochefoucauld*

CHAPTER THIRTY

"THE DEMOISELLE CRANE IS THE highlight of the Menagerie, prized for its elegance, grace, and beauty. It was a gift from a foreign ambassador and one of the king's favorite animals," Prince Louis said as he stood in front of the bird pen. "Don't you think that it's a wonderful animal?"

"It is a wonderful bird, Monseigneur," Diane said, perhaps a tad too eagerly. "Quite unique."

I suspected that Diane found the bird to be as interesting as I did, which wasn't very. It was a strange little beast, with red eyes and a long gray neck. I liked when it bobbed about the pen on its spindly legs, but it wasn't even doing that. The crane was just standing in the corner, staring at the wall. Maybe it was bored. I know I would be, trapped in a pen with other birds and nothing to do while various nobles oohed and aahed over them.

"It *is* unique, isn't it? I confess that it isn't my favorite animal, but I can admire its beauty."

A few of the girls smiled at the dauphin and nodded vigorously. It seemed that the king wanted to find a bride for his eldest son quickly, as this outing at the Menagerie came only a few days after the royal hunt. And it wasn't a typical event either, where the dauphin spent time alone with each of us, but a group event where we traveled around the Menagerie together making awkward small talk while examining each animal enclosure.

Perhaps the king thought this kind of event would save time, but in reality, it just meant that the pushiest ladies surrounded the prince while the less forceful were relegated to the back. That was fine with me, as my thoughts were consumed with Auguste. I kept hoping I'd run into him, but he was nowhere to be found.

The Menagerie was located in the southwest section of the grounds, far from the palace itself, walled in and accessible only through the main gate. At the center of the park was a lovely little stone pavilion where refreshment-laden tables had been set up. Surrounding the pavilion in a circular layout were seven long enclosures where the animals were kept. A walking path took visitors past each enclosure in a wide loop. If only I'd been able to explore by myself. The Menagerie housed animals I'd only read about in books. Lions and tigers and odd, massive birds that Diane told me were called ostriches, with long necks and legs.

But I could hardly even get close to the gates without being elbowed out of the way by Severine and pushed to the back of the group. And it didn't help that the pavilion was packed with onlookers from court staring at us as if we were the animals in a cage. Maybe I could come back when the Menagerie was less crowded. Maybe with Auguste. My cheeks flushed at the thought of Auguste. I hadn't seen him since our kiss in the stables.

And I wanted to see him so badly, I couldn't sleep. Hence, I was sleepwalking through the day.

"Are you all right, Lady Cendrillon? You look a little flushed. Is the heat getting to you?"

Startled, I turned to see the duchesse from Bavaria, Maria Anna Victoria, standing beside me with a concerned expression on her face. She was small and dark-haired and so quiet, I hadn't even realized that she was there. Or that I'd stopped walking, letting the rest of the group wander on ahead. That wouldn't do. I needed to be present and involved, not lost in daydreams like a child.

"I'm fine. Thank you for your concern, Duchesse."

"I'm the last person who would judge someone for feeling tired or ill. I've experienced far too much of it from others to behave that way. You needn't be ashamed of being tired. I could escort you into the pavilion if you'd like."

Duchesse Maria was a slight girl, nearly overwhelmed by the voluminous skirts of her cream silk dress and the height of the fontange her dark curls were pulled into. Sweat beaded her brow, and the dark circles under her eyes were quite prominent.

"It might be nice to step inside the pavilion for a while. Have some refreshments."

At the duchesse's smile, we made our way to the pavilion, easily slipping away from the rest of the group. The dauphin was too engaged with the other girls to notice. But Severine noticed and grinned mockingly at me again before turning back to Prince Louis and laughing exaggeratedly at something he said. I released the exasperated sigh I'd been holding in all day for fear of Severine hearing me.

"Do you know Lady Severine?" the duchesse asked, the gentle lilt of her Bavarian accent unique and pleasing to the ear. I'd never met someone from Bavaria before.

"She's my stepsister."

"How unfortunate," she said, the barest hint of a smile on her lips.

I laughed in surprise. I couldn't help it. No one was willing to speak badly of Severine. Not to my face, at least.

"Why do you say that?" I asked.

"Do you deny that she is quite unpleasant?"

"No. I don't deny it. I'm just surprised that you would know."

"I spoke with your stepsisters briefly on the first day of the competition, when we were all gathered in the Hall of Mirrors. The younger one, Alexandre, is lovely, but Severine was not particularly kind when she heard my accent. It was only when she found out that I was a duchesse that she tried to be nice to me, but I was no longer interested."

We entered the pavilion through one of the double doors thrown wide to let in the summer breeze. The shade was wonderful after the heat of the sun, but the crowds of courtiers shooting furtive glances at us over the rims of their glasses wasn't. Duchesse Maria clutched at her stomach and took a few deep breaths as we sat down on an unoccupied marble bench near the doors.

"Are you all right? Would you like me to get you something to drink?"

She nodded quickly. I stood up and hurried to the refreshment table, bringing back a small glass of wine. Water would be better, but it was all they had. The duchesse didn't seem to mind, eagerly taking a few sips before resting the glass on her lap with a sigh.

"Thank you, Lady Cendrillon. Walking too far tires me, especially in the heat. I appreciate you coming inside with me. I only hope no one noticed. The gossip about the sickly foreign duchesse would be never-ending."

"Rest assured, I won't tell anyone."

She smiled weakly and continued sipping her wine. I hoped that Duchesse Maria was truly all right. She seemed kind, and her candor was refreshing in this place where no one ever truly spoke their mind.

"Have people been unkind to you here?" I asked tentatively, afraid of upsetting her with a question that was too personal. "Would you rather be home in Bavaria?"

"Gossip and rumors run rampant through the halls of any palace. Duchesses who are plain and sickly often bear the worst of it. People looked down their noses at me just as much in Bavaria as they do here, but Bavaria is still the only home I've ever known. So, yes, I would prefer to be home. But the choice isn't mine. For my father, a potential political alliance is more important than what I want."

I could understand the duchesse's sadness over her lack of choices. While my situation was not the same as hers, I was still participating in the competition for reasons beyond my own desire. If Papa had still been alive, would he have tried to make me participate in the competition? I don't think he would have forced me if I didn't want to, not like the duchesse's parents were doing to her. She must have been very lonely indeed.

"Ah well," she said. "At least Louis seems amusing."

"Do you think you could love him?" I asked. Many of the girls chosen to court the dauphin professed their ardor.

She looked at me with a shrewd smile. "Love does not factor in this kind of marriage. But he seems tolerable." She sighed. "I wish that we could rest here longer, but we should be getting back to the tour, if you're willing. I feel well enough to return, and the dauphin might be missing us."

Even though we'd been inside the pavilion for close to fifteen minutes, the group was still standing in front of the bird enclosure, Prince Louis at the center of the crowd of ladies and looking quite pleased with all the attention.

"Perhaps we should escape back to the palace since the dauphin is distracted," Duchesse Maria said with a little frown. "It is still terribly hot."

How Diane saw us standing a ways down the path from her spot in the middle of the group next to the dauphin, I don't know, but she did. And she made her discovery known, waving furiously at me and calling out, "Cendrillon! I was wondering where you were. Come and join us!"

All eyes landed on us, including Severine's disappointed ones. There was no going back now. Pasting smiles on our faces, the duchesse and I made our way back to the group, lingering around the outskirts.

"Where were you?" Diane asked. "It was as if you two disappeared into thin air."

"The sun is quite strong today," I said quickly. "I needed a small rest, and Duchesse Maria was kind enough to accompany me into the pavilion."

The dauphin smiled warmly and said, "I assume you're feeling better, Lady Cendrillon?" He hardly glanced at Duchesse Maria.

"I am. Thank you, Monseigneur, for your concern. I just needed a little shade."

Severine's tone was nasty as she said, "You've missed quite a lot of the conversation while you were taking a rest."

I glanced at the dauphin, but he was still smiling, seemingly unbothered by our disappearance. That was all that mattered, not Severine's never-ending displeasure.

"Not too much, I hope."

"Not much at all," Prince Louis said. "Lady Paulette expressed discomfort with the attention we're getting from all the courtiers, and I was explaining that the future dauphine must become accustomed to such attention. The life of a royal is carried out almost entirely in the public eye."

Poor Paulette. Her cheeks flushed a bright red, and she refused to make eye contact with anyone, staring intently at the ground instead.

Louis didn't seem to realize how terrible he was making her feel, he was so wrapped up in the adoring attention of all the girls.

"There are some among you who haven't spent much time at court, so I was explaining some of the royal family's daily rituals," he said. "The lever, the waking-up ceremony, and the coucher, the going-to-bed ceremony, are held every day, as are public suppers in front of courtiers and commoners visiting the palace. There are other ceremonies as well, but this isn't the proper venue for such a discussion," he said with a lascivious wink.

I ignored it. "Do you ever tire of the attention?" I asked. "All the eyes on you constantly? It sounds taxing to never have a private moment."

The dauphin looked at me like I was a silly child who'd asked a question that should have been obvious.

"I spend some time alone in the afternoon and evenings. But it is the duty of the king, and consequently, his wife and children, to remain visible and accessible to his people. And why shouldn't I want my subjects to see me? When their king isn't present, the people start to become rebellious. We can't have that, now, can we?"

I smiled and nodded, keeping my disquiet to myself as the conversation moved on. A life lived so publicly sounded horrid. There would be no running off to the stables for a quiet place to read if I became the dauphine.

And I would be married to a man who wouldn't understand my unease, one who actively courted and reveled in the attention. He would never understand my desire for peace and quiet. I wasn't even sure he would want to try.

Auguste understood me in a way I wasn't sure Louis ever would. I didn't want to become just another animal in the Menagerie besieged by ever-judging, always-watching, demanding eyes.

"Lady Cendrillon, will you walk with me?" the dauphin asked, wading through the crowd of girls to offer me his arm. "I wanted to show you the tigers. Marvelous creatures. Absolutely marvelous."

I smiled and gazed up at him from underneath my lashes, because it didn't matter what I wanted. "I would be overjoyed to see the tigers with you, Your Highness."

"Wonderful!" The dauphin tucked my arm against his chest. "My undivided attention is now yours alone. We'll be back shortly, mesdemoiselles," he threw a glance over his shoulder at the group of disappointed young ladies as we set off down the path together.

I walked with Louis, and my heart sank as I realized Auguste couldn't factor into my plans for the future. Only the dauphin. Even if I wasn't entirely happy, a life with him as dauphine would be leagues ahead of the drudgery I would face with my stepmother. If only there was a way that Auguste could ask for my hand, but he was illegitimate. He had no name, no title, and no future. He could not save me, especially while I was in a race for his brother's hand. I had to become the next dauphine to save myself and my friends, whom I loved. I had to take care of the three of us.

CHAPTER THIRTY-ONE

"I won't go if you don't want me to," Diane said worriedly.

"I want you to go."

"Are you sure? Because I'll stay behind."

"I don't want you to stay behind. Go. And have fun."

"I just don't want you to feel left out."

Diane's insistence on staying with me was sweet, but she kept shooting anxious glances at the barge floating at the edge of the canal, as if it would leave without her if she took her eyes off it for a moment. She wanted to go on the group outing with the dauphin, and I wasn't about to stop her.

"I promise that I won't feel left out, Diane. I'm used to being alone. I prefer it most of the time."

"But—"

"No!" I said with a laugh. "There is no way I'm going to let you miss out on a barge ride down the Grand Canal with the dauphin. If you don't get on right now, I'll drag you there myself."

"I thought for sure that the dauphin would invite you too. He seems to be so taken with you."

"I'm sure he just wants time with some of the other girls too. I'm not worried. And that doesn't matter right now. What does matter is that the dauphin's ardor for you is clearly heating up. He has consistently invited you on group outings, and you're not going to miss this one," I insisted.

"Are you really, really sure?"

I rolled my eyes and gave Diane a gentle shove toward the barge. "Yes! Now go!"

"All right. But I'll come find you right after and tell you absolutely everything that happened."

Diane threw her arms around me for a quick hug, then ran off toward the barge. She was the last to board, and it launched just after she stepped on. A round of applause arose from the crowd assembled around the Canal to watch the departure. A large fête was being thrown in the gardens that day, and the dauphin had encouraged the courtiers to view his entourage.

As the barge started to make its way down the Canal, cutting smoothly through the water, the group of courtiers split off into two groups. Each group took one side of the Canal to walk down as they followed the barge. Prince Louis really did adore attention.

While most courtiers took off after the barge, some remained in the gardens to enjoy the fête, their brightly colored justaucorps and dresses like flowers amongst the riotous green of the lawns and hedges. All the fountains had been turned on, a rarity saved only for special occasions, what with the difficulty of transporting water to Versailles. Even the king's favorite attraction, the water bower, was running in the Grove of the Three Fountains.

I was absolutely fascinated by the water bower. It was one of the most talked-about waterworks at Versailles. Even Papa had loved it, and he was never the kind of person who enjoyed outdoor endeavors. At the entrance to the Grove of the Three Fountains, multiple jets on either side of the path sent water arcing over the heads of those who passed underneath. It was said that not a single drop of water touched those heads.

I had to see it for myself. The groves would provide a delightful distraction for the next few hours until Diane came back from the outing.

I snaked my way around the remaining courtiers milling about to get to one of the little paths hewn through the hedges that led to the groves, helping myself to a lemon tart off the tray of a roving servant. The king had put a great deal of effort into this fête: the dauphin must be close to choosing a bride. Why else would so much emphasis be put on the courtiers observing the outing? They wanted the nobles to see their future dauphine, whomever she may be.

It was clear that Prince Louis had favorites. Anna de Medici, Princesse Henrietta, and Duchesse Maria had been chosen for every group outing so far and solo outings on other occasions. Duchesse Maria explained her high position in the matter had to do with her father's political wrangling and nothing to do with affection, but I hoped for her sake that there was some fondness between them.

And I was still torn between trying to win the competition and trying to find a way to be with Auguste—surely there had to be a way for us. Though he was officially fatherless, he was still the king's son.

"No! We're doing this! Don't argue with me."

The hushed whisper emanated from an opening in the path just ahead of me. I stopped to listen. I immediately recognized the voice. And my curiosity was piqued by this clandestine meeting in the gardens.

"We'll get caught. It's not worth it!" said another voice, also incredibly familiar.

With tentative steps, I moved closer to the opening. I was certain who was speaking, but the crass answering shout confirmed it.

"It *is* worth it!"

"But they haven't been on an outing together for some time now!"

"It doesn't matter! I'm barely noticed in this competition, and you have *never* been noticed. And you know he likes her—she cannot win, or Mère will be furious! We have to do this!"

The girl who had dropped all pretense of being quiet and just started yelling was Severine. I would know that whiny sound anywhere. And the other girl had to be Alexandre. But why were they arguing in a secluded area of the gardens? If Lady Catherine was going to be angry about something, it would be about her daughters hiding away and not mingling with the other nobles.

"If you want to do this, you're going to have to do it alone," Alexandre said, her voice strained as if she were trying not to cry. "I'm not going to be part of it."

"That's not how this is going to go. We're doing this together. Mère said—"

"I don't *care* what Mère says! It's never about us. It's always about her."

"Fine. Give it to me, then. Come on! Hand it over."

I crept as close as I dared to the sounds of the struggle—grunting, the scuffling of feet, and the slap of a hand on flesh. Should I have intervened? It was never pleasant to be caught up in Severine's wrath. Just as I'd decided to intercede from a distance, a vial rolled out of the alcove and bounced off my foot. The vial was small and made of thick glass, with a metal lid that had a chain threaded through it so it could be worn as a necklace. It was the perfect size to hide under clothing. The liquid inside was a rich amber that gleamed when I held it up to the light. It was strangely beautiful, the glass itself cool in my palm. I didn't want to take my eyes off it.

"Come back! Alexandre!"

Alexandre burst from the alcove, tears staining her cheeks. I froze with my hand still in the air, but she didn't even seem to see me. She brushed past me without a word and disappeared into the maze of paths within seconds.

A sigh of relief had barely escaped my lips when Severine ran out of the alcove after her sister. I wasn't so lucky the second time.

"What are *you* doing here?" Severine said, spitting the words at me. "Are you spying on me? Following me around, sticking your nose where it doesn't belong?"

"No, I—"

"You're obsessed with me! You've been jealous of me since we first met. Jealous that my mother is still alive, jealous that your father loved me like his own, jealous of my beauty and charm. It was only a matter of time before you tried to ruin everything for me!"

When Severine saw the vial in my hands, her eyes narrowed dangerously. She ripped the vial from my hands and stormed off, bumping my shoulder with her own so hard, I reeled back into the hedge. I managed to right myself just before she disappeared.

The entire interaction left me feeling uneasy. Not Severine's taunts; I knew those weren't true. But the argument, Alexandre's tears, Severine's desperation, and the strange liquid inside the vial . . . something was wrong. It was clear Lady Catherine wanted them to do something, and it had everything to do with whatever was inside the vial.

I shivered, suddenly cold even though I stood in a bright patch of sunlight. That glass vial held something that would alter the outcome of the competition, and I knew Lady Catherine would do anything to get what she wanted. What did she want her daughters to do? What were they plotting?

A hand landed on my shoulder, and I jumped.

CHAPTER THIRTY-TWO

"AUGUSTE! DON'T SCARE ME LIKE that!" He was tall and blocked out the sun when he stood so close behind me.

"I'm sorry. I didn't mean to scare you. Why are you so jumpy?"

I thought about telling him what I'd overheard, but I wasn't completely sure what I heard. And while I had no affection for Severine, I didn't want anything to happen to Alexandre. In the end, there was nothing to tell.

"I've been looking for you everywhere," Auguste said as he took my hands. I should have pulled away and put some distance between us. That would have been the sensible thing to do. But I liked the feel of his warm hands in mine. I let him take a step closer, until we were standing nearly flush against each other. My pulse jumped at his touch, but I felt secure tucked against him all the same.

"Come on, I want to show you something," he said, guiding me into the maze of paths.

I hesitated. My desire to be with him was complicated by my reason for being at the palace. I was vying to be his brother's bride.

I couldn't wander off alone with another boy, even if that was the dauphin's brother. *Especially* if it was the dauphin's brother.

He saw the expression on my face.

"Just listen: Now is the perfect time to be in each other's company. Louis is on his group outing, which the majority of the court are spectating, and my father is in meetings for the next few hours. No one will notice our absence. Can't we just live in the moment and worry about being proper and decorous later?"

Auguste wiggled the fingers of his outstretched hand at me. My own hands trembled at my sides. We were walking down a dangerous path, one that could end in pain if we weren't careful.

But a walk through the gardens was perfectly innocent as long as I ensured that my boundaries stayed in place. Which I would do because I was careful. Auguste took my hand—a perfectly innocent gesture—and led me down the garden path.

"Is this what you wanted to show me? The water bower?" I asked as Auguste and I stood at the entrance to the Grove of the Three Fountains, our hands still clasped together.

"This is it. Do you like it? I've never found it particularly interesting. It's just jets of water. They don't even do anything interesting, not like the fountains."

"I think it's lovely."

Auguste shrugged. "If you say so."

I'm sure the water bower would bore someone who'd seen it a thousand times before, but I'd never seen anything like it. Jets on both sides of the path sent water shooting up into the air, higher than I could reach even if I jumped. The water arced over our heads and terminated in basins that ran alongside the gravel walkway. We were boxed in on all sides, as if we were traveling through a tunnel made of water, the streams the walls beside us and the vaulted ceiling above. Not a single drop fell on us as we walked, our steps slow and measured as I took my time looking around. The effect was magical, like we were entering another world. I understood why Papa and the king loved it so much.

"I'm sure you don't want to walk this slowly," I said.

Auguste had released my hand and was trailing a few steps behind me now, scuffing the red heels of his shoes in the dirt. I felt bad that he was so clearly bored, but I didn't want to rush for fear of missing anything.

"You can go on ahead," I said. "I'll be along in a few minutes."

"I've seen all this before, Cendrillon. I'm here because of you. I'd like to stay with you, if you don't mind."

"Actually, sir, I do mind." I glanced at Auguste with a mock frown as I reached a hand toward the wall of water. "I really shouldn't be associating with someone so unrefined. It simply isn't proper."

My fingers barely brushed one of the streams of water, but it was enough to send a spray spurting directly into my face. Lukewarm water ran down my throat and shot up my nose. Coughing and spluttering, I stumbled backward. Auguste smacked me on the back far too many times for the amount of water that I'd swallowed.

"Enough! Enough! I'm fine," I said, only gasping for air a little.

"Thank heavens! I thought I'd lost you there for a minute."

"Oh, hush."

Strong arms wrapped around my waist and pulled me back against a chest that was rumbling suspiciously.

"Are you laughing at me?" I asked, but I couldn't really be upset with him, not when I couldn't control my own giggling.

"No. Not at all. Whatever gave you that idea?"

A huff of cool air brushed against the shell of my ear as Auguste snuggled me tighter to his chest and pressed his cheek against the

246

side of my head. Suddenly, I wasn't laughing anymore. Nor could I breathe. But I didn't mind it. Not one bit.

"Let's keep going. I'm tired of looking at the water bower," I said, wriggling out of Auguste's arms and hurrying ahead of him into the grove proper.

It had felt far too good in Auguste's arms. Too safe. Too right. I couldn't let myself get used to the feeling, not when it couldn't last.

"Are you sure you're feeling all right?" asked Auguste, his green eyes narrowed with worry.

"I'm fine. Is there anything here you'd like to show me, or should we move on?"

My voice was high-pitched and strained, as if I'd been screaming for hours. It was embarrassing. Only a few days prior I'd spent a not-insignificant amount of time kissing Auguste in the stables, and now him holding me against his chest for mere seconds had me running about like a nervous child with her first crush. Which I suppose he was. Did he know what his touch did to me? He must, given the crooked smirk on his handsome face.

He cleared his throat. "Yes, actually. I wonder if it's still here. Follow me."

Auguste smiled and set off, his long stride quickly putting him far ahead of me. I had to run for a few yards to catch up. He'd been apathetic at best about the grove just moments ago. I nervously anticipated seeing whatever it was that had sparked his interest so.

The grove was organized into three different levels, each one separated by a set of grassy steps and a small waterfall cascade. On the lowest level, where we started out, the fountain jets created the shape of a fleur-de-lis in the pool. It was ingenious, and I wanted to stop and take a look, but Auguste hurried up the steps without sparing it a second glance. After our awkward moment under the water bower, I wasn't going to call him back and insist he wait for me again.

Auguste stopped climbing on the second level, past the rectangular pool with the jets that mimicked the water bower. But he didn't stop walking. No—he continued walking right into the waterfall cascade at the base of the steps to the third level.

"Wait! What are you doing? You're going to get soaked!"

Auguste's eyes sparkled mischievously as he said, "I know. It's very refreshing. You should join me."

"Absolutely not. My dress will be ruined."

"All right. But you won't get to see what's hidden here."

"That's fine with me."

Auguste actually had the nerve to wink at me before turning back around to wade farther into the basin. The water barely lapped at Auguste's ankles, but the depth of the pool wasn't the problem. My overskirt that day was a cream-colored silk with an elaborate appliqué of gold birds and flowers. I wanted to follow Auguste into the pool more than anything. It was terrible to stand still and watch as someone else had all the fun.

But Auguste had the luxury of being a boy. And the king's son. The only articles of clothing getting wet were his shoes and a small bit of stocking. Both would dry quickly, and if anyone noticed that he was wandering about with wet shoes, as the dauphin had made clear to me, no one would dare mention it.

A spark of inspiration struck me. I pulled a gold ribbon from my hair, letting the loose waves fall about my shoulders, then got to work bunching the front of my dress up into a little ball.

While I was busy fussing with my dress, Auguste had climbed up onto the second level of the cascade, just behind the fountain, where an iron structure in the shape of a seashell lay between two waves.

"Cendrillon, I found it! Oh . . ." he said, trailing off when his eyes landed on me.

"You were right. The water *is* refreshing. A little chilly, but nice on such a hot day."

Auguste's eyes darted down to my stockinged legs and back up to my face, his cheeks reddening. My own face started heating up when I remembered that revealing my stockings to a gentleman who was not my husband was shockingly inappropriate. Here I was trying to avoid a scandal, and I had walked right into one.

Lady Celia would say I should be ashamed of exhibiting such indecent behavior, and I was a *little* ashamed. But a greater part of me was excited at the power my bared stockings held over Auguste. He certainly wasn't smirking anymore. After his little display under the water bower, a comeuppance was in order.

"What is it you wanted to show me?" I asked, making my way toward him.

He held out his hand. "Something I hid here years ago. It's been here so long, I nearly forgot about it. I assumed that it would have been lost or taken by now, but it was just where I left it."

In Auguste's outstretched hand was a small sculpture made of wood. I picked it up gently and held it in the palm of my hand. Flecks of white paint were still speckled across the body of the horse, but most of the coating had worn away. The wood itself was cracked and swollen with water, spongy in places. But for being hidden in a cascade for years, it was in remarkably good condition. I could still see the all the details of the face—two little eyes and a mouth yawning.

"This is what you wanted to show me? What is it?"

Frowning, Auguste snatched the horse from my hand. "What do you mean, what is it? It's a horse. Can't you tell? I thought I did a pretty good job with it."

Auguste held the horse at eye level and peered at it closely, turning it over and over in his hands. The expression on his face was wounded as he glanced between me and the little horse. It was sweet. Amusing, but sweet.

"I meant, why did you want to show it to me? Did you make it?"

With a small smile, Auguste said, "I did. When I was eight or nine. With help, of course. Have you heard of Madame de Maintenon?"

The king's mistress, of course. I remembered the last time I saw Auguste before the ball over a year ago, when Madame de Maintenon and the king's affair was brought up by our classmates. He'd stormed out of the Grand Commons and canceled our plans to see each other later. I nodded.

"She was my tutor. My brother's too. She was more than just a tutor to me, though; she basically raised me. I lived with her in Paris throughout most of my childhood."

"What about your mother?"

"Madame de Montespan? She died when I was young. And my father was too busy for me. But of course, he is the king and has many concerns."

Auguste's voice was low and bitter, but his eyes shone brightly. I reached out and squeezed his forearm. My heart ached for the pain I saw on his face. I knew what it was like to lose a mother.

"Did Madame de Maintenon help you make the horse?" I asked.

"She did. I'd seen a woodworker carving toys at the market one day and said I wanted to learn how to make my own toys."

His voice was full of warm affection. "We spent the entire summer learning to woodwork. Madame de Maintenon managed to persuade my father to hire the woodworker from the market to come to our home and teach us.

"That year, the king split his time between the palace and the house in Paris, so most of the time it was just Madame de Maintenon and me. That was my best summer. I've never had another like it."

"Did you make a lot of toys?" I asked, tracing a finger lightly over the rough body of the horse.

"Not at all. It was a bit of a disaster. Neither one of us was very good. The horse was the closest I came to making something decent. It was my prized possession for the longest time."

"You should be proud. The horse is adorable."

"You don't need to flatter me. I know it's messy, especially now with all the water damage."

"I'm not trying to flatter you!"

Auguste looked at me skeptically. "You asked me what it was."

"Like you said, it's water damaged! I couldn't tell at first. But now I know, and it's very well made, particularly for such a small child."

I meant what I said. Mostly. I hoped Auguste would believe it. His face had never been gentler than when he talked about Madame de Maintenon. It was clear that he loved her deeply, and that the memories of his childhood with her had a special place in his heart.

"How did it end up hidden away in a cascade?"

Auguste shook his head. "Louis. We were visiting Versailles while it was in the process of being built. I was about twelve and he thirteen. He was making fun of me for still playing with toys and threatened to throw it in the Grand Canal. Louis chased me all over the gardens. This grove was one of the first to be built. I evaded him and tucked the horse away in the cascade, where I knew he'd never look. He hates getting wet. We left before I could come back and retrieve it. I was sad for a while, but I moved on and mostly forgot. Until you dragged me in here, that is." Auguste winked at me.

"I did not *drag* you in here! What happened to wanting to spend time with me?"

With a laugh, Auguste tucked a loose strand of hair behind my ear. My skin burned where his fingers brushed my cheek.

"I guess you're . . . uh . . . excited to have the horse back," I said, my throat dry and scratchy.

"I am. Thank you for bringing me here. I missed Frederick."

"Frederick?"

"I'd read the name in a book. It seemed fitting at the time. Don't judge me."

"I would *never.*"

"Right, right."

Auguste was doing it again. Looking at me like I was the most important person in the world; like I was the only person in the world. When his green eyes were locked on mine, I felt special for the first time in a long time, and I didn't want him to look away.

A soft pressure on my hand drew my eyes down. Auguste had placed the little horse in the palm of my hand and closed my fingers over it. I looked up, confused.

"What are you doing? Don't you want Frederick?" I asked, putting extra emphasis on the horse's name.

"*Frederick* is a dignified name. The name of a great leader. And no. I want you to have him."

"Why? After all these years, you've finally been reunited, and now you want to give him up. To me?"

"Yes, you. Who else?"

"I don't know. You, maybe?"

Sighing, Auguste said, "I'm trying to give you a gift. Can't you just say thank you and leave it at that?"

"Of course not. You should know me better by now."

Auguste released my hand and leaned back against the stone wall of the cascade. It was only after he'd put space between us that I realized that my skin was wet where he'd touched me. He'd dripped on my dress, too, leaving dots of water scattered across the silk. Somehow I didn't mind if I got wet anymore.

"You're going to think it's ridiculous," he said, so quietly I could barely hear it over the sound of rushing water.

"You won't know until you tell me."

He took a deep breath before speaking. "Cendrillon, there's nothing I want more than to court you myself. But with my brother courting you right now, it's impossible. Not only can I not make you dauphine, but I have nothing to offer you. I am the king's son, and while I was raised at court, I have no land and no title. I am no one. I have nothing to offer you."

I wasn't prepared for him to be so honest and vulnerable, and I realized it was time to tell him the truth about my feelings as well.

"Auguste, I don't give a whit about land or title," I told him. "I just want you." I felt a desperation taking over me.

"No. Even if Louis doesn't choose you, because you were favored by him, other high-ranking lords will want your hand. You deserve a better life, a life that I cannot offer," he said softly. "I can't take that away from you."

"No . . . no!" I said. "We have to find a way."

Auguste shook his head. "I brought you here because I want you to have something to remember me by. You deserve so much more than a silly little toy, but it's all I have to give you right now."

The thought of losing him just as we discovered each other was too much. I threw myself against him and pressed my lips to his. Our bodies were flush against each other now, my arms around his shoulders, the cold water from Auguste's soaked clothes seeping into my dress, but I didn't even feel the chill; my entire body was on fire. We kissed until my lips were sore—minutes or hours, I couldn't tell. Only then did Auguste pull away, gasping.

"We can't," he said, chest heaving in a mirror of my own. "Cendrillon, we can't."

I buried my face in the crook of his neck and felt the tears fall down my face. "Yes we can," I said. "You are the only happiness left in my life."

"Oh," Auguste whispered, his breath warm against my cheek. He placed a feather-light kiss on my jawline and another on my neck. I shivered and held on tighter. "Then we'll find a way. I promise."

We stood in the cascade's pool, wrapped in each other's arms as water lapped at our ankles and sprayed cool droplets onto our already-damp clothing.

Anyone could have come along and spotted us. We weren't even watching our immediate surroundings, much less the entrances to the grove. It was incredibly reckless, but that thought couldn't spur me into leaving Auguste's arms. I was so very tired of not getting what I wanted.

CHAPTER THIRTY-THREE

FOR THE NEXT WEEK, AUGUSTE and I spent as much time together as we could. I barely paid attention to the competition and merely smiled politely at Prince Louis. As far as I was concerned, there was only one king's son that mattered.

I didn't know what I was thinking. Perhaps we had been too naïve, too innocent. While I was getting ready to meet Auguste in the maze once again, there was a commotion in the Place d'Armes.

The courtyard was so packed with people—nobles and commoners alike—that the carriage couldn't get through the main gate. No matter how much the coachman yelled and pleaded with the assembled crowd to move out of the way, they refused to budge. I had to climb out and make my own way into the courtyard while the coachman took the long way around to get to the stables.

There was still plenty of time before I needed to meet Auguste for our rendezvous in the little alcove where I'd seen Severine and Alexandre arguing, so I stayed to watch what was happening. I wanted to clear my head before I saw him again anyway.

We had decided we would find a way for us to be together—no matter what. The thought thrilled me and scared me at the same time. Even if he had no land or title, the king would never allow a son of his to suffer. Surely we would be able to make a home in the country somewhere. I was used to cooking and housework, and we would not need very much. All I had to do now was make sure Louis did not pick me to be his bride. That couldn't be too hard. There were twenty-four other girls who would die to be chosen.

Once again, I was grateful for my small stature as I made my way forward. While a carriage might not have been able to pass, I was able to push through the throng with ease. No one paid me any attention anyway, too fixated on the spectacle taking place in the center of the courtyard.

Inside the loose ring formed by the crowd was a carriage. Standing beside it were two women. One had her head in her hands, shoulders shaking, while the other stood in front of her as if attempting to shield her from the crowd. I wasn't close enough to make out who they were, and it was so tightly packed at the edge of the circle that there was no way I was getting any closer.

"What's happening?" I asked the woman standing next to me, a wicker basket filled to the brim with cabbages perched precariously on her hip.

The woman glanced at me and looked away, only to snap her head back to stare at me.

"Aren't you one of the ladies the dauphin is courting? Lady Cendrillon? The one who ran away from the ball?"

"That's right. Do you know what's happening here?" I asked again, wanting to move away from questions about my controversial reputation.

"You'll be happy to hear this. Two girls have just been banished.

You missed the first one being forced out, but you're right on time for the second."

"Do you know why they've been banished?"

"The first one is said to have been caught using a love spell on the dauphin. Nothing new about that. Everyone and their mother has been trying to use so-called magic spells on the king and the dauphin."

"Who was it?" I asked.

"Paulette's the name, I believe."

I gasped.

"And this one was having an affair with another noble."

Now all the breath fled from my lungs in a rush. It made sense that having an affair with someone else while courting the dauphin would be an offense worthy of banishment, but I hadn't thought I would see it enacted right in front of me.

"The king demanded that this girl, Mathilde, and her family leave immediately, but her father decided to argue the punishment instead. Eh, I'm not complaining. Court goings-on were getting awfully stale. We've needed a little livening up."

Lady Paulette and now Lady Mathilde. Both of them were friends of Diane. Paulette was a little too obsessed with witches and magic, and Mathilde just wanted someone to pay attention to her. Diane was going to be devastated. She and Mathilde and Paulette had been friends since childhood. Would Diane even be allowed to see them again? I couldn't imagine being forbidden from seeing Elodie or Marius.

"Look," the woman said, pointing toward the front of the court-yard. "There's the girl's father. I don't know why he thought arguing with the king was going to go well for him."

Two expressionless guards were holding a lavishly dressed noble-man by either arm, dragging him toward a carriage. He wasn't putting up much of a fight, but he was unleashing a litany of abuse aimed primarily at the guards, a safer proxy than the king, who had handed down the punishment. Laughter erupted from the crowd. No one would dare laugh at a noble in his hearing distance, but he was so thoroughly disgraced that there would be no consequences.

The guards deposited Mathilde's father in front of the carriage and returned to the palace without a backward glance. The nobleman yelled something at their retreating backs, then turned his anger on Mathilde when the guards ignored him. After a bout of yelling that only made Mathilde sob harder, her father ushered his family into the carriage. There was to be no begging people to get out of the roadway this time. The carriage set off at a speed that was, frankly, unsafe, and didn't stop for to wait for people to move, forcing them to scatter so they weren't run over.

"She's getting what she deserves," said a familiar voice from right beside me.

I jumped when I turned to see the woman I had been talking to gone and Severine in her place, an uncomfortably chipper smile on her face. I had to take a few embarrassingly audible deep breaths to calm down enough to speak.

"Do you really have no heart?" I asked, focusing less on the question and more on coming up with an escape plan. The less time I spent talking to Severine, the better for my sanity.

"I have eyes," said Severine. "You really should be paying more attention to what's going on around you. Does something have you distracted?"

I didn't like the superiority in her tone. Severine had nothing to feel smug about, not after I had come upon her and Alexandre plotting to use a love potion of their own.

When I didn't respond, she continued. "The dauphin is rightfully very possessive of his things. You, me, Mathilde, and all the other girls he's courting belong to him. That's the way he sees it, like it or not. The only one to blame for Mathilde's banishment is herself. She's actually quite lucky. The king could have ordered her to be executed for the disrespect to his son. Monseigneur was furious enough that the option was surely on the table."

My palms were cold and clammy, my stomach queasy. I kept my face turned away from Severine. She would pick up on my distress immediately, and I couldn't have that. I couldn't be weak in front of her or Lady Catherine.

"I have to go," I said absentmindedly, taking off into the quickly dispersing crowd before Severine had a chance to reply.

I needed to get away from her. I needed to find Auguste.

CHAPTER THIRTY-FOUR

AUGUSTE WAS WAITING EXACTLY WHERE he said he would be, in the forgotten alcove tucked away among the twisting paths of the gardens, on a cracked marble bench pushed up against one of the hedges. As soon as he spotted me enter the alcove, he stood up, eyes bright, and reached for me.

"No. Just . . . please stay there for a minute," I said, pushing my hands out as if I could ward him off with such a simple gesture.

Auguste stopped walking, but I could see the confusion in his eyes. "What's wrong?"

I moved a few paces into the alcove, but that was as close as I could get to Auguste. A distance between us needed to be maintained. This wasn't going to work otherwise, not when all I wanted to do was dive into his arms and never let go.

"Did you hear about the banishments today?" I asked.

"I did, yes."

"Both girls were friends of a friend. I didn't know them well, but my friend Diane adored them."

"I'm so sorry. That's terrible."

"A horde of people watched Mathilde crying in the Place d'Armes as her father was dragged from the palace by guards. Do you know why she was banished?"

"No," he said, his eyebrows raised. "I've been with my tutor all day."

"She was banished because she was having an affair with another noble."

Auguste's face fell, and he came closer to put his arms around me, and this time, I didn't push him away. "I will talk to my father. I will tell him about us. I will tell him everything."

His words shocked me. I pulled away from his embrace. "No! You can't! You have no idea what he would do! I can't let you risk that!" I shook my head. "We can't see each other anymore. This has to end. For our safety. I'm sorry."

Auguste looked at me as if I were tearing his heart from his chest, the depth of feeling in his eyes nearly overwhelming. He was stooped low but was still so much taller than me. He made me feel so special. So wanted. When he held me in his arms, I felt safe, like the ills of the world couldn't touch me. But that was an illusion. A lovely illusion, but an illusion all the same. Auguste needed to know the truth. The entire truth. Maybe then he would realize why our relationship had to come to an end.

"Sit with me, please. I need to tell you something," I said, guiding Auguste toward the marble bench.

Barely an inch of space separated our bodies as we sat, arms and thighs pressed together and hands still entwined. It might have been selfish, but if this was the last bit of contact we were going to have, I was going to take full advantage of it.

"When we met in the stables, I told you my stepmother was unkind, but that I could handle it. Then I changed the subject. Because you were right—I didn't want to talk about it then."

Auguste was stroking my palm, the gentle touches calming my nerves. I'd never experienced such affection before. The thought of giving it up was unbearable. "You can tell me anything," he said. "I'll listen."

The dam in my chest burst, allowing the words to pour out. There was no stopping them.

"The truth is my stepmother is very cruel. As soon as my father was buried, she made me her servant, forced me to wait on her and my stepsisters hand and foot. My friend Elodie is a seamstress and was trapped with me in Lady Catherine's château. And Marius—an orphan boy we took in who is like my brother—was sent away. Now he works on a farm where he is beaten. I had no family other than Papa and no money or possessions that weren't Lady Catherine's. I had nowhere to go and no choice but to do what she wanted. I thought that Lady Françoise would be able to save me, and she promised that she would, but—"

My voice hitched. My godmother's passing was too recent to talk about without getting emotional. Auguste let go of my hands, nearly sending me into a panic, but he instead wrapped an arm around my shoulders and tugged me against his chest. Gratefully, I leaned into his warmth and shut my eyes.

"You're taking part in the competition in order to escape your stepmother?" Auguste asked quietly.

I nodded. The silk of his justaucorps was soft against my cheek. If only we could stay like this always.

"I didn't have a choice. But I thought I could live with it, until . . ."

"Until?"

"Until I saw you again," I said. "But it can't be, Auguste. Your father and your brother are too powerful. It would hurt Louis's pride too much, and who knows what they would do to you, to us."

Auguste tightened his hold on me and said, "I am the king's son too. My brother may be the dauphin, but that does not mean the king doesn't love me. I know we can find a way. I can't lose you again."

I wished I could believe him, but I had lived in France for too long. The king's word was law, and nobles who fell out of favor were soon reduced to peasants, if not worse. "Your brother could have both our heads if he found out about us. I don't know about you, but I would very much like to keep my head, and I prefer yours exactly where it is."

"I would never allow it. You won't be beheaded. Don't even say that. And my father may not recognize me as his legitimate son, but he wouldn't have me executed. Punished, yes, but not executed."

"You can't know that for certain. Mathilde's punishment was banishment for herself and her entire family. What would my punishment be for having an affair with the dauphin's brother? If Louis found out, do you think he'd just smile and give us his blessing? If you truly believe his reaction would be thus, I would be more than happy for you to court me publicly."

Auguste brushed a soft kiss against the crown of my head. "My brother would give his blessing because he would have no choice. I would protect you."

I pulled back to look him in the eyes and said, "I know you would want to."

"But you don't believe I can."

"I don't want to hurt you, but I need you to come to terms with what is happening. It's too dangerous for us to be together right now. We've been reckless, and all over a foolish dream. This has to be our goodbye."

"No, I can't say goodbye to you." Auguste tenderly kissed the corner of my mouth.

"You have to," I whispered.

But turning my head slightly, I met Auguste's lips with mine.

He groaned low in his throat at the contact. The sound sent a thrill racing through my body. I burned to bury my fingers in his hair, to sink deeper into his embrace. The taste of honey flooded my mouth. I wanted—no, I needed—this one final kiss. I would remember this forever, as it was the last kiss we would share.

After, Auguste cradled my head in his hands and kissed my forehead like a blessing. "I know you don't believe me. But I promise I will find a way for us to be together."

"There isn't one. I made the decision to enter the competition, and now I have to see it through to the end, wherever that takes me."

We said nothing more. There was nothing else to be said. I left him then.

CROWN

Men always want to be a woman's first love.

That is their clumsy vanity.

We women have a more subtle instinct about things:

What we like is to be a man's last romance.

—*Oscar Wilde*, A Woman of No Importance

CHAPTER THIRTY-FIVE

"Do you know why the dauphin asked us to meet him in the Hall of Mirrors?" I asked Diane as we stood off to the side of the rest of the girls milling about the gallery.

"No idea. He was supposed to be taking us each out on one-on-one outings today. Maybe he has an announcement to make. Perhaps he's sending someone home. Hopefully not us."

Diane nudged me with her shoulder and smiled cheekily. My answering smile was much less enthusiastic. I'd ended my affair with Auguste out of necessity, but I couldn't stop dreaming of him, of what our lives might have been like if he was the one courting me instead of Louis. It was incredibly frustrating. Surely a little time apart would lessen my ardor for him.

"The dauphin isn't sending one of us home," Duchesse Maria said, appearing at our sides so suddenly that Diane and I both jumped. "He's sending all of us home. All but one."

Diane's face paled. She grabbed my wrist and squeezed so tightly, I was sure there would be bruises tomorrow. In truth, I appreciated the contact. It kept me grounded after the shock of the duchesse's news.

"What? How do you know?" Diane asked, her gaze boring into the duchesse with an intensity I'd never seen from her before.

All talking in the room ceased as the dauphin made his entrance into the gallery. His appearance was so unexpected that some curtsies were more delayed than others, girls dipping and popping up in a decidedly ungraceful manner. When I rose from my own curtsy, I realized that the dauphin wasn't alone on the red-velvet-lined dais. Auguste stood at his side, resplendent in a blue justaucorps and silver waistcoat that gleamed brilliantly in the sunlight, his eyes fixed on me. I tore my eyes away and focused deliberately on the dauphin, who thankfully hadn't noticed his brother's interest in me. What was Auguste doing here? I needed to remain perfectly composed in front of Louis, and I wasn't sure that I could do so with Auguste so close, observing every move I made.

"Mesdemoiselles, thank you for meeting me here on this glorious day," the dauphin said, arms spread wide, looking every inch a king in his red justaucorps embroidered with the fleur-de-lis. "I know that we were scheduled to go on outings today, but the plan has changed. I've decided that I cannot wait any longer. France must have her dauphine, and I must have my wife. It is imperative that the realm be made whole. So, today, I will choose my bride."

Gasps and shocked cries erupted from the assembled ladies. Diane squeezed my hand even more viciously, her entire body trembling. I glanced at Duchesse Maria, who only inclined her head at me, surprisingly serene for the occasion. Did I appear as calm as she did? I hoped so, because inside I was trying very hard not to throw up. And it was a struggle. How unbecoming it would be for Lady Cendrillon de Louvois to vomit all over the marble floors of the Hall of Mirrors.

"Please know that every single one of you who remains is absolutely worthy of becoming my wife. Both myself and the king offer you our deepest thanks for participating in the competition and will hold you always in the highest esteem as valued members of the court. But only one can win my hand."

The dauphin paused and cast his eyes across the gallery. What a showman he was. But if he didn't hurry up and reveal the winner, many of the girls, including me, were going to faint from the anticipation.

"I'm not sure how many of you know this, but I haven't always been the charming, compassionate prince that you see before you. I'm not too proud to admit that I was once spoiled and selfish, preoccupied with my own gratification. The lady that I've chosen once bore the brunt of my selfishness."

Ice water flooded my veins at the dauphin's words.

"But in all her elegance, grace, and kindness," he continued, "she was willing to forgive me and look past my youthful indiscretions, capturing my heart in the process. Qualities such as these are exactly what France needs in her future queen, which is why I will be taking to wife Lady Cendrillon de Louvois."

Diane squeaked and pulled me into a quick hug, one I didn't reciprocate.

"Congratulations, Cendrillon. I'm so happy for you!"

"Yes, indeed. Congratulations. You will make a wonderful dauphine," Maria said with a warm smile that did nothing to soothe me.

The dauphin, Diane, and Maria were the only happy people in the room. I could see the glares of all the rest of the girls reflected back at me in the mirrors running down the walls, trapping me in an endless parade of anger and disappointment. Severine started to sob openly, Alexandre's ministrations doing nothing to soothe her.

And Auguste. His face was tight and his jaw clenched as he looked everywhere but at me. This was worse than banishment. Worse even than death. I would see him every day but never be able to love him.

What was I thinking? I should never have entered the competition knowing my heart lay elsewhere.

I had loved Auguste since the very first day at the Orangerie, when he was kind to me. I had always loved Auguste.

An invisible force was pressing down on my chest, stealing the breath from my lungs. I should have been the happiest girl in all France. I was being given the privilege of marrying the dauphin. It was a privilege many would kill for. Many of the girls in the gallery looked like they wanted to kill for it. They could have it.

Except . . . Lady Catherine and Severine would never treat me poorly again. They would never even dream of whispering a word against me. I could set up Elodie and her shop and get Marius away from that terrible farmer who beat him. Maman and Papa would have been so proud if they could've seen me. Maman especially would have been beside herself with joy. Becoming the dauphine of France was so far beyond even the life as an influential courtier that she'd wanted for me. And Lady Françoise . . .

The dauphin held his arms out to me and said, "Lady Cendrillon, please join me on the dais and take your place by my side."

I didn't move. A wave of whispers spread throughout the crowd. Auguste finally looked at me, his brow furrowed. The sunlight streaming in through the windows cast him in a golden glow, illuminating the strong planes of his face. He was the handsomest man I'd ever seen.

"Lady Cendrillon," Prince Louis said again as he climbed down from the dais and started to make his way toward me.

Before we came to Versailles, Lady Françoise told me that I didn't have to worry about disappointing Maman and Papa, because if I was happy, they would be happy. She would have wanted me to be happy too. If I married the dauphin, I would be safe, but I wouldn't be happy.

I couldn't do that to myself. Or Auguste. If only things could have been different. I'd fallen in love with the wrong prince.

But I still had a choice.

I could still make my voice heard.

The dauphin of France had chosen twenty-five girls to court him, but I had never chosen *him* to be my future husband, and I think, no matter what, that mattered. I wanted to be happy, and maybe Auguste was right. Maybe we would find a way to be together.

One day.

But I would never know if I didn't speak up for me, for us, for my happiness and my future.

"I'm sorry, Monseigneur," I said, backing away as Louis moved closer. "I cannot accept."

"Cendrillon!" I heard Auguste cry out as I turned and fled from the Hall of Mirrors.

CHAPTER THIRTY-SIX

I WAS SOBBING WHEN I walked through the door of Lady Catherine's château. Stumbling through the hallways, I managed to make it to the sitting room, collapsing into Papa's old armchair and allowing my tears to soak into the fabric as I struggled to catch my breath. I wanted Maman and Papa and Marraine here to tell me that I'd made the right decision, because nothing was ever going to be the same again.

I could never go back to court. My reputation was ruined. The dauphin was no doubt furious at me for the embarrassment I'd caused him. I'd been so close to becoming the dauphine, and I willingly hurled the proposal back at him. But it had to be done. I couldn't marry someone that I didn't love, not when I was in love with that someone's brother.

"You're certainly making a name for yourself as the girl who bolts from palaces with royalty hot on her heels."

I jerked upright at the intrusion. Through the blurry film of tears, I saw Lady Catherine standing in the doorway. She looked predictably lovely in a red silk dress with roses embroidered on the bodice and underskirt, her silver-blond hair tied back in a simple chignon. Amongst all the commotion of running away from the palace, I hadn't thought about my Lady Catherine situation. And now she was here, and I was trapped with her once again.

"Goodness, ma chérie, you look an absolute mess. Stay there," she said, disappearing in a cloud of rose perfume.

Before I had finished debating whether or not I should get up and run, Lady Catherine reappeared with two cups of tea in her hand. She handed me one, and the warmth of the cup was wonderfully soothing to my chilly hands.

"Drink up, Cendrillon. It will fortify you," she said as she took a seat in the chair across from me.

My stepmother took a sip from her own cup. "I just got back from the palace. Severine told me what happened. Why did you refuse the dauphin's proposal?"

"Why do you care?" I asked, the words leaving my mouth before I could stop them. "I would think that this outcome would please you. It means that Severine and Alexandre still have a chance."

"I'm your stepmother. Of course I care. But I know I haven't been the kind of mother that you needed, the kind you deserved."

This was not the reaction I was expecting from Lady Catherine. "I'm not sure I believe you. You never had a problem causing me pain before. What's changed now?" I asked, deciding to remain bold.

Lady Catherine winced. "What's changed is that I realized how abominable my treatment of you has been. And I want to apologize to you for that."

"You want to apologize? To *me*?"

"Of course. I almost lost you to the dauphin, never to see you again, and I realized that I was never going to be able to make amends for the harm I caused you if I didn't act now. Seeing you become more independent and take your first steps away from the château opened my eyes to many things."

I was so taken aback that I needed something to drink. I raised the cup to my lips and took a sip. The tea was sickeningly sweet and quite awful, the sugar doing very little to hide the bitterness of the leaves.

"I was very young when my first husband died, leaving me to care for two young girls alone. I had to struggle to manage myself, my daughters, and my home. For so many years, I thought that I would never find love again. But then I met your father. Michel swept me off my feet. It was love at first sight. He was so strong, so caring. The man of my dreams. Then he died. And I was alone again."

Drawing in a shaky breath, Lady Catherine pulled a handkerchief out of her bag and began dabbing at her eyes. The only other time I'd ever seen her cry was at Papa's funeral, and that had been theatrical, attention-grabbing keening. I'd never known how much of that was real and how much was performance. I still didn't know, but that didn't stop me from feeling slightly bad for her. Her life before Papa was something I had never considered before. Maybe she, Alexandre, and Severine had struggled more than I realized. That would explain some of their behavior.

Sitting forward in her chair and staring intently at me, Lady Catherine said, "You are so much like your father, Cendrillon. Strong, capable, hardworking. I was lost after Michel died, and there you were, holding it together while I was falling apart. It was easy to rely on you to take care of day-to-day tasks at the château, because you were so good at it. But I am the adult and you are the child. I should have taken care of you instead of relying on you so much. For that, I am sorry."

I couldn't believe what I was hearing. This had to be a dream.

"Cendrillon, can you ever find it in your heart to forgive me?"

Lady Catherine asked. "I know I don't deserve it. My behavior toward you has been reprehensible, but I want to make it up to you. I've ruined the mother-daughter relationship we could have had, but I want us to be friends at least. Do you think that could happen one day?"

I looked at my stepmother, handkerchief clasped in her hands, cheeks wet with tears, and I didn't know what to do. In my wildest dreams I never would have thought to hear an apology come out of her mouth. And I never would have thought I would be considering accepting the apology.

I didn't know what to do or what to feel. Instead, I decided to pick up the cup of tea again and slowly drink the rest, ignoring the sticky sweetness coating my tongue. At least then I had something to hold.

Because holding on to all this anger and resentment wasn't good for me. My stepfamily was the only family I had left. And now that I'd ruined my reputation at court, I would need the support that an atoned Lady Catherine could give me. And Papa wouldn't want me to let this anger fester. He was always willing to forgive.

"I could forgive you. One day. It might take a while, but I would like to try to forgive you."

It was all I could muster at the moment, but Lady Catherine didn't seem to mind, her face lighting up as she beamed at me.

"I'm so happy, Cendrillon! Rest assured, I don't expect anything right away. It's enough to know that you *want* to forgive me. I'll do everything in my power to prove to you that you're not making a mistake. Would it be too presumptuous of me to ask for a hug?"

A hug? The last time I'd hugged Lady Catherine was the day she and Papa wed. She wasn't a particularly affectionate person, even with her own daughters.

Just as I started to stand up, I was hit with a dizzy spell that sent me right back down into the armchair. The teacup slipped from my fingers and shattered to pieces on the floor as my suddenly numb fingers couldn't grasp the smooth surface any longer.

"Are you feeling all right, ma choupette? You seem awfully pale."

I mumbled something unintelligible. My tongue was heavy and sluggish in my mouth. I couldn't get it to work right. A chill wracked my body, like someone had dumped a bucket of icy water over my head. Something was wrong, but I didn't have the strength to ask for help.

The form of Lady Catherine looked like a splotch of blood staining the walls. I tried to stand up, to make her understand that I was sick, but my legs gave out beneath me, heavy and numb, just like my fingers. I tumbled to the floor, unable to feel the impact of the wood on my body.

Darkness crept in from the edges of my vision. The floor was soothingly warm and eased some of the chill in my limbs. I wanted to lie there forever and let the warmth seep into me.

Faintly, as if from a great distance, I heard a voice calling my name. I didn't answer. I couldn't answer. My eyelids were heavy and starting to close without my permission. What was the point in fighting them? A little sleep might make me feel better. I let them close and sank into the darkness.

CHAPTER THIRTY-SEVEN

"THEY'RE NOT JUST ON HER neck anymore. They're spreading. Look at her arms! Look at her arms!"

The words were muffled, as if Elodie had her face pressed into a pillow, but I could still hear the fear in her voice. Was she talking about me or to me? That was ridiculous. I needed to reassure Elodie, but when I tried to move, strong hands pressed me back down into the bed. How did I end up in bed? I was in the sitting room, talking with . . . with . . . someone who's face was cast in shadow. Why couldn't I remember who it was?

"Don't move, Cendrillon. Everything's going to be just fine. The doctor will be back shortly. Everything is going to be just fine."

That was Auguste. I'd know his voice anywhere, so deep and kind. What was he doing here? He was supposed to be back at the palace, where I left him.

I shivered violently, my whole body shaking as a wave of cold passed through me. The blankets I could feel wrapped around my legs and waist were doing nothing to warm me. I needed to pull them up. That would help. But when I reached for them, those same hands grabbed mine and forced them back down by my sides. I groaned in frustration.

"Please, Cendrillon, don't try to move. It will only make things worse. I need you to stay still for me. Can you do that, mon amour? Just stay still?"

It was a silly request, but Auguste sounded so upset that I reluctantly relaxed into the mattress. If he didn't want me to move, I would look at him instead. But when I tried to lift my head from the pillow, a sharp, throbbing pain in my chest and stomach made me stop right away. It felt like there was a chain wrapped around my chest, digging into my flesh and making it difficult to breathe. Was I tied down? Why would he do such a thing? I intended to ask him, but the pain discouraged me from speaking. Surely I could open my eyes at least?

Though there seemed to be weights on my eyelids, holding them closed, I managed to force them open only to be met by a fuzzy, indistinct world. Maybe I really did need a doctor. Something was very wrong.

Blinking a few times helped clear my vision. Slowly, my bedchamber came into focus. But that wasn't right. This wasn't my attic. This was my old bedchamber, the one Lady Catherine made me give to Severine. I would recognize that beautiful velvet-topped window seat anywhere. Two people were in the room with me. Auguste was on my left, leaning over me, and Elodie was on my right, sitting on the bed, holding my hand. Funny. I couldn't feel her hand in mine.

Perhaps the chilly air in my chambers was to blame. It would be nice to have a fire on. Why hadn't anyone lit a fire? But when I let my gaze drift across the room, I saw a large orange flame flickering merrily in the fireplace. How strange that I could feel none of its warmth.

Elodie was staring intently at me, her cheeks streaked with tears.

Oh no. She wasn't still upset with me, was she? I couldn't stand another argument, especially not when I felt so poorly.

"Her eyes are open," Elodie cried. "How are you feeling, Cendrillon? Does anything hurt?"

Ice was creeping through my veins, originating in my stomach and traveling up my body, through my shoulders, and down my arms, freezing the blood solid. How did one articulate such a concept? I'm not sure that I could have, even if I had been of sound mind and body.

"Gentle, Elodie. Gentle. Keep your voice down, and don't ask her too many questions," Auguste said as he brushed a damp cloth across my forehead.

I didn't appreciate it when people talked about me like I wasn't there, but the cloth was blisteringly hot against my icy skin. It felt so amazing that I was thoroughly distracted. Until Elodie's next words, that is.

"When is the doctor going to get here?" she asked in a whisper that wasn't quiet enough to evade my ears. "Look. They're getting worse."

I followed Elodie's pointed gaze, desperate to know what was going on. The light was dim, emanating only from the fireplace and a few candles scattered about the room, but it was just bright enough to illuminate the skin of my arm. If I'd had the strength, I would have started crying at the sight.

My right arm was covered in purple-blue spots the size of a livre. They looked like bruises, dark and vivid against the ghastly pallor of my unblemished skin. Each spot's center was marked with an angry red welt the color of blood. I couldn't take my eyes off one spot in particular, the one with the deepest of reds at its center. It made my stomach roil, but there was something about that color that was significant, if only I could remember.

"The doctor thinks it's the pox; he's coming back with leeches," said Elodie anxiously.

My mind was swimming in a fog. But it wasn't the pox. I knew it wasn't. Instead, I focused on the red.

A red dress. Roses. Sugar with a bitter edge on my tongue. And I remembered seeing something—in my mother's mirror, my last heirloom. Lady Catherine had moved it from the attic and placed it in the sitting room. I remember seeing Lady Catherine holding a glass vial above my teacup in my mother's mirror. I had been too distressed by what happened at court to register what I'd seen, until now. The thread of lucidity in my mind snapped taut where only moments before it had been slack. I remembered what happened to me. I needed to tell Elodie and Auguste.

The thread was beginning to fray. I didn't have much time. "Lady . . . Lady . . ."

Auguste brushed his hand against my cheek. "You don't need to talk. Save your strength."

My body ached with every movement, but I needed to get the words out. This was my only chance. "No," I said with as much force as I could manage. "Lady Catherine. The tea. Lady Catherine."

"What did she do?" asked Auguste, his voice barely containing his rage and worry. "We need to know. The doctors think it is a disease, but if it is something else—"

"She had a vial, a vial of . . ." I rasped. I couldn't find the word. I shook my head in frustration. "Poison," I finally whispered.

"Poison!" said Auguste. "Poison in the tea!"

Then I blacked out again.

When I next came to, Alexandre had burst into the room, her blond hair escaping from her fontange to fall messily around her shoulders.

"I found it! I found the antidote," she said, rushing toward the bed and handing the vial to Elodie. "This is the antidote. I watched Maman buy it."

Elodie stared at Alexandre for a few moments before she faced me again, a determined set to her face.

"All right. Open up," Elodie said as she uncorked the vial.

Elodie emptied the white powder into my mouth. It was tart on my tongue, like freshly sliced lemon. I swallowed quickly. The powder burned on the way down. As soon as I felt it fill my throat and chest with a delicious warmth, I let the darkness take me once more.

CHAPTER THIRTY-EIGHT

I OPENED MY EYES TO brilliant sunshine streaming in through the windows of my old chambers, dazzling, brilliant sunshine that hurt my eyes so much, I had to squeeze them shut immediately. I groaned and clapped my hands over my eyes. Someone laughed from right beside me.

"It's a beautiful morning," Elodie said from the armchair pulled up to my bedside. I could hear the smile in her voice. "How are you feeling?"

"Hot."

The word passed my lips before I even realized what I was saying. But it was true. I was hot. Too hot. A fire burned in the fireplace even though it was daytime in the middle of summer. Warmth was preferable to the cold, but I still felt smothered by the heap of blankest piled atop me.

"That's good. I'm glad. I'm so glad." Elodie sighed heavily and scrubbed at her face with her hands. She looked exhausted. Dark circles rimmed her bloodshot eyes. Her hair was unbound, tumbling down over her dressing-gown-clad shoulders. I hated that I was the one to cause her such strain.

"Are you feeling all right?" I asked.

Elodie smiled tiredly and reached for my hand, clasping it gently. The relief I felt at such a simple gesture was immense. My limbs weren't numb anymore. I could feel her palm against mine. All my fingers and toes were accounted for.

"I'm not the one who was sick. Do you feel anything besides hot? Is there any pain? Discomfort?"

There was a twinge in my stomach. It was nothing like the pain I'd experienced there before, more of a dull ache—a ghost of previous pain—than an angry throb.

"My stomach . . ."

At the look of panic on Elodie's face, I hurried to say, "It isn't bad. Really. It's just a little sore, like I pulled a muscle."

Elodie sighed in relief and got up to sit on the edge of the bed.

"That's good. The doctor mentioned that you might have some lingering pains for a short while. It's been a week, so I'd hoped—"

"A week," I said, startled. "What do you mean it's been a week?"

"The doctor thought this might happen as well. Cendrillon, you've been slipping in and out of consciousness for the past week. You were sick. Very sick."

The long sleeves of my nightgown covered my arms up to the wrists. Dread pooled in my stomach at the thought of those horrible spots afflicting my skin. If they were still there, I just might fall unconscious again.

Noticing the direction of my gaze, Elodie said, "The spots disappeared not long after I gave you the antidote. Do you remember anything about what happened?"

My thoughts still felt fuzzy and muddled, but the image of Lady Catherine in a red dress, beaming at me, was fixed in my mind.

"Lady Catherine. She poisoned me, didn't she?"

Elodie whispered, "Yes. She did. You were able to tell us what she did. Luckily, Alexandre knew where to find the antidote. How did she poison you? You said something about tea?"

I laughed humorlessly. "She was apologizing for the way she treated me, and she served me tea. I'd never heard an apology from her before, so I hardly believed it. At first. But she was *so* convincing. She begged for my forgiveness. And then she turned away, and I saw something in the mirror . . . I saw her . . . How could she?"

"It's all right. You don't have to talk about it anymore. I know most of it already."

"It was bad, wasn't it?" I asked even though I already knew the answer.

Elodie's eyes shone wetly as she said, "You nearly died, Cendrillon. If Alexandre hadn't found the antidote, you wouldn't be here now. And if Auguste hadn't come after you and forced his way inside the house, Lady Catherine would have gotten away with it."

I started at the mention of Auguste and instantly regretted it. My muscles screamed at the movement, as if I'd been running for ages instead of lying in bed for a week.

"Auguste was here? It wasn't a dream? Is he here now? And I don't appreciate your smirk," I said, my cheeks warming. "I am still ill after all. Just tell me what happened that day, please."

Elodie kept me in suspense for a few more seconds, but the smile dropped from her face when she started telling the story. "Please remember that I heard a great deal of this secondhand. I was visiting Marius in the village when you came back. Auguste told me that, after you ran from the palace, he chased after you and followed you back to the château in his own carriage. When he arrived, he heard a commotion inside and forced his way in to find you lying on the floor of the sitting room, covered in those horrid spots, with Lady Catherine standing over your body, doing nothing to help. Marius accompanied me back to the château, and we came upon you unconscious and Auguste restraining Lady Catherine."

I gasped, hardly able to imagine such a scene. It was almost too fantastical to believe.

"It was quite shocking," Elodie continued. "Everything became extremely messy when Auguste ordered Marius to return to the village to fetch the constabulary and a physician, and Severine and Alexandre returned from the palace. Alexandre was crying, the physician was tending to you, and Severine was screaming at the constabulary for detaining Lady Catherine and bringing her to the palace. Severine went with her mother, and since then, the only people in the château are you, me, Marius, and Alexandre. I thought it fitting that you have your old chambers back.

"And before you ask," Elodie said, "Auguste had to return to the palace to inform his father about what happened. He wanted to stay, believe me. He wouldn't leave your bedside until the physician assured him that you were going to be all right."

My heart warmed at the thought of Auguste chasing after me, of his staying to watch over me while I slept. Without him, I would be dead. Lady Catherine would have murdered me. Just a week prior, I'd been on death's door. The thought filled me with dull horror. I'd been perhaps minutes away from joining Maman and Papa and Lady Françoise in the afterlife. Because my stepmother tried to murder me. She poisoned me with a smile on her face and sweet words on her lips. I'd always known that she never liked me— that she maybe even hated me—but I never imagined she would want me dead.

"I am so stupid," I said loudly, my parched throat protesting the volume.

Grabbing a glass of water off the nightstand, Elodie leaned over and helped me drink a few sips. Water dribbled down my chin and dripped onto the neckline of my nightgown, which Elodie promptly wiped up with a handkerchief. I hated this. Elodie had done so much for me already, staying and putting up with Lady Catherine's mistreatment for my sake, and now here she was, coddling me like a child.

"Don't say things like that," she said as she deposited the glass back on the nightstand and returned to her perch at the edge of the bed. "Why would you even think that?"

"Because I should have known that something was wrong! We lived with the woman for a year, and in all that time, she never once showed us even an ounce of kindness. Why would she start now? I should have known something was wrong as soon as she made me tea, especially after she started apologizing. She wanted either Severine or Alexandre to marry the dauphin at any cost; I bet she'd been planning to poison me for weeks! I even overheard Severine and Alexandre arguing about it. She was worried he would propose, and when he did, Lady Catherine realized she had to get rid of me once and for all."

"Oh, Cendrillon," Elodie said, "it's only obvious in hindsight. It was obvious that Lady Catherine would be angry over the dauphin's proposal, but it is ridiculous for us to imagine she would *murder* you."

I was interrupted by the door to my bedchamber flying open. Alexandre came running in, cheeks flushed and eyes wild. When her eyes found me, she burst into tears. "Cendrillon! Thank goodness you're all right!" she cried, running up to the bed and throwing herself on top of me.

I gasped in surprise as she buried her head in my neck and continued crying, her tears soaking my nightgown. I wasn't at full strength, so the added weight of Alexandre leaning on me emptied the air from my lungs.

"I'm so sorry! I'm so sorry! I knew what she wanted to do, but I couldn't stop her in time. The best I could do was give the antidote to Elodie. I—"

Alexandre's words dissolved into more sobs. I disentangled my left arm from underneath the pile of blankets and patted her back, slightly confused at this surprising turn of events.

"You don't have to apologize, Alexandre. I'm not quite sure what happened a week ago, but I'm fairly certain you saved my life. Without that antidote, I would be dead. You did everything that you could. Thank you. Truly." Just as I suspected, the strange vial that she and Severine were arguing about was for *me*, not Louis. Lady Catherine and Severine had wanted to poison me from the beginning.

By the end, I was gasping for air. Noticing my distress, Elodie took Alexandre by the shoulders and pulled her gently away.

"It's all right. It's all right," she said soothingly. "Why don't we leave Cendrillon alone for a little while so she can rest? I think she'll be ready for visitors tomorrow."

Alexandre nodded and rubbed her eyes as Elodie led her to the doorway. Before leaving, she spun back around. "You shouldn't be thanking me," she said, sniffling. "I don't deserve it. I might have given you the antidote, but it was the first thing I ever did to stop her. I suspected she had something to do with your father's death, but I was too scared to say anything. I should have done something."

My eyes widened. I wasn't sure that I'd heard Alexandre correctly. I couldn't have heard her correctly. Elodie ushered Alexandre out the door with a few whispered words I couldn't hear and turned back to me, a concerned expression on her face.

"Did Alexandre . . . did Alexandre just say that Lady Catherine did something to Papa?"

I didn't even need to ask. I already knew. And the tears rolling down Elodie's cheeks confirmed the truth of Alexandre's words.

"Lady Catherine poisoned my father, didn't she?"

Elodie only nodded as she returned to the bed, scrubbing furiously at her eyes. I wanted to cry too. Or maybe scream. Or hit something. My emotions were twisted up around each other like vines. I couldn't get a handle on just one. I was feeling everything, and it was overwhelming me.

"Are you sure?"

"Nearly positive. Alexandre showed Auguste and the palace guards Catherine's logbooks. In them, she recorded the dates and times of the meetings she had with various enchantresses to buy love potions and . . . and poisons." Lady Catherine was always meticulous about expenses and recorded everything.

"Do you think she used a love potion on Papa?" I asked. It did seem odd, the way he had decided to marry her so quickly.

"Who can say? No one knows if love potions really work," said Elodie. "Alexandre told me that her mother mentioned that Lady Françoise was a fool who took too long to declare her love for your father, which made him easy to seduce. But poisons are real."

That tea she was always giving him. That blasted tea she said the doctor had prescribed. Most likely the exact same tea she gave me, but delivered slowly over months. How poetic it would have been for father and daughter to die by the same hand. Lady Catherine must have been thrilled before it all went wrong.

"But you don't have to worry," Elodie said. "A letter from Auguste arrived yesterday. The king has the logbooks and the testimony from Alexandre that she gave at the palace a few days ago. Alexandre's words and the books convinced him of the truth. He ordered Lady Catherine's inheritance of Monsieur le Marquis's effects revoked. The château and everything inside it are yours now, as are all your father's assets."

I said nothing. Elodie climbed onto the bed and lay down beside me. We snuggled against each other, like we did when we were children. It seemed like so long ago that we were young and innocent. So much had happened since. I let myself cry then. For all that I'd lost and all that Lady Catherine had taken from me.

CHAPTER THIRTY-NINE

"Do you need me to go in with you?" Elodie asked Alexandre and me as we stood side by side before the door to the king's throne room. "We can try to convince the king that you need extra moral support."

"I'm sure it will be fine, right? And quick. Is that correct?" Alexandre's voice was soft as she spoke, and she grew quieter by the second, until her voice was nearly inaudible. Her eyes darted between Elodie and the wooden double doors, as if they were going to burst open and suck her inside. In truth, Alexandre did need moral support. Without Elodie grasping her arm, I feared Alexandre may have bolted before we even stepped foot in the palace. But I knew that the king wouldn't allow her to accompany us.

"That's correct. The king only asked you here to sign some documents and request that you speak during the trial, I believe. It shouldn't take long," said Elodie.

King Louis had graciously waited another week after I awoke before calling us to court. Barring occasional bouts of exhaustion if

I exerted myself too much, I was practically back to full health. This trip to court was the first time I left the château since the poisoning.

I was eternally grateful to my friends for their tender care of me during my illness, but lying in bed all day with nothing to do but read or sew was dreadfully boring. Even though my destination was Versailles, I was just happy to be up and about and doing anything other than grieve and stare out the window at the same admittedly lovely garden day after day.

Elodie whispered something in Alexandre's ear, and though she was still pale and jumpy, my stepsister nodded and allowed Elodie to disentangle their arms and move over to my side. We'd all been trying to treat Alexandre as gently as possible. She'd been incredibly brave, but she'd lost her entire family in the process.

When Severine found out that Alexandre had turned Lady Catherine in, she needed to be restrained from attacking her sister. It was a difficult time for all of us, but the one who was suffering the most was Alexandre. She remained in the château with us, as I would never ask her to leave, and Elodie had been sticking by her as much as possible, which was a balm to be sure but not enough to entirely soothe the ache.

I hated Lady Catherine for putting her own daughter in such a terrible position. She'd never been a particularly loving mother, always favoring Severine, but those two were all Alexandre had for the longest time. I could only hope, and vow to show her, that she wasn't alone.

"Ready?" I asked with what I hoped was a reassuring smile.

When Alexandre nodded again, I led her to the double doors and waited as the guards standing on either side shoved them open and gestured us inside.

We were greeted by the sight of the king sitting on his great wooden throne atop a red-velvet dais to match the canopy above him, surrounded by advisors and other court dignitaries. The dauphin stood by his father's side, looking splendid in a purple velvet justaucorps accented in gold. When he saw us enter the room, he offered me a small, tentative smile that nearly made me trip, I was so surprised. I'd expected that he'd still be angry with me, but he didn't seem upset at all. Was it all an act for his father, or was it possible that he'd forgiven me?

The king, however, looked down his long nose at us, lips sternly pressed together. If I hadn't known better, I would have assumed that *we* were the ones in trouble. Maybe we *were* the ones in trouble. Perhaps Lady Catherine had convinced him that she was innocent and cast the blame on me instead. It was far-fetched, but I wouldn't put anything past her, and the king was known to be temperamental. All kinds of horrible fears along a similar vein ran through my head until I realized that the king wasn't looking at us at all. His gaze was fixed on something just behind us. I turned my head slightly to the left and spotted someone out of the corner of my eye whom I'd hoped never to see again.

"Lady Catherine," I gasped involuntarily.

I wouldn't have thought it possible, but Alexandre paled even further, her face turning a sickly white when she caught sight of her mother being escorted into the throne room by two guards.

Escorted was a gracious way to describe the way two guards dragged a bedraggled Lady Catherine into the room. Her dress was ripped at the hemline and covered in stains, while her hair hung loose and tangled around her shoulders. It was a far cry from the sophisticated, refined image she had invested so much effort into presenting at court. She must have hated looking such a mess in front of so many important people. But you wouldn't be able to tell it from her face.

Lady Catherine's lips were trembling and her eyes so downcast that she didn't even notice Alexandre and me until the guards deposited her in front of the dais, across the room from us.

She spotted me first. There was a flash of something in her eyes that I couldn't place. Probably veiled rage. But when she caught sight of Alexandre, her eyes filled with tears. "Oh, ma fille chérie. I'm so happy to see you," Lady Catherine said, her voice choked with tears. "Are you all right? I've been so worried. I tried to get in contact with you. Why aren't you staying with your sister?"

I felt Alexandre's arm stiffen, but she didn't even glance at her mother, keeping her eyes on the king instead. All I could do was make sure to keep a firm grip on her arm and pat her hand encouragingly. It was woefully inadequate to soothe the tumult Alexandre was surely feeling at being in the same room as her mother.

Why was Lady Catherine here? We were only supposed to be signing documents and confirming our stories. Something else was clearly going on, and I didn't appreciate it being sprung on us so suddenly. It was odious to be anywhere near the woman who murdered Papa—who tried to murder me.

"This is all going to be over soon, ma coeur. I promise," Lady Catherine called out, undeterred by her daughter's lack of response. "Just as soon as I clear up these . . . misconceptions about me, fueled by the egregious lies someone in this room has been spreading."

The king ignored Lady Catherine. "I've brought the Ladies Cendrillon and Alexandre here today to confirm their stories. Accusations such as the ones leveled against Lady Catherine are not to be taken lightly. Often, I find it is most revealing to hear them in person instead of indirectly. And to hear them in front of the accused."

This was a test. The king wanted to make sure that we weren't lying by throwing us into a room with Lady Catherine to see if our stories changed when we were face-to-face with her.

It wouldn't bother my stepmother in the slightest, but I'm sure telling the story—even though it was true—would be hard for Alexandre. It ensured her mother's continued imprisonment, which was an awful burden to bear, made doubly so by having to look her in the eye while reporting to the king.

It was cruel to make her do this, especially after how brave she'd already been. But the king wasn't known for kindness.

"Lady Cendrillon de Louvois," he said firmly, turning brown eyes that were nothing and everything like Auguste's on me. "Is the woman standing across from you, Lady Catherine de Louvois, your stepmother, the person who poisoned you?"

"Yes, Monsieur le Roi. Lady Catherine gave me a poisoned cup of tea and left me to die. It was the same poisoned tea she used to kill my father, Michel le Tellier, Marquis de Louvois."

The king nodded once and turned his severe gaze on Alexandre.

"Bald-faced lies, Monsieur le Roi," Lady Catherine said with a wounded expression on her face. "I don't know why my stepdaughter, the girl I housed and cared for after my dear husband passed away so suddenly—of a long, protracted illness, might I add—would turn on me like this, but she is lying to you."

"This is not the time to plead your case, Madame de Louvois," the king said. "You will have a chance to defend yourself at the trial. Now is the time for your daughter to speak."

I squeezed Alexandre's arm as she began to tremble, attempting to impart some comfort or peace of mind in any way that I could.

"Lady Alexandre, did the woman standing across from you, Lady Catherine de Louvois, your mother, poison your stepsister and stepfather, her husband? Did she also attempt to use a love potion on my son, Monseigneur le Dauphin?"

An uncomfortable silence descended on the room as Alexandre stood completely still next to me, her eyes locked with the king's. I would have thought that he would lose patience with her, but he met her stare with a pensive one of his own and waited for her to speak.

The advisors arrayed behind him fidgeted and pressed their heads close together to whisper amongst themselves. Prince Louis tugged at his lace cravat and frowned at Alexandre.

I was nearly about to poke her to make sure that she was still breathing when Lady Catherine's voice rang out, so loud that I flinched.

"It's all right, ma jolie fille. Just tell the king the truth, and all this can be over."

Her tone was soothing and gentle, as if she were talking to a frightened child. I was suddenly unsure for the first time since entering the throne room. Lady Catherine was putting on a magnificent performance. She seemed to be a loving mother who only wanted what was best for her child.

What if Alexandre couldn't go through with it? We would all be in trouble then, and none more than me.

"If you tell him the truth," Lady Catherine continued, "we can go home. You, me, and your sister. We can put this nightmare behind us and move forward. You don't have to be afraid, ma coeur. I know that you care for Cendrillon, but that doesn't mean you should lie for her. She isn't your real family. I am your—"

"Maman, that's enough!" Alexandre said. She tore her arm from mine and stepped in front of me to glare at her mother. "Cendrillon isn't the one trying to manipulate me. *You* are. Did you think that you could just ply me with a few pretty words and I would lie for you again? That isn't going to work this time, Mère. You tried to murder Cendrillon, and you would have succeeded if I hadn't stolen the antidote from you and given it to her. I watched you buy the poisons, and I overheard you telling Severine that you murdered the marquis.

I should have said something then, but I didn't, and I will regret that decision always. If I'd been braver, Cendrillon might have been spared all the pain you put her through."

Alexandre's words petered out as she stopped to catch her breath. I'd never seen her like this before. There was such anger in her eyes and conviction in her voice. The only person who had ever stood up to Lady Catherine was Severine, and that was only when her mother denied her something that she wanted. Never Alexandre. Until now.

"I will not let you hurt Cendrillon. She isn't lying about what happened, and neither am I."

Lady Catherine didn't seem upset by her daughter's outburst. The expression on her face remaining placid, as if carved from stone. Frighteningly placid. It was never a good thing when Lady Catherine was so still. There was nothing she could do to harm any of us here, but that didn't stop me from taking Alexandre's arm and guiding her back to her previous spot beside me, where I could shield her from her mother's gaze.

"I see," said Lady Catherine at last. "And I suppose you choose your illicit friendship with the servant over your own mother as well?"

"I'm proud of who I am and whom I love," said Alexandre. "It's more than I can say for you." If only Elodie were with us to see Alexandre at this moment.

"I believe I have heard all I need to," the king said, a small smile curling his lips upward. "From this moment forward, Catherine Monvoisin de Louvois shall be stripped of her title and status at court. Even if she is declared innocent at trial, she will no longer count herself amongst the nobility of France. Guards, remove her."

The same two guards reentered the salon and approached Catherine. She didn't resist as they took hold of her arms and drew her toward the door. Alexandre turned her face away as her mother approached, the trio's path from the salon bringing them uncomfortably close to where we stood. Just as it seemed like they were going to leave without incident, Lady Catherine broke free from one of the guards and grabbed my arm roughly. Her nails bit into my skin as she wrenched me forward until our foreheads nearly touched.

"You must be overjoyed to have finally won," Catherine hissed, her breath cool against my ear.

Even after spending so long imprisoned, she still carried the faintest whiff of rose on her skin. The scent turned my stomach, bringing back the memory of falling to the floor in the sitting room as bruise-dark spots spread across my body. I tried to pull away, but her grip was surprisingly strong, and I was still frustratingly weak.

"You just couldn't leave anything for anyone else, could you? You had to have it all! You've even stolen my own daughter from me."

"Is that how you see it?" I asked. "That *I've* stolen from *you*? I haven't stolen anything. Papa's assets are rightfully mine. You made sure that I had no access to them after you killed him. If anyone here is a thief, it's you. In addition to being a murderer. Everything you took was always mine in the first place. Except for Alexandre. She isn't mine or anyone else's. She is her own person, something you never cared to acknowledge as you used her for your own ends."

"Guards, remove her now," the king said, his voice booming across the salon.

The guards easily overpowered Catherine and hauled her from the room. She stopped fighting them, but her eyes never left me. The only thing to break her hateful stare was the closing of the double doors behind her.

Before they shut, I caught a glimpse of a panicked Elodie arguing with one of the valets standing watch just outside. I wasn't looking forward to having to explain all this to her.

"Are you all right?" Alexandre asked, clinging to my arm worriedly.

Unfortunately, she clung to the arm that Catherine had grabbed. I could see little crescents in the skin where her fingernails had dug in. They stung a little and were probably going to bruise. Once again, I bore the marks of Catherine's anger, hopefully for the last time.

"I'm fine," I said with a smile. "She didn't hurt me. I'm more worried about you. You were very brave."

Alexandre tried to smile back, but it deflated quickly, leaving a trembling lip and watery eyes behind. I wrapped an arm around her shoulders. Catherine was absolutely delusional if she thought that this was winning.

"I apologize for that uncouth behavior, Lady Cendrillon," the king said, causing me to jump as I realized that Alexandre and I still had an audience. "That should not have happened in my throne room. You are uninjured?"

"I am uninjured, sire. Thank you for your concern."

The king cleared his throat and said, "I also owe you another apology, Lady Cendrillon."

"Excuse me, sire?" I said. The king never apologized to anyone.

"I apologize for neglecting you. Your father was once my closest advisor and dearest friend, and I should have ensured that his daughter was being taken care of properly. But I did not. I assumed that Lady Catherine was treating you well, and that assumption allowed my friend's murderer to remain free for a year, mistreating his daughter and almost killing her. I failed you. And for that I am sorry."

An apology from a king was a rare and precious thing. I'd never expected to receive one, and I would probably never receive another. I collapsed into the deepest curtsy I possibly could.

"I place none of the blame for what happened on you, sire, but I appreciate your apology all the same and accept it gratefully."

I rose and turned to Prince Louis, who was at his side. "I regret that I was not able to accept your proposal, Monseigneur le Dauphin. I hope we can always be friends."

Elodie had told me that after the ruckus I had caused, the dauphin had proposed to Duchesse Maria, and she'd readily accepted the political alliance her father had desired. I only hoped the duchesse would find some happiness in her marriage.

Louis gave me a small smile. "Maybe it's the spirit of wedded bliss that's taken over the palace now that we have two upcoming royal marriages, but I agree, it's best to put the past behind us and be friends again."

"Forgive me, Monseigneur, but while I offer you my sincerest congratulations on your upcoming nuptials, I'm afraid I haven't heard of this second royal wedding."

After a glance from the king, the dauphin said, "That reminds me. The Duc de Maine wishes to speak with you before you leave, Lady Cendrillon."

"The Duc de Maine?"

"That's right. Duc de Maine is our dear Auguste's new title. The king was gracious enough to grant him a dukedom after legitimizing him, in recompense for saving your life and helping to uncover Catherine's misdeeds. It is his upcoming marriage that is to be the second royal wedding. I think he wanted to invite you to attend."

The bombardment of information set my head spinning. Auguste was getting married? To whom? That didn't make any sense. Auguste cared for me. I knew he did. He chased after me the day of the proposal and spent days by my side while I was unconscious. He'd made his intentions toward me clear. Or at least, I thought he had. Maybe it was not that he was a fickle rake, but a condition of his legitimization. But that wasn't much better. It still meant that we couldn't be together.

"If I see Auguste on our way out, I'll be sure to congratulate him on his new title," I said with as sweet of a smile as I could muster even as I felt my heart breaking. The king had legitimized him! He would no longer be considered fatherless. But now he was marrying someone else?

When the dauphin and the king said nothing more, I dragged Alexandre into a curtsy alongside my own and ushered her to the door. I breathed a sigh of relief when Elodie came into view. It was over.

Elodie, Marius, and I were going to be together and safe at last.

And Auguste. All was well for him too. Being illegitimate hurt him greatly, and I was happy that his family realized how important he was and made it known to everyone at court. But no matter how happy I was or how grateful I was to him for saving my life, I still couldn't face him. Not when I knew he would be getting married to another, and so soon. Our last goodbye would have to remain as such.

CHAPTER FORTY

"WHAT HAPPENED IN THERE?" ELODIE asked as soon as the doors shut behind us. "I saw the guards bring Lady Catherine in and then bring her out again, and she looked furious."

I let Elodie take charge of Alexandre, taking her hand and drawing her into the crook of her arm. As soon as Elodie touched her, Alexandre relaxed. It was sweet how the tension evaporated from her body as she rested her head against Elodie's shoulder. A pang of longing surged through me. I wanted what they had. I'd had it briefly and lost it just as quickly. But I was happy for them.

"Alexandre was like Jeanne d'Arc," I said with a smile. "She stood up for us—and you." Everything would turn out all right. I had my life back, and soon all of us would be safe, including Marius.

Elodie looked mystified, while Alexandre looked shy. The coachman opened the carriage door, and I was about to step inside when I heard Elodie say loudly, "Oh. I'm so sorry. I didn't even see you there, Lord Auguste!"

I backed up quickly and ducked behind a startled guard. Elodie and Alexandre were standing in the doorway leading to the Salon of Mercury. He stood on the other side of the doorway, towering over their heads, his broad shoulders making it impossible to see into the salon.

"You just appeared out of nowhere, Lord Auguste, I mean, Duc de Maine, Your Highness, Your Grace. What should I call you?"

Elodie was speaking so loudly, the king could probably hear her back in the throne room. She was trying to warn me—alert me to his presence. Elodie really was the best friend anyone could ask for. In more ways than one, I wouldn't be where I was without her.

"Are you unwell, mademoiselle?" the guard whispered, but he obligingly didn't move, keeping me shielded from view.

"I'm fine, thank you," I whispered back. "If you don't mind, I would appreciate it if you would allow me to remain here until my friend comes back."

I had no doubt that Elodie would come up with something to keep Auguste away. If Elodie had to fake a fainting spell to get him to run for help so we could make our escape, she would. Did I want her to get rid of him? Part of me did. Another part wanted to run to him, to throw myself into his arms and let him hold me. But I couldn't do that. Auguste was a loyal person. Louis had said that he wanted to invite me to his wedding. It was too upsetting to realize he was so ready to move on, even though I was the person who ended our relationship after all. I had no one to blame but myself. But still, I couldn't face him.

"I'm very well, Elodie, and you know you ought to call me Auguste." He turned to the coachman. "Gabriel, you seem to have sprouted an extra elbow. That is a very concerning development, un- less you have someone crouched behind you."

I pulled my elbows tightly against my sides and silently cursed my clumsiness. If I hadn't been so careless, Gabriel's massive frame would have completely hidden me from view. Maybe if I remained silent, he would just give up and go away.

Gabriel laughed, and said, "Alas, as amusing as that would be, I have only the two. Perhaps the owner of the third elbow will emerge sometime soon."

I sighed heavily and stepped out from behind Gabriel, glaring at him unhappily before turning to face Auguste. Elodie and Alexandre had moved out of the doorway, allowing him access into the salon. And suddenly there he was, standing right in front of me, just as handsome as ever. His green eyes locked on mine, unwavering in their intensity. I hadn't seen him since the day I'd been poisoned. It had only been two weeks, but those two weeks without him felt like years.

"Lady Cendrillon," Auguste said, his deep voice sending a chill running down my spine. "I'm glad to have caught you before you left. You've been through quite the ordeal. I wanted to make sure that you were all right. You look well."

I didn't look at all well, and I knew it, but he was too kind to let me know if he was alarmed by my pale and weak appearance.

"Thank you. As do you. And please allow me to thank you for your interference with my stepmother, Catherine. Without you, I would not be here now. I owe you a great debt."

"I would do it all again in a heartbeat. And more. So much more. Perhaps we could take a walk and speak on it? I have something to ask you."

"All right." When I realized what I said, and how quickly I said it, I silently cursed my weakness in all matters of Auguste and added, "Just a short chat. We really need to be going."

"Just a short chat," he said, looking a little mystified as he extended his arm to me.

I glanced back at my friends for the first time since Auguste had entered the room. Elodie was glancing between me and Alexandre, a worried expression on her face. She wanted to intervene, I could tell—offer to come with us and chaperone, maybe—but she also wanted to stay with Alexandre. I couldn't separate them, not when Alexandre was still so fragile. I could handle Auguste for a little while.

"You can head back to the carriage, Elodie. I'll be along shortly," I said.

"Are you sure? I can come with if you want."

"No. It's fine. You stay with Alexandre. I'll be back before you know it."

I took Auguste's arm and let him lead me away.

"The Orangerie? You've brought me to the Orangerie?" I asked as Auguste and I walked down the long, wide white steps.

I hadn't recognized the path until we made it to the stairs and the orange trees came into view. It had been over a year since I'd been here last, and Elodie, Marius, and I entered through the interior gallery. I'd never used the main entrance before. The grand wrought-iron gates had been locked the last time. They were locked this time, too, but Auguste pulled a large key from an interior pocket in his dark green justaucorps and began to fiddle with the lock.

"Are we supposed to be in here?" I asked skeptically as the lock clicked.

Auguste swung the gates wide open and gestured me inside with a flourish. Despite myself, I smiled at his antics and walked through the gates. The familiar sweet scent of citrus wafted over me, chasing away any lingering hint of roses. I breathed in deeply, letting the calm of the Orangerie fill me up.

I could do this. Hear Auguste out, congratulate him on the upcoming wedding, decline any invitation to his nuptials, and leave. I would have to stay away from court for a while, but that suited me. I was looking forward to saying goodbye to Versailles.

"The Orangerie being off limits never stopped you before," Auguste said teasingly as he held the door for me.

He closed the gates behind us but left them unlocked. I started walking toward one of the paths that curled through the geometric lawns. The tree branches bowed under the weight of the oranges that glistened under the sunlight. If I could get some fruit out of this outing, maybe it wouldn't be so bad after all. I even spied a few pomegranates. Elodie would love those.

"I was much more naïve then. I didn't realize—"

Before I could even finish my sentence, I was spun around and enveloped in strong arms. Auguste pressed me tightly against his chest and buried his face against my neck. I should have shoved him away. I should have told him that this wasn't appropriate and gone back to the carriage. I should have done anything but grab hold of his waistcoat and burrow closer. But I wanted this just one more time.

"You're safe. You're safe," Auguste whispered, his breath hot against my skin.

"I'm safe. I'm here," I whispered back.

"When I broke into the château and saw you lying on the floor covered in those awful spots, I thought you were dead. There were so many times over those next few days that you were still far too close to death's door. I nearly lost my mind with worry. If something had happened to you, I would never have been able to forgive myself."

"It wasn't your fault. You saved me. If you hadn't arrived when you did, I would be dead."

"Still, I promised to protect you and—"

"No. I'm tired of people blaming themselves for Catherine

Monvoisin's actions. She's the murderer, not you. You're a hero. Your father clearly thinks so, too, or he wouldn't have granted you the dukedom."

"You heard about that?"

"I heard about that. The *Duc de Maine*. Like Elodie said, do I call you Your Grace now? Should I even be talking to you? I think I'm too far below you in station. Do you have an extravagant estate?"

Auguste rolled his eyes, but I could see him trying to smother a smile. When he held his arm out to me, I accepted, and we set off down one of the fruit-tree-lined paths. A warm glow burned inside my chest.

"Even if you weren't allowed to speak to me, that wouldn't stop you," he teased. Then his face became more serious. "But I did talk to my father. I told him what was going on between us. I told him he could banish us both and I would accept it, but I hoped he would consider my plan instead."

"Your plan?"

"My father had been promising me a title and land ever since I was brought to court. I finally told him it was time to live up to his promise. It turns out that's what he was waiting for all along. He wanted me to demand my own inheritance. That way he knew I was his own son and not a simpering courtier."

"Fathers are tricky," I said.

"Yes." He blushed then. "He told me that my mother—my mother was one of his favorites. The love of his life, he called her. But he could never show that, not at court; it would put her in too much danger. Anyway, as it turns out"—his voice caught a little—"I am his favorite too."

"Your father loves you," I whispered. My father loved me too. We were never in danger, I realized. Not with a father's love and protection. That was why Lady Catherine had murdered mine.

Auguste nodded. "I knew he did. That's what I was trying to tell you. That even if the court dismissed me, he never did. He loved my mother, and he loves me. He could have sent me away years ago, but instead I was always right by his side, with Louis."

"I should have believed you," I said. "You told me to trust you. That you would find a way."

"I did," he said, smiling. "But you are very stubborn."

We laughed together.

He continued his story. "And I do have an estate. It's been a challenge learning how to manage it in the last few weeks. But I'm glad to have it. My new duties will require me to reside there for most of the year. I'll be able to get away from Versailles for months at a time. What heaven that will be."

"It sounds like the perfect place to start a family. I'm sure you'll be very happy there."

Auguste looked at me strangely. There was surprise on his face. Had I said something rude? I didn't think so. What I said was perfectly neutral, and I would remain so throughout our conversation.

Maybe he was just nervous about my reaction to the news. He didn't have to worry. I would take it bravely and cry about it later. There was no use making him feel guilty about something that was beyond his control.

"That's what I wanted to talk to you about," Auguste said in a choked voice. After he cleared his throat, he continued. "Why don't we sit? Let's sit."

Auguste led me to a bench nestled between two large orange trees and lowered himself quickly, staring at me expectantly until I took a seat beside him. The moment I'd been dreading. I had a whole speech worked out in my head detailing why I couldn't attend the wedding. I would be regretful but firm, offer him my warmest congratulations, and take my leave, begging fatigue as the reason.

But this day once again did not go according to plan. As soon as I sat down, Auguste leaned forward and kissed me. I kissed him back, and it took me a moment to realize what was going on, but when I did, I grabbed his shoulders and pushed him away.

"What are you doing? Are you mad?" I cried as I scooted to the other end of the bench.

Auguste held his hands up placatingly and said, "I'm sorry. I'm far too impulsive, but seeing you makes me want to kiss you."

"What are you talking about? Your behavior is completely inappropriate for a man about to be wed."

Auguste seemed confused.

I was confused.

There was no reason for him to be confused. He was the one behaving strangely, not me.

He tilted his head at me. "It isn't *that* inappropriate. No one is going to begrudge a betrothed couple stealing a few kisses in the gardens."

"Yes, a betrothed couple. Not one half of the couple and someone else. It isn't right."

"I don't understand you, Cendrillon. What are you saying?"

"I'm saying that it's inappropriate to kiss me when you're about to marry another woman." I spoke slowly so that there would be no way Auguste could misinterpret my meaning, but he still looked confused.

"Another woman?" he asked, recoiling from me as if I'd said something revolting.

"Are you . . . ? You're not . . . ? Aren't you marrying another woman in a few months?"

"No! Of course not. What in the world gave you that idea?"

I felt like I was trapped in the middle of the Labyrinth, hopelessly turned around, with no one to guide me to safety. Auguste and I were having two different conversations, and I wasn't sure whose was correct, or if either of them was.

"I just came from a meeting with your brother and the king in the throne room. After all of the matters with Lady Catherine were sorted, Louis told me that you wanted to see me so that you could invite me to your wedding. I assumed that it was a condition of your legitimization. Was he lying? Are you not getting married?"

Auguste dropped his head into his hands and groaned. "That idiot. That spoiled, selfish idiot," he mumbled into his hands.

When Auguste didn't emerge from his hands, I tapped him on the shoulder a few times. My mouth was painfully dry, and my stomach was beginning to turn. It was a terrible feeling to not know what was going on. I couldn't handle any more surprises. My nerves were strained enough as it was. "Auguste, if you don't tell me what's going on right now, I'm going to get up and leave."

He finally lifted his head up from his hands and looked at me. "Louis was making a joke when he said that I wanted to invite you to my wedding. He's always thought himself to be quite funny. He isn't funny, but he's the dauphin, so everyone puts up with it."

"So, you aren't getting married, then."

"It's a little more complicated than that."

Auguste sighed and scooted closer to me, taking my hands in his. I allowed it, but only as long as he actually told me what was happening. My threat to leave was serious. I was in no mood for games.

"As part of naming me a legitimate heir, the king required me to agree to get married right away. A duc needs a duchesse, and he thought, after all the turmoil of the last few weeks, two royal weddings would sufficiently placate the skittish nobles, who are always looking for weakness in the royal family. But he has allowed me to pick whom I want to marry. Luckily, he enthusiastically approved of my choice. He considered allowing this marriage to be part of his efforts to make amends to a girl and an old friend that he allowed to be hurt under his watch. He also thought it was amusing that I had won the heart of someone Louis wanted for himself. I told you: I am his favorite."

"So you have to be married." I could feel my heart beating out a staccato rhythm inside my chest as it sent blood surging through my veins. My breath hitched in my throat. I involuntarily squeezed Auguste's hands. He squeezed back. His grip was firm, but I could see the fear in his eyes. I'm sure it matched my own, if the burning in my cheeks was anything to go by.

His green eyes shone. "Yes, the wedding date is set, all the bride has to do is say yes."

"What are you saying?" I could hear how wispy and weak my voice was. I wasn't even sure how I was managing to speak at all. My head felt light and airy, as if I'd had a little too much wine at dinner. I was so mixed up, I could barely summon a coherent thought. "Tell me or I might scream."

"Please don't scream. That would make this proposal even worse than it already is."

"Is that what this is, a proposal?"

"Yes."

"An invitation to your wedding. Louis really does think he's funny, doesn't he?"

Auguste laughed a little and began fumbling around in his pockets. "I had everything perfectly planned out. I was going to bring you to the Orangerie and tell you how much I loved you. I was going to tell you that the best day of my life was the day we were reunited at the ball, and that I couldn't bear to be apart from you for even another minute. I was going to mention how I told my father that if he didn't accept my terms, he would have to banish me or throw me in the

Bastille or execute me, because I wasn't going to marry anyone but you."

Auguste pulled a little wooden box out of his pocket and promptly dropped it on the ground. He lunged for it, but I was faster, his fingers brushing mine as I scooped it up and gripped it tightly in my hand. I knew what it was, but I couldn't bring myself to open it.

"I was also going to mention that you were under no obligation to say yes," Auguste said quickly. "I would never want to pressure you into doing anything that you didn't want to do. Father's decree isn't a binding contract for you. If you were to say no, I would completely understand. This is all very sudden and not at all traditional. I know that. Father wouldn't force you either. Not after everything you've been through."

My palms were slick with sweat. It made opening the box a bit difficult, but I managed to get a firm grip on the lid and lifted it to reveal the contents. On a bed of red velvet lay a gold ring. It was a lovely, delicate thing. Not new, based on some spots of wear, but beautiful nonetheless. Tiny sapphires were studded all across the band. I loved it immediately.

The ring wasn't perfectly circular. It was molded into the shape of two hands clutching a heart, a common design of rings intended to be given to a lover. Papa had given Maman a ring like this when they were courting. I'd seen it in her jewelry box and tried to wear it, but it slid right off my child-size finger. Maman had whisked it away before I lost it.

There was something inscribed on the ring. I lifted it from the box carefully and held it up to the light. Along the inside of the band the words *My heart is yours* were carved.

I looked back up at Auguste. He was so vulnerable in that moment. Every emotion he was feeling was written across his face. Love, fear, desire, anticipation. I could see them all. I felt them all.

"This is a beautiful ring. Where did you get it?"

"Madame de Maintenon. When she found out that I was planning to propose, she gave me the ring. It was a gift from my father. She wore it for years."

"On the left-hand ring finger, yes? Over the vena amoris?"

"Did you . . . Do you want to put it on?" Auguste asked cautiously.

"But I haven't actually been proposed to yet. I only heard about someone's plans of how they *wanted* to propose, not the actual proposal."

I smiled at the nervous, hopeful expression on Auguste's face. I couldn't stop smiling. I was so happy. So blissfully happy. And terribly afraid. My stomach still flip-flopped out a rhythm to match the thudding of my heart against my ribs. I had to grip the ring tightly so that it didn't slip. I probably looked a little mad. Maybe I was a little mad. I certainly felt like I was spinning out of control.

"Are you sure you want me to propose?" Auguste asked the question as if he didn't believe that I was serious. I suppose the expression on my face would give someone that impression.

"I wouldn't ask you to go through with it if I wasn't sure, Auguste. What kind of girl do you think I am?"

"If you married me, you wouldn't be a princesse. My official title is *duc*. The highest you'll ever be is a duchesse."

"Oh," I said, pretending to be disappointed.

His face fell, and I elbowed him with a laugh. "Auguste, I've never wanted to be a princesse! And I've worked as a maid." I tapped my chin, remembering our etiquette lessons from a year ago. "Plus, if I'm a duchesse, I can finally sit down at the table when the king is there. I wouldn't have to stand!"

But he still looked anxious. "I was serious when I said that my duties will keep us away from court for most of the year. Would you be all right with that?"

"Staying away from Versailles is just as much a boon for me as it is for you."

"We'll be together for the rest of our lives. Just us two. Well, until the children arrive," he said, reddening again.

Children! We would have children. I thought of Maman and Papa and how happy we were. I could have a family with Auguste. The thought was so sweet, I could hardly believe it.

He cleared his throat. "I want to warn you—"

"Auguste, if you add on any more clarifications to this proposal, I'm going to go find Louis and ask him to reconsider marrying the Bavarian duchesse."

Auguste laughed and shook his head sheepishly. "I'm sorry. I don't mean to be difficult. I'm just nervous."

"I know. Me too."

He held his palm out for the ring. I gave it to Auguste. As soon as it was in his hand, he climbed off the bench and got down on bended knee in front of me.

"Cendrillon, Lady de Louvois, I've loved you from the moment we met at the Orangerie. I can't imagine my life without you. Would you do me the great honor of becoming my wife?"

I didn't even need to think about the answer. It was ready to leave my mouth as soon as Auguste started his proposal. "Yes!"

"Yes?"

"One thousand times yes! You know I love you, you foolish boy!"

Auguste laughed as he slipped the ring onto my finger. I loved the sound of his laugh. I wanted to hear it for the rest of my life.

"Cruel woman, wounding me while I pour my heart out to you."

"I thought you already knew how much I loved you. But if you need a reminder . . ."

I leaned down and silenced his doubts with my lips. Auguste wrapped his arms around my waist as he climbed back up onto the bench, pulling me onto his lap as he deepened the kiss. Each time we parted for air, I whispered a declaration of love against his mouth.

"Oh! I almost forgot," he said when we caught our breath. He reached into the pockets of his coat once more.

"Another surprise?" I asked. But I gasped when I saw what it was.

He held in his hand my brocade slipper with the glass crystals. "You left it on the terrace. I found it that night, when I was looking for you. I've kept it all this time."

I marveled at the exquisite slipper before me. A most precious gift from my beloved godmother. I had given it up for lost.

I'd nearly lost Auguste too. I'd come to meet him thinking that I was going to have to give him up. But now that he was here and safe in my arms, I was never going to let him go.

Auguste was not a prince, but he was my prince.

And together, I knew we would live happily ever after.

AUTHOR'S NOTE

WHILE THE STORY IS FICTIONAL and based on a fairy tale, I was inspired by stories of the court of Louis XIV, the Sun King. Michel le Tellier, Marquis de Louvois, was the king's closest advisor. Louise de la Valliere (who inspired Lady Françoise) was one of the king's first mistresses. Louis, the dauphin of France, married Duchesse Maria of Bavaria. Louis-Auguste, Duc de Maine, was an illegitimate child of the king with Madame de Montespan, the king's favorite mistress. He was legitimized at the age of four and given title and land. Auguste was told to choose his bride from one of three daughters of a noble family close to the king. Madame de Maintenon, a governess to the royal children, was another of the king's favorites. She never had children herself but was known as the secret queen of France. Catherine Monvoisin was known as Le Voisin, an enchantress who counted the noblewomen at court among her many clients. She was arrested, tried, and executed for selling poison. And of course, this story is inspired by the one from Charles Perrault, who worked at Versailles and then collected folktales and fairy tales into a Mother Goose collection, which included "Cinderella," or as it was known in French, "Cendrillon."

ACKNOWLEDGMENTS

WHAT WOULD I DO WITHOUT Ari Lewin??? Thank you to my awesome editor, who always makes me laugh! Thank you to the *Penguinos*: Jen Loja, Jen Klonsky, Elyse Marshall, Elise LeMassena, Felicity Vallence, Anne Heausler—it's always a party! Thank you to Richard Abate and Martha Stevens, my agents and dear friends. Pandemic life was hard, but we survived together. I'm proud of all the work we've done together to bring fun books to the world. Thank you to all my amazing and loyal readers. Please don't tell me how old you are anymore. Or how many kids you have. And how you were kids when you started reading my books. LOL! Kidding! I never age.

I would be nothing without my family and friends who are family. I would not be here without my two: Mike and Mat. Everything begins and ends with you.